The Road to Lattimer

Virginia Rafferty

Milford House Press
Mechanicsburg, Pennsylvania

MILFORD HOUSE
an imprint of Sunbury Press, Inc.
Mechanicsburg, PA USA

NOTE: This is a work of fiction. Names, characters, places and incidents are the product of the author's imagination or are used fictitiously, and any resemblance to actual persons, living or dead, business establishments, events or locales is entirely coincidental.

Copyright © 2019 by Virginia Rafferty.
Cover Copyright © 2019 by Sunbury Press, Inc.

Sunbury Press supports copyright. Copyright fuels creativity, encourages diverse voices, promotes free speech, and creates a vibrant culture. Thank you for buying an authorized edition of this book and for complying with copyright laws. Except for the quotation of short passages for the purpose of criticism and review, no part of this publication may be reproduced, scanned, or distributed in any form without permission. You are supporting writers and allowing Sunbury Press to continue to publish books for every reader. For information contact Sunbury Press, Inc., Subsidiary Rights Dept., PO Box 548, Boiling Springs, PA 17007 USA or legal@sunburypress.com.

For information about special discounts for bulk purchases, please contact Sunbury Press Orders Dept. at (855) 338-8359 or orders@sunburypress.com.

To request one of our authors for speaking engagements or book signings, please contact Sunbury Press Publicity Dept. at publicity@sunburypress.com.

ISBN: 978-1-62006-213-5 (Trade paperback)

Library of Congress Control Number:

FIRST MILFORD HOUSE PRESS EDITION: August 2019

Product of the United States of America
0 1 1 2 3 5 8 13 21 34 55

Set in Bookman Old Style
Designed by Chris Fenwick
Cover by Chris Fenwick, Drawing by Stephanie Grossman
Edited by Chris Fenwick

Continue the Enlightenment

This book is dedicated to my great-grandparents
Stephen Dusick and Maria Schreida.

The tragic massacre at Lattimer in 1897 and the subsequent trial of the deputies are historical events. The four families are a composite of genealogical records and the imagination of the author, as is the fictitious patch town of Ario.

Coal patch towns near Hazleton, Pennsylvania

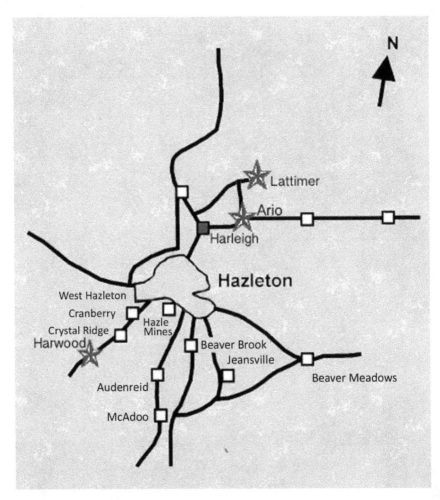

Map designed by Brooke Lundy, Greg Richardson, and Will Hills.

Beneath the starry banner

Though they came from foreign lands,

They died the death of martyrs

For the noble rights of man.

From **Ballad of the Deputies**

The Hazleton Daily Standard, September 17, 1897

Cast of Characters

Four families emigrated from rural villages in Eastern Europe in the late 1800's and settled in the anthracite coal region of Pennsylvania.

Stefan (1863-1939) & Anna (1867-1939) Dusick
Children
Stephen (1887-1918)

Rose (1890-1942)

Lucia (1893-1894)

Robert (1894-1965)

Lillian and Izabela (1895-1895)

Rudolph (1897-1922)

Joseph (1898-1971)

Peter (1900-1900)

Istvan (1901-1901)

John (1906-1960)

Cyril (1856-1900) & Adriana (1866-1910) Banik
Children
Jacob (1877-1942)

John (1882-1918)

Louis (1884-1935)

Patrik (1885-1965)

Elizabeth (1889-1920)

Helena (1891-1911)

William (1893-1955)

Iva (1896-1963)

Jan (1860-1930) & Katarina (1863-1940) Chuba
Children
Tomas (1880-1914)
Alex (1884-1918)
Cecelia (1886-1922)
Edward (1889-1940)
Irene (1891-1965)

Emil (1873-1965) & Edita (1875-1956) Tesar
Children
Alica (1897-1970)
George (1900-1962)
Andrew (1902-1980)
Susan (1905-1925)
Adeline (1908-1976)

Prologue

Hazleton, Pennsylvania, 1939

Anna

That is my casket covered with roses and carnations. The bouquet of wildflowers on the ground was placed there by my grandchildren. Last week I stood on that very spot as they buried my husband of fifty-two years.

Listen, the priest is about to begin. "Let us commend Anna to the Mercy of God," he prays. Soon, I will be lowered into the ground and laid to rest next to my Stefan.

Although it is March, everyone is still wearing their winter coats, and the babies are covered with heavy woolen blankets. The sky is hazy, and it looks like rain. I miss the smell of the rain on an early spring day.

My family is here among the mourners. Rose, my sweet daughter, is standing there next to her children. Her hair, streaked with gray, once thick and lustrous like mine, trails down her back. She is a grandmother, you know; that makes me a great-grandmother. Imagine that!

Mary Magdalena, my son's widow, is over there with her children. With the mines and steel mills shutting down, I don't expect they will stay in Hazleton much longer.

My sons, Robert, Joseph, John, and Rudi are here with their families. They make me proud.

My friends, Adriana and Katarina and their husbands, are gone now. Emil and his wife, Edita, have moved to California. We came to America together, and we settled in a coal patch town not too far from Hazleton. I am afraid our story will be forgotten. While I was alive, I did not want to talk about the past. We wanted to forget the struggles. Now, I know the story needs to be told. What happened during those years needs to be remembered. It is up to me to tell our story.

Our story started in a small village in Eastern Europe, where I lived with my family. I can still see the tiny homes, huddled together, surrounded by fields of green and gold that stretched toward the distant Carpathian Mountains. The mountains were mighty and dangerous, a reminder of God's power and presence in our lives. Many in our village, and other villages like ours, were tempted to cross those mountains, to see the world beyond. My husband's cousin Adriana, and her husband, Cyril, were among the first of our family to venture across the ocean to America

**1876-1889
Austria-Hungary**

Chapter 1 - 1876

Cyril and Adriana

Washday, the women gathered at the communal spring that was a short distance from their homes. There was endless chatter as the women gossiped while they filled their wooden buckets with ice-cold water. A young girl, one hand resting on her hip, and a stick in the other, coaxed a reluctant cow to move away from the stream. Goats nibbled on the tall grass. Chickens roamed freely, their heads bobbing and beaks pecking at the earth. Young children played with only occasional reprimands from their mothers.

Adriana stood at the water's edge, a washboard held in one hand, lye soap in the other. The pile of clothes to be washed waited in a bucket by her side. She scanned the stream's edge delaying the task and the frigid water. *Is this all there is? Will I live here forever?*

Her mind drifted to far off places. *America. I will go to America. A steamship will take me across the ocean.* Possibilities for adventure and a better life existed there. She had seen pictures of the massive transatlantic steamers on postcards and posters. *What an adventure, waves crashing against the sides of the powerful ship, wind blowing through my hair. Will the saltwater sting my face? Will I see a whale?*

"You need a husband and babies, not fantasies," her mother insisted when Adriana spoke of her desire to go to America.

"And who will marry me, Mother?"

"She's too tall," the old women in the village would cluck when they were together. They would remark on her hair that lacked luster and fullness. Her voice was loud and harsh, she walked with a stride that did not flatter.

Adriana knew that the qualities of meekness, obedience, and a willingness to follow the rules, expected by many of the men in her village, were not in her nature. *Perhaps even someone like me could find a husband on the ship. Perhaps someone in America will understand and accept me as I am.*

Adriana abhorred the poverty, starvation, and discrimination that was all around her. Villagers ostracized the gypsies who lived at the edge of the community. The ragged children, living in filth and deprivation, were starving, and Adriana's heart hurt for them.

She wanted to help. Neighbors gossiped about her. Her family was mortified. More than once her father had forbidden her from visiting the gypsies, but she defied him, bringing food to the children and sharing the gypsy celebrations.

"The children are hungry, and besides, I love to listen to their music and watch the women dance," she explained to her parents, only to find herself the recipient of a few lashes from her father's belt. Her mother wanted to intervene but knew the punishment was needed. What her willful daughter had done was dangerous, and far outside the unspoken rules of the village.

The aristocrats treated the peasants the same way the villagers treated the gypsies. Adriana resented their wealth and arrogance. When they passed through the village in their extravagant carriages, she held her head high refusing to show proper deference. "Why should I bend my head?" She would ask anyone who would listen. "They have done nothing to earn my respect."

What man would want a woman like my Adriana? her mother lamented.

Who would share my passions and my dreams? Adriana could not envision spending her life with any of the men she knew.

"Finished!" Adriana sighed as she lifted the heavy basket of wet clothing. With a slow, steady pace, she walked back to her home. The voices of the women and children at the spring faded away, replaced with the chirping of a bird and a gentle rustling of the leaves as a small animal scampered away. The snowcapped mountains in the distance beckoned her. Beyond them was the Port of Bremen and the ocean. *America. I will get there someday.*

The basket of wet clothing began to feel heavy, her arm ached. *I need a rest.* Lowering the basket to the ground she stretched her muscular arms. Lost in thought, *The ocean, America, adventure,* she did not hear the man approaching.

"Hello, there!"

Startled, she picked up the basket and turned to confront the voice behind her. A stranger stood only a few yards away. *I should run.* Her mind raced as she looked for help that was not there.

"Hello," he said again without moving. He did not want to frighten her.

He doesn't seem dangerous. His unkempt droopy mustache reminded her of the one her brother had recently grown, and his blue eyes seemed kindly. *He's just a traveler.*

"I didn't mean to frighten you."

"You didn't." She turned and started to walk to the village.

"May I walk with you?" He hastened his steps to catch up with her.

She nodded her head. "If you want."

"Is the village far from here?"

"No."

"I have a sister about your age."

"Oh." She adjusted the basket on her hip.

"May I help you with that? It must be heavy."

"I'm fine." Adriana, not accustomed to being helped, continued walking. *He seems congenial. Just a tired wanderer. Perhaps he is running from conscription.* Men in her village had left for America to do just that. She turned to the man with new respect.

"What's your name?"

"Cyril."

"Adriana."

"Where are you from, Cyril"

"I'm from Silica."

Adriana had heard of the village but had never been there. *He must have been walking for days.*

"Where will your journey take you?"

"America."

"Oh." She wasn't surprised to hear that he was going to America. He was not the first traveler to pass through their village on the way to Bremen or Hamburg.

"I plan to work in Bremen until I have enough money for a ticket."

"I'm going to America." She blurted out this information without thinking.

"Soon?"

"Well, no." *I should not have said anything. He will think I am foolish.*

"Are you going with your family? With your husband?" She thought his questions were rather impertinent.

"I'm going alone." *Why did I tell him that?*

"I see." They walked together in silence until the first houses of the village were visible. "Is there a place where I can rest in your village?"

Maybe he can give me information about America, she thought. "We can ask my father. Perhaps you can sleep in the barn."

"I would be most grateful. I can work to pay my way."

The man's name was Cyril Banik. The conscription order had come on his twentieth birthday. Father Bernatyak read the document to him. Like many other young Slovak men, Cyril had only attended school for a brief time before his family needed him to help in the fields. He could barely read or write. Working with his hands was all he knew.

"You are to report to the regiment in Kosice," the priest informed him. "Three years of service are required."

"Thank you, Father. I will do as ordered."

"It is your duty."

"Yes, Father."

"Remember, being obedient to authorities is God's command."

The priest suspected the young man had no intention of obeying the order. Cyril's brother had died fighting for the glory of the empire, while another had returned home blinded by an artillery shell.

Without ceremony or discussion, Cyril went home and packed his few possessions into an old sack and tied it with rope. When it was dark, he kissed his mother and left his home. No one heard him as he walked down the dirt road leading toward the mountains. Loneliness tugged at his heart. He walked until exhaustion would not let him go any farther. Resting on the side of the road, he planned his future. He would walk to Bremen, where a ship would take him to America. There, he would be free from conscription and the authorities. *I am strong, and young, and willing to work. America. I will be a free man in America.*

He had been walking for three days, sleeping along the road, begging food from strangers. Tired and hungry, he needed a place to stay for the night. A barn would provide shelter and perhaps some bread could be purchased. He had little money, yet he might fix a fence or patch a roof to pay his way. Then, in a day or so, he would again head out for the mountains and, eventually, Bremen. He had not anticipated meeting a woman like Adriana.

When he saw her in the road, his first thought was to not frighten the young woman holding the basket of clothing. Having sisters of his own, he knew the presence of a male stranger approaching on a deserted road might elicit screams for help. He needed to find shelter for the night and did not need to face the wrath of an angry father or brother. Yet the girl had not appeared to be afraid when she turned and looked at him. There was strength in her voice and a determined look in her expression he found intriguing.

Adriana had been cautious when she first met the stranger. But when he spoke of America vigilance was replaced with excitement. *America. The man had plans to go to America. Would it be possible to join him? Should I? Can I trust him?* She studied his face and liked what she saw. *Will he like me?*

Adriana, stumbling with the basket, used her shoulder to push open the door, "Matka, this man needs a place to stay tonight." It was a statement of fact not a request. Her mother was at the table, preparing green beans she had just picked from their small garden. Before Adriana's mother could answer, a tall man, a stranger, entered the house.

"I beg your pardon," Cyril, hat in hand, felt awkward facing the tiny woman sitting at the table. "I don't want to impose."

"No, no. It is all right," Adriana said, not giving her mother a chance to reply.

"I was just passing through. If I could rest in the barn for a while, I would be gone by daybreak."

"Matka, he could sleep in the barn."

"I could work to pay my way."

"We shall see what my husband says when he returns. You can rest in the barn until then." Her daughter did not rule the house yet.

Cyril stayed, fixing a fence, roofing the barn, offering to help anywhere he saw a need. It was the evenings that kept him in the village, the evenings with Adriana.

"How will you get to America?" she asked, watching him carefully as he ate the meager meal offered by her mother. She needed information.

"I will walk to Bremen."

I can walk with him. A plan beginning to form. "What then?" she asked.

"I will book passage to America when I have saved enough money."

I know how to cook and clean. Perhaps there is a family who needs a servant.

"What do you know about the ships that cross the ocean?"

He told her of the shipping lines that brought immigrants to great ports like New York and Philadelphia.

"Are you sad that you will be so far from home, away from your family?"

He did not answer.

Days passed. Adriana's parents watched but did not interfere with the intimacy that was growing between their daughter and this stranger.

"What do we know of him?"

"We know he works hard."

"Can he manage our Adriana?"

"Our Adriana won't be managed."

"Have you spoken to the matchmaker?"

"Of course. There is an older man in Kosice who has nine children. He needs a wife to care for the children and offer him solace. Adriana refused him."

There was no further discussion.

Tonight, I will tell her I am leaving. I cannot stay any longer. It is time to say goodbye.

He waited for her outside the barn, as he had done every night since arriving in her village. The air was warm and inviting, with the sweet smell of summer flowers drifting on the breeze. She was smiling as she approached him, and there was a warm, inviting flush on her cheeks. She held a bowl of sauerkraut soup.

"I am leaving in the morning, Adriana," he blurted. He could feel her watching him, but he just looked down at the bowl in his hands.

"I am going with you, then." It was not a request.

He was astonished and confused. *How would they manage? What were her expectations?* These questions flooded his mind.

"I'm going to America." Her voice was defiant, leaving no room for argument.

"I have no money, Adriana." There was sadness and regret in his voice.

"Neither do I."

"I'm walking to Bremen," he pleaded.

"I can walk."

"What will your parents say?"

"We don't need to tell them."

She had an answer for everything, and he was unable to say no to her. In the night, when everyone was asleep, she left her bed and found Cyril waiting for her outside the barn. Her mother heard her leave, and quiet tears fell on her pillow. She understood her daughter and wished her well.

"In Bremen," Adriana later told her friend Anna, "I worked in a boarding house, and Cyril worked on the docks. We lived wherever we could find a bed. Without Cyril, the journey would have been impossible. There were many who wanted to take advantage of unwary travelers. A woman traveling alone would have been vulnerable to unspeakable horrors. Cyril protected me."

It took months, but eventually, Cyril and Adriana had enough money to buy tickets for the SS *Rhein*. They were married at Castle Garden in New York City.

Chapter 2 - 1878

Emil the Peasant Boy

"Buttercup! Wait!" the five-year-old boy called to the brown-and-white goat springing playfully through the meadow. "Wait, Buttercup. Wait for me." But the goat continued jumping over yellow and white wildflowers as though they were mountains waiting to be conquered. The boy's eyes sparkled as he felt the fresh, cool air from the mountains on his face and the damp grasses tickled his bare feet. "Buttercup!" The goat had slid to a halt, something noteworthy having caught her attention. "It's not going to bite you." The boy laughed.

His name was Emil, and he was the youngest of eleven children. Emil's appearance as he chased the goat was not noteworthy. Tangled shoulder-length hair, brown eyes, sun-bronzed skin, loose-fitting clothing, and bare feet marked him as a peasant. His place in the family was to accept the food that was offered, to sleep wherever he could find space in the crowded one-room house, and to mind the goats. Emil's sister oversaw the house, while the others worked as day laborers in the village. She would offer Emil bread and cheese when he was hungry and chastise him if he got in her way as she washed the clothes for the family and prepared their meager meals. Emil spent his days with the chickens and the goats. Although he was alone, he was not lonely. The goats were his companions and his friends.

"Good morning, Biela." Biela, a bundle of soft white fur with a pink nose and big brown eyes, was just six months old, and Emil's favorite. As he did every day, Emil stroked her tummy, and she rewarded him with a look of contentment.

Flower, Biela's mother, gently nudged Emil's hand. "You are always hungry." Emil giggled, as Flower's soft lips touched his fingers. "Listen! Listen, Flower." Emil heard a thunderous rumbling in the distance, and the ground trembled. "Can you hear it, Flower? Can you feel it?" Much to Flower's dismay,

The Road to Lattimer · 13

Emil pulled his hand away as he turned his head to listen. "Horses, Flower. I hear horses, lots of horses."

"Hussars!" his sister called from a window in the house. "Hussars are coming, Emil. Hurry." Her voice was loud and filled with excited urgency.

"Stay here, Flower," Emil commanded. "I will tell you about the horses when I get back." The goat, whose only interest was food, nibbled the grass, while Emil ran as fast as he could to join the others gathering along the road. Everyone from the village was there.

"Lower your eyes, take off your hat, show respect," his sister roughly directed when he reached her. Emil's heart was pounding as he took off his hat and tried, without success, to lower his eyes. Hussars! He had heard stories of daring fighters skilled with horses. His grandfather had told him of dashing young men with long mustaches, uniforms with gold braid, black boots, and curved sabers that hung menacingly at their sides. "Someday I will take you to see them," Emil's grandfather had promised.

The Hussars were getting closer. Emil could see them, the horses racing towards him, hooves kicking up a cloud of dust. He could clearly see the soldiers with their shiny black boots and red breeches. Their military head-dress, a busby, made of black fur was topped by a wind-swept feather. The Hussars barely touched the reins as they guided their horses into the village.

"I want to ride a horse like that. I want to be a soldier," Emil proclaimed.

"How dashing they are," a girl whispered.

"That one smiled at me. I am sure of it." Her friend giggled, blushing.

"Magyars," a few of the men mumbled in contempt. The Magyars were the despised Hungarians who had conquered the Slovak people centuries ago.

Emil watched them until they vanished into the horizon, and then he went back to his goats. He told Flower what he had seen and how he wanted to be a soldier. Flower ignored him. Emil knew he needed to practice. He needed to be prepared for the day when he became a soldier and, displaying his skill and his magnificent steed, rode past cheering villagers.

"I need to practice," he explained to Buttercup, who was nibbling on a patch of grass. "You will be my horse." Trusting that Buttercup understood the mission, the boy wrapped his arms around the goat's neck and prepared to mount his steed. Buttercup, much to Emil's surprise, was not pleased with this arrangement and bolted away, dragging the little boy beside her. Unable to hold on any longer, Emil let go, and Buttercup resumed her meal, this time a crop of wild daisies. "Now stand still," Emil ordered. "I am a soldier, and you must obey me." The goat ignored his master and moved to a patch of clover that looked more appetizing than the daisies. Emil decided a discussion with a goat was useless, so he took a running leap onto the goat's back. Once again, Emil found himself in the dirt as the goat bounded away.

Flower, equally uncooperative, jumped shaking him off when he repeated the attempt. "Please, Flower, I just want to pretend you are a horse," he pleaded, hoping the hay he offered would put her in the right frame of mind. But Flower, who would eat from his hand, and nuzzle his cheeks, wanted nothing to do with a rider on her back.

"Biela, I know you would like to be my horse," he explained to the kid goat. "But you are just too small."

"Flower, you are a wise old goat. Do you think if I walked to the manor house, I could watch the horses grazing in the fields?" The nanny goat nuzzled her face against the boy's hand. "All right then, that is what I will do." For a moment, he considered telling his sister about his plan but then thought better of it. *She will just swat me around the ears and forbid me to go. I will leave now and be home before dark. No one will miss me.*

It was a long walk for a little boy, but there was much to amuse him along the way. He watched a vulture devouring the remains of a hapless fox; he cheered when a rabbit escaped the claws of a hawk by disappearing inside a hollow log. A brief rest at a shallow pond with tadpoles and frogs proved to be a pleasant diversion when he needed to rest.

Just as the sun was setting on the horizon, he saw the manor house, a beautiful yellow structure with more windows than he could count. Next to the house, in a fenced pasture, was a pretty mare with her colt. *No one will care if I watch them for a while,* he reasoned as he nervously looked around. *I am little. If I lie down in the grass, no one will see me.*

Time passed unnoticed. Emil's fascination with the horses was greater than any concern for food or the distance he was from home. Dusk engulfed the pasture. Sounds of evening, the soft neigh of a horse, the hoot of an owl, soothed the boy. His eyes grew heavy, and he rested his head on his folded arms. Visions of the colt and its mother filled his dreams.

The stable master saw the boy asleep in the grass but left him alone. He was certain the boy would be gone in the morning and no harm would be done. *The boy must have been watching the horses,* he thought, remembering nights when he had slept in the pasture behind his father's house. He did not expect to see the boy again.

Emil's mother noticed that he was not asleep on the floor next to the stove in the space he had claimed as his own. *He's sleeping with his goats in the shed. No need to check on him,* she thought. *Where else would he be?*

The neighing of a horse, unfamiliar voices in the distance, intruded into the boy's dream. "Flower! Buttercup! Biela!" They needed him, but he could not find them. The men will take them away.

Emil shivered. The cold mist in the early-morning air dampened his skin and clothes. The dream faded. Men, not too far from him, were talking and laughing. They were getting closer. Emil listened; his empty stomach churned with fear. *Were they looking for him?* He pressed his body closer to the ground. *The grass is tall.* The thought gave him little comfort. *Still, be still.*

The voices were gone. Only the occasional neighing of horses and the screech of a hawk interrupted the stillness. Hungry and cold the little boy started on the long walk home.

"I will be back," he promised the colt bounding with delight along the edge of the pasture. "I will be back."

When he reached home, his sister offered him some bread and cheese. She did not ask where he had been.

Emil frequented the pasture, watching the horses and spending the nights sleeping in the cool grass just outside the pasture fence. The mare and her colt recognized him and accepted the treats he offered. The stable master told his wife about the boy who visited the pasture and slept on the grass outside the fence.

"Perhaps he is an orphan," she suggested.

"No, I made inquiries. He is a peasant boy from the village. Seems he wanders here just to be near the horses."

"Not unlike you my dear husband."

"Hmm."

No one missed the boy. He would run an errand for his sister or help a neighbor in the garden and then go to visit the horses. His sister assumed he was caring for his goats or playing in the hills. His mother and father were too tired to notice the frequent absences of their youngest son.

Three years passed, and the scrawny child with the tangled hair and bare feet turned into a strong, agile boy. *It is time,* thought the stable master.

Emil was in the pasture stroking the nose of the colt, who had grown into a handsome stallion. He did not see the stable master approaching.

"What are you doing here?"

Emil was startled by the harsh voice behind him. "Th-The horse, sir," he stammered. "We, we are friends."

"Friends, huh! Hmm."

"Yes, sir. See?" Emil stroked the horse who rewarded him by nuzzling closer.

"I see." The stable master's expression softened. "Do you want to work?" Emil did not know that for some time the man had been thinking of hiring him to work in the stables. He had even spoken to Emil's father. It was already arranged.

"Y-yes, sir," he stuttered. "I would like to work with the horses, sir."

"All right, then. Go to the stables. Ask for Max. He will tell you what to do."

Emil, stunned by the new developments, stared at the man who had just offered him a job.

"My father."

"He has approved. You will sleep in the stables."

Emil looked at the man with disbelief. He could sleep with the horses!

"Go!"

"Yes, sir." Emil ran toward the stables afraid the man would change his mind.

The stable master stifled a laugh when the little boy, in his childish excitement, tripped over his own feet and tumbled to the ground. "He will do just fine. Just like me, he is. Just like me."

Chapter 3 - 1886-1889

Stefan and Anna

Anna

We were not always old, although some of you will only remember us with gray hair and wrinkled skin. Try and picture my Stefan. He is wearing a white tunic with wide trousers, standing barefoot in the fields, his body moving with strength and skill as he swings the scythe. My heart would race, and my face would flush whenever he was near. Oh, the desire I felt for him was not that of an experienced woman, but that of a young girl just beginning the passage into womanhood. I wanted him to smile at me, perhaps pick a wildflower and leave it at my door. But he never seemed to notice me; it was like I was not even there. He could not see the longing in my heart. In church, when his eyes wandered from the missal, he did not look in my direction. I was much younger than he was. He would have thought of me as a child, you see, if he thought of me at all.

What a sad day when he left to join the army. What a fuss everyone made. The women cried, the men shook his hand and wished him well. Standing off to the side, my heart felt a pain I did not understand. "I will pray for your safe return," I promised, but no one heard me.

Monika, everyone knew that Stefan was in love with her. "Their mothers approve of the match," the old women of the village would say as they gathered around the well to gossip. "They will have beautiful children," was the consensus. I would hear them talking, and my heart would break.

Monika was a beautiful girl, so radiant she looked like an angel. She would tease Stefan with her glances, encourage him with her smile. They would walk hand in hand next to the stream, where no one would see them. I am sure they shared a kiss, perhaps more, when no one was watching.

I was jealous. In confession, Father Emery would remind me that jealousy was a sin. Yes, I felt remorse, and Father Emery was patient, still, I was a sinner and could not help what was in my heart.

On the day the conscription notice came, Monika's cheeks were wet with tears as she promised to wait for him. He would be gone for three years in service of the empire, but their love was strong, she told all who would listen. They would be married when he returned.

As he left our village, looking so handsome in his uniform, I watched Monika give him a flower, a token of her affection. But the beautiful Monika did not wait for him. A year after Stefan left, a merchant from the city noticed her, and the promise of wealth was enough to gain her affection. She married the merchant and left our village. I have not seen her since that day. I am not even sure she wrote to Stefan telling him of her change of heart.

Perhaps you don't know what conscription means, or the pain it caused our families. The empire required three years of service in their Army. We had no interest in fighting for the glory of Emperor Franz Josef, you understand. Some men left for America to escape the conscription. Others hid from the authorities. Still, when Stefan walked out of our village that morning, the expression on his face did not contain any evidence of resentment or anger. It was his duty to go, and he accepted his fate. I was so proud of him.

But enough of that. I want to tell you about Stefan and the day he first looked at me the way a man looks at a woman. When he returned home from the army, everyone noticed there was a sadness about him. Something had happened that seemed to haunt his thoughts.

"A young man needs a wife," the women clucked when they were gathered at the spring washing clothes.

"Why not me?" I would think, but the words were never spoken. I can still see him, lost in thought, walking down the dirt road of our village. There was worry and anguish on his face, and it hurt my heart. What could I do?

I was sitting under the linden tree near the church. My little brother had scraped his knee, and I was comforting him. It was not a significant injury, mind you, but the big tears on his tiny face would soften anyone's heart. I had been so engrossed in my task; I had not heard the approaching footsteps.

"May I help?" I remember him asking. My heart stopped when I saw it was Stefan. I told him everything was all right.

Would you think I am foolish if I told you the church bells began to ring at that moment? I am sure a bird began to sing, and the flowers around me suddenly bloomed. Of course, none of those things happened, but that was how I felt. Stefan had noticed me.

The Soldier Returns

Stefan came home. His uniform was dusty, his boots pinched his feet, but it did not matter. After three years in the Emperor's Army, he was home in his village, with his family.

The dirt road, with its wagon ruts and memories, meandered over the gentle hills toward the village in the distance. Fields of green stretched to the horizon, where they met the snowcapped mountains. A hawk circled idly below the clear blue sky of an early spring day. The land and the fields were owned by the Magyar aristocrats, but Stefan's family had toiled in those fields for generations. They were part of him, the planting, the harvest, the sweet smell of hay. Things had changed while he was away. His father had died, and his Monika had married another. *I have changed,* he thought.

Bosnia! The memory, the nightmare, would not leave him. *Allahu akbar.* Even now, as he walked to his home, the words echoed in his mind. *Allahu akbar.* He covered his ears with his hands, hoping to stop the fearful cry that would not leave him alone. The metallic smell of blood filled his nostrils, and the gray earth beneath his feet turned red. He tried to scream, but there was no sound. Josef's head lay severed from his body.

They had been on patrol, Josef and Stefan, when the nightmare began. It was dusk, and shadows danced on dingy walls of dwellings that crowded the dark alley. A woman, shrouded in black, huddled in a doorway with her children. Her piercing dark eyes, the color of obsidian washed by rain, followed the soldiers' movements. Was there a warning in her eyes? The soldiers, preoccupied with their own thoughts, ignored her. She was unimportant, and certainly not a threat.

The day had been routine, and the soldiers were laughing, their rifles slung carelessly over their shoulders.

"A beer tonight?" Josef queried. "Some girls, maybe?"

"Your sweetheart back home will not care?"

"She will know, and she will care," Josef answered, laughing.

"Allahu akbar!" The shout startled the soldiers, and they reached for their rifles.

Even now Stefan could feel the weight of his rifle in his hands and the revulsion he felt as his bayonet found soft flesh. It happened over a year ago, yet Stefan felt his body tremble at the memory. His palms grew moist as he clenched his fists. "I killed a man and watched my friend die." Stefan's face paled at the memory, and he was filled with regret and sadness. "Josef, I am so sorry."

It was noon as Stefan reached the outskirts of the village where the Roma, the gypsies, lived in dilapidated huts. Muddy water littered with debris trickled through a narrow ditch on the side of the road. The smell of sickness and decay permeated the air. *How can they live like this?* he wondered without sympathy.

"Thieves," Stefan mumbled to himself, averting his eyes from the dark-skinned children dressed in rags who huddled in the doorways. His hand fell to the pouch hanging from his belt. He had some small gifts for his family, and he knew well the reputation of the gypsies. "Thieves," he mumbled to himself again.

"Please." A woman, bent, crippled, her face sallow from hunger, approached him. "Please, food, for my children." The soldier ignored her. She was not worth his time, and surely not his sympathy.

Children surrounded him, pulling on his clothing, begging.

"Please, bread, a coin?" A little boy stood in front of him, blocking his way.

"I have nothing to give you." Stefan roughly pushed the child aside, avoiding the dark eyes that stared at him. "*Sviňa,*" he muttered, hastening his pace. "Swine."

Almost there. A smile crossed his face as he saw the first wooden houses nestled together in the village. *Mrs. Novak's chickens are still running wild.* The stream on his left trickled and tumbled cold and clear from the mountains. *Monika!* On the first day of spring, when the returning sparrows were spotted, the stream belonged to the young girls of the village. The bushes and tangles of vines had hidden the boys who watched them. He had been among those boys, but he was only watching Monika, *I loved you.* How his heart had raced when she looked in his direction, an inviting smile on her face. *That smile was for me.*

That was long ago now. His sister had written that Monika had married and moved to another village. It had only been a fantasy of a boy, and he was a man now.

Church bells rang and dogs barked as the soldier reached the dirt road lined with thatched cottages. He was home. Curious villagers pushed aside window curtains, doors opened, and the street filled with people. Men slapped him on the back with words of welcome, young girls handed him flowers. Old women, who had known him since he was an infant, smothered him with kisses.

A girl, holding her skirts above her ankles, her face flushed with excitement, ran toward him. *Lucia?* For a moment Stefan was baffled—*was the young woman running toward him his little sister?*

"Stefan!" She was in his arms, kissing his cheeks, laughing. He held her close and stroked her hair, marveling at the changes in his little sister. *When I left, she was a girl still playing children's games.*

"Stefan, do you remember Karol?" Lucia turned to an awkward-looking boy who was standing next to her. "He worked with us in the fields," she said, taking the boy's hand.

"Karol, yes, I remember you."

"We plan to be married," she proclaimed as Karol shuffled his feet. "In a few years, of course. Mother and Godmother have approved." Lucia beamed with excitement, while Karol seemed to want to fade away.

"Well, congratulations to both of you."

"His mother! The soldier's mother is coming," someone shouted. Everyone fell silent and moved away from the soldier. A woman, dressed in a faded black skirt and a blouse made of rough homespun cloth, her silver hair covered with a tight-fitting white cap, was standing in the street. Her body was bent forward as though it bore a heavy weight. His brother, Marek, and his brother's pregnant wife, Terezia, were standing next to her, supporting her. *Marek was there for her when I was not,* Stefan thought with a mixture of gratitude and remorse. Stefan had not been there when his father had died. He had not been there to support his mother in her grief. Now, when he saw the love in her eyes, his guilt was magnified.

But this was not the time for sadness. His mother was in his arms. "Matka, I am home," he said, hugging her as tightly as he dared. "I am home. I am finally home."

That night, Stefan took off his uniform and stowed it away. He was in his own bed. *I am home.* Content, he drifted off to sleep.

Bosnia. He is on patrol with Josef. They are laughing, happy. They will be back in the barracks soon. "Allahu akbar," the words echo in the mist. "Allahu akbar," Josef's mutilated body covered in blood, lay on the road. He felt his bayonet enter the soft flesh of their attacker and heard the anguished cry as the man fell lifeless to the ground.

Dark, red blood flowed through the street. The woman in black was there, as she was every night, her eyes watching him. "What do you want from me?"

A Brother's Guilt

"A man needs a wife," the woman fussed as she put the bread in the communal oven.

"He should marry, and soon," declared another.

"You can see he is lonely."

"His mother should talk to the matchmaker."

The animated chatter was the same wherever the women gathered. It was the responsibility of the women, they believed, to be sure that the young soldier, so soon returned to them, should find a wife.

Stefan knew what was expected, but he could not think about a wife, or providing for a family. Nightmares interrupted his sleep, and memories of Bosnia intruded whenever his mind was idle. Only when he was working, patching a roof, tilling a field, or helping a neighbor repair a wagon, was he able to forget. He could not talk to anyone about the sadness and regret. "Why was I allowed to live? Josef, forgive me."

"You have changed, Stefan." The brothers were sitting in the saloon. They had been banished from the house when Terezia had gone into labor.

"Maybe."

"Do you want to talk about it?"

"No." How could he explain the life of a soldier to his brother, who had never left the village?

"I should have been with you."

"You were needed here, Marek, and besides, your leg." The brothers fell silent, each with their own thoughts. "I am sorry," Stefan wanted to say. "We were only children," his brother would have protested if asked. But the words were never spoken.

There had been an accident when Marek was two years old. His mother, for reasons that were a mystery to her family, would often tell the story. Even strangers would hear in painful detail about the accident that left Marek with a limp. It was hurtful to Stefan, and an embarrassment to Marek, but she did not seem to notice.

"It was terrible," their mother said, her voice cracking, her eyes glistening with moisture. Somehow, her children noticed, the tears came right on time and never failed her.

"Oh, Sofie, you were so brave," the listener comforted her. "To see your little boy so damaged." Everyone shook their heads in sympathy.

"Marek was playing near the door, and Stefan, still an infant, was in my arms, crying. He was just an infant, you understand. What could a mother do? I am only one person."

"No one is blaming you, Sofie."

"Thank you," she whispered between sniffles.

"Marek was just a toddler," someone intervened. "You were not responsible."

"But before I knew it, my little boy, my Marek, was in the street, horses all around him, men shouting. Stefan, still a baby, was in my arms, crying."

"It was the Magyar's fault, not yours, Sofie. We have all seen them on their horses racing through the village. What do they care about our children?"

"Yes, the Magyars," all agreed.

"I know, I know, but still, it breaks a mother's heart to see her boy like this."

It's my fault, Stefan thought each time the story was told.

Mrs. Ciernik

"I am fine," Stefan's mother insisted. "I just need to rest."

"You are not fine," Stefan protested, looking at the withered, pale woman huddled under her blankets. He had never known his mother to stay in bed like this.

"Can I get you some warm tea?" Terezia asked while fussing with the blanket.

"No, Terezia, mind the children. I will just rest a little longer."

"We need Mrs. Ciernik," Marek said, taking charge, as always.

"I'll go," Stefan volunteered.

There was no doctor in the village. They did not need one—they had Mrs. Ciernik. She had a remedy for every ailment. The shelves in her home were lined with labeled infusions and dried herbs. If you had a cold or sore throat, dried linden blossoms offered relief. The sap from red milkweed was valued for its effectiveness to treat serious cuts. Burdock was administered to burns, an ointment made from pot marigolds was applied to wounds, and cumin given for nausea.

Mrs. Ciernik made opium out of poppies to soothe the pain and comfort the sick. As she had learned from her mother, she scored the immature seed pods by hand, collecting the sticky yellowish residue. The residue was dried and stored in small, carefully labeled vials to be added to a warm, soothing tea when needed.

Years before, Mr. Ciernik had found a lump developing on his back. "We will watch it," his wife declared while examining the suspect protuberance. Four days later the abscess had doubled in size and started to turn white. "It needs to be drained," his wife proclaimed with authority, as she went for her darning needle and prepared the tea laced with opium, honey, and wine. "This will help."

Weeks later Mr. Ciernik, always garrulous and willing to share every detail of his life would tell his friends, "She gave me that tea, and I slept for three days."

Now, with their mother ill, Mrs. Ciernik was the one who would know what to do.

Stefan walked down the main street of the village toward Mrs. Ciernik's cottage. The snow-covered mountains rose in the distance, their peaks touching the clouds in the blue sky. The smell of baking bread from the communal oven tantalized his senses.

Mrs. Toth, planting potatoes in her small garden, smiled and waved to him as he walked past her cottage. The cooper paused from his work to ask about his mother's health, and the blacksmith nodded a greeting. Stefan could hear children singing in the schoolhouse, and for a moment imagined his child might be there someday.

The church and the schoolhouse were just beyond the bend in the road. His mother had suggested he talk with Father Frederik. "He knows about war, Stefan. Confession and absolution might end your suffering."

"Yes, Matka," he had answered. "Just not today." Stefan could not speak of what he had done, and he was not ready for forgiveness. "Someday soon," he told himself. "Soon I will say my confession and accept my penance."

He paused for a moment to look at the well-worn path leading up the hill to the church. He imagined his father's funeral procession. The parish priest with his raven-black robes, a purple stole over his shoulders, and the altar boys with their candles, leading the mourners up the hill. His mother was weeping, supported by Marek and Lucia. His father's wooden casket was carried by young men of the village. *I should have been there for her*, he lamented.

On the hill, sitting under a linden tree, was a woman, shrouded in black. Her black eyes emotionless, almost frightening as she watched him. He wanted to look away, to run from her, but he could not. Sorrow filled his heart as he remembered the woman he had seen in Bosnia. The woman, with her children, who had watched as he killed a man.

"Leave me alone," he pleaded. The woman did not move. "What do you want from me?" There was only silence as his voice echoed among the trees scattered on the hill. "I will be here for my mother." His voice was subdued and filled with pain. "I will be here for her," he repeated, but still the woman did not move. "I will be here for my mother, for my family." But no one was there to hear the anguish in his voice.

"Matka, you need to take half of this right away," Stefan called as he entered the house. "Terezia will make some tea to help it go down." His mother puckered her lips and frowned in disgust as she drank the dark liquid.

"She is to drink half tonight and half in the morning," Stefan said, handing Terezia the vial that now contained half of the dark liquid.

"Rest now, Matka."

"You need a wife," his mother chided as her son fluffed her pillow.

"Yes, Matka." But Stefan was not thinking of a wife. He was just glad to be home. *I will be there for you this time, Matka*, he thought, caressing her warm cheeks. *I will not leave you again.*

"You cannot hide from your demons," Stefan chastised himself the next day as he slowly walked down the road to the church. "You cannot avoid life." The church was there on the hill, peaceful, silent. "You see, nothing to fear." Still, the feeling of dread would not leave him. He did not want to see the woman in black with her sorrowful eyes accusing him. The apparition was not there. In her place, a young woman was kneeling under the linden tree comforting the little boy of perhaps five years of age who stood before her. Her hair, the color of deep chocolate or freshly tilled earth, floated in shimmering satin waves down her back. She was not wearing the white cap of a married woman, and Stefan wondered why this was important. *I am not looking for a wife,* he reminded himself.

"May I help?" Stefan asked, relieved to see a real woman rather than the dark-veiled lady.

"He is fine," she answered, giving him a smile of recognition before turning back to the boy and wiping away fresh tears. "He fell and scraped his knee."

Stefan stood there for an awkward moment, not sure what to say. Unexpected yearnings caused him to hesitate. It had been a long time since he had felt the gentle touch of a woman.

"I am Anna. Do you remember me?" she inquired, looking back at him with soft green eyes and a sweet smile.

"Good to see you again, Anna." He was trying hard to remember her. Perhaps, yes, he had seen her in church and while they harvested the wheat, but she was just a child then, easy to ignore. *Now, not so ignorable,* he thought. He imagined touching her hair or kissing the hands that were comforting the boy. The slight flush on his cheeks went unnoticed, or so he hoped.

"Welcome home, Stefan."

"Thank you," he answered, embarrassed at his presumptuous thoughts. "Are you sure the boy is all right?"

"Yes, he's fine. Just a scrape. He fell on the church steps."

"All right, then." Stefan nodded.

As he walked down the road, he struggled not to look back at Anna. "You have seen women before," he mumbled to himself. "You do not need a wife." His body was telling him something very different.

Anna watched him as he disappeared around the bend in the road. She was amused by his reaction when she had smiled at him. This was not the boy she watched harvesting hay years before. He had not noticed her then, or her admiring glances, but today had been different.

Time passed before they saw each other again.

Courtship

Stefan, his head buried in his hands, listened to the sounds of the water cascading over the moss-covered rocks in the streambed. As a child, he had come here on hot summer days to play. He had laughed with his friends and teased the young girls who ventured near. Now he was here seeking solitude.

There was no one in the village who would understand the cause of Stefan's melancholy. Bosnia. The eyes of the man he had killed would haunt him forever, but Stefan did not feel remorse. A soldier was trained to kill the enemy. It was the death of Josef, the soldier who had walked with him that night, that filled Stefan with guilt. *Why am I still alive? Josef, why didn't I protect you?* The words were a primal scream that tormented him relentlessly.

There was a rustling in the leaves behind him. Startled, he reached for the rifle he no longer had. The enemy was not standing there, only a woman with soft green eyes and flowers in her hair.

"I-I did not mean to startle you." It was Anna, the woman he saw under the linden tree.

"No, no, it is fine. I was just far away."

"Sometimes I like to come here." Her voice was soft, almost musical. "It's quiet, and I love listening to the water."

Somehow—Stefan was never sure how it happened—they were there together, sitting by the stream and listening to the water. He felt happier than he had in years.

"May I walk you home?" he asked when she got up to leave.

"Anna, will you marry him?" Nathanial, Anna's little brother, asked. He had been watching from a window as the man had walked his sister to the door. "I like him, and Matka says you need a husband."

"Yes. Yes, I will marry him."

"Matka, Anna's going to marry the soldier," the child shouted to his mother, who was working in the garden behind the house. She was not upset by the news.

Stefan was dreaming, he knew, but still, he did not want to let the moment pass. She was with him, the woman with the chestnut hair and green eyes. He reached for her, and his body responded with desire as she surrendered into his embrace. The dream faded, and the soldier opened his eyes. The emptiness returned.

Anna

So many memories are lost to me now. Age will do that, you know. However, some things a woman never forgets. Treasured moments that remain as static pictures in our minds are as real as a photograph.

I remember our wedding day as if it were yesterday. My mother and sisters are in the room, arranging a table filled with pastries and ham and kielbasa. Sunshine filters through the windows. The room smells of fresh flowers from the meadow and the garden. I am sitting in a chair in the center of the room, while my dear friend Katarina arranges my hair. A crown, made of flowers and ribbons, made by Katarina awaits on the small table.

My father is in the room standing next to my mother. Katarina puts the crown of flowers on my head and arranges the ribbons that cascade over my hair and down my back. I feel beautiful and happy. Soon, I will be Stefan's wife.

I am kneeling in front of my parents, thanking them for providing and caring for me. Although my parents are still young, there are strands of gray in their hair. Mother placed her hands on me with a blessing. Father bent and kissed me. There was joy and sorrow in their voices as they wished me and Stefan well. This is how I will always remember my mother and father. I would not be there to watch them grow old.

The image in my memory changes again. The priest has blessed our union, and the ceremony and dancing are over. Surrounded by friends and family my mother removes the crown of flowers and binds my hair under a white cap. From that moment, only my husband, Stefan, would see my hair loose and flowing down my back, covering my shoulders. I am a married woman. I am married to the man I have always loved.

Outside I can hear the jingle of bells, the clip-clop of horses' hooves, and the crunch of wagon wheels on the dirt road. The wagon is coming for me and my belongings. I am leaving this place, my home, where I spent my childhood.

A Love That Would Last a Lifetime

Stefan, hat in hand, opened the gate to Anna's home. He was uncomfortable. The collar on his shirt felt tight on his neck, his new shoes pinched his feet, and he was about to meet Anna's parents. He was there to ask permission to visit with their daughter. *I am acting like a child.* Stefan knocked on the door.

"Yes?" Anna's father stood in the door. He did not look pleased to see Stefan.

"I am Stefan Dusick."

"I am aware."

"With your permission, I would like to speak with Anna."

"Hmm."

"I would be honored…"

"Come."

The room was hot and dark, cluttered with the belongings of a large family and the necessities of life. Like most of the village homes, the house had two rooms. The family lived in one, and the other, connected by a hallway, was used for storage. From the hallway came the sounds of children giggling and a woman's voice whispering a quiet reprimand. A small head peered around the corner of the doorway, and Stefan smiled at Anna's little brother. It seemed the entire family was expecting him.

"Anna, you have a visitor," her father called, his voice unnecessarily loud.

Anna came into the room with her mother. *They must have been waiting.* Had his mother and godmother already discussed the possibility of a union between their children? *It is the custom. It seems I am the only one who did not foresee this day.*

"Good morning," Anna's mother greeted him, while Anna stood by her side. Stefan noticed they had the same green eyes.

"Good morning, Mrs. Schreida."

"Good morning, Stefan." Anna's voice was soft and warm as she smiled at him. There was a silent, awkward moment before Stefan had the courage to speak.

"Anna, with the permission of your mother and father, would you care to take a walk?"

"Yes, Stefan," Anna replied with a fleeting glance to her mother. "I would like that."

They left the house, with a stern look from Anna's father, a wide smile from her mother, and the giggling of children fading behind them.

Stefan became a frequent visitor to Anna's home. He walked her to church on Sundays. Tentative kisses that grew warmer over time were exchanged when they were alone. In the fall of 1887, they informed their parents they wished to marry.

The mothers arranged for the wedding, and the banns of marriage were announced in church. Everyone agreed that the young married couple would live with the groom's family. Anna sold her share of the family plot to her brothers in exchange for a small dowry.

On the day of the wedding, after the ceremony, it was time to leave her home for the last time.

"Dear child, these are for your new home and new life," Her mother placed a large feather bed and pillows near the door.

With a smile she watched her father and Nathaniel carry a chest of drawers into the room. "I made this for you and your husband."

Villagers, walking next to a wagon loaded with gifts, and decorated with flowers, ribbons, and bells, came to her house singing love songs. "We are here to help load the wagon with the bride's belongings."

Anna thanked her parents for taking care of her all her life and bid them a ritual farewell. She left the home of her childhood and went to live in her husband's home.

Chapter 4 - 1887

Decisions Are Made

Anna

Well, so you see, I was happy that summer of 1887. We lived with his family, and they were good to me. His mother entertained us with family stories in the evenings, although at times there were recollections that were embarrassing and sometimes hurtful to her children. But I liked to hear the stories of Stefan as a little boy. "He had hair the color of wheat at harvesttime," she would tell everyone. "A bit shy, unlike my other children." I think he must have been a precious little boy.

Terezia, Marek's wife, was only a year older than I was, and we soon became close friends. We laughed and gossiped as we did the laundry, made the noodles for dinner, or sat outside and shredded cabbage for sauerkraut. I was never lonely in those days.

You might wonder how we managed in such a small house with so many people. It was not something we thought about. We cooked, and ate, and slept in one room of the house. The other room was used for storage. The same was true for nearly everyone in the village. It was the way of things.

Stefan and I shared a small bed in a corner of the room next to the stove. At night, when everyone was asleep, Stefan and I would whisper our love to each other. When the only sounds were the soft murmurs of a restless sleeper or the hoot of an owl outside the window, we would find each other and share the closeness of a husband and wife. In those early months, that was all that mattered to either of us.

Do you know what it is like to be hungry? We were often hungry, but it was the way it had always been, and the way it always would be. Many left the village looking for work. They left their villages, their homes, crowding into rickety old wagons pulled by oxen. Some even left for America. It seemed the entire village was leaving.

Stefan would leave, sometimes for weeks, looking for work. My heart ached when he was gone, but when he returned the lovemaking was ardent, and I would be all aglow for the next few days. Yes, Terezia would tease me, Marek tried to ignore me, and Stefan's mother would frown—perhaps she was jealous that she was no longer young. On the day I told Stefan he would be a father you could see pride and love in his face. We were content, or so I thought.

And then, the day of the fire, Stefan changed. He would come home at night sullen, thoughtful. Sometimes he would touch me and wait for the baby to kick, but all I could see in his face was worry. At night, in his sleep, I could feel his body tense, and he would mumble words I did not understand. I suspected it had to do with the war, although he never spoke of it. He would not talk to me, and I was afraid. Perhaps he did not want the child.

A few weeks after the fire Stefan told me we were going to America. I was not happy. This was my home. Soon I would be a mother. What did I know of America?

"Why?" I asked him. "Why must we leave our families, our friends?"

"There is work in America, Anna." I can still see his face as he begged me to understand.

"You can find work here," I protested."

"Do you want our sons to fight for the Emperor?" Stefan asked, and the sadness in his voice spoke of the horrors he had seen in the war. There was a wound in his soul I could not reach or hope to heal.

"But we will hide them," I had answered in desperation.

"And they will be found and put in prison." The image of my child in a prison weakened my resolve. I trusted my husband and eventually agreed that we should go.

The Fire

Anna gazed at the white clouds drifting beneath the blue sky. The rows of potato plants stretched before her, their green leaves contrasting with the brown soil in which they grew. From here the village seemed to be asleep, nestled in a tiny valley beyond a curve of the road. She felt close to God when she was here in the fields, her soul at peace.

Familiar sounds surrounded her. Women chattered, while children laughed and shrieked as they chased each other across the fields.

On the rutted dirt road just to her left, a wagon rumbled and creaked on its way to the village. A hawk screeched overhead. With her hand on her lower back she deeply inhaled the scent of freshly turned earth. She stretched gently bending backwards and took in the cool mountain air.

"Anna, do you feel all right?" Katarina knew that Anna was expecting a baby.

"Fine, Katarina. I'm fine."

"You should sit and rest." Katarina, the mother of three children, seven-year-old Tomas, three-year-old Alex, and two-year-old Cecilia, knew all too well the discomforts that came with pregnancy.

"I felt the baby move."

The sky was gray, the mountains in the distance shrouded in dense fog as Anna and Katarina bent over to once again tend to the young potato plants. Katarina's daughter, Cecilia, was sitting next to her mother, playing with a tiny rag doll. Her son Alex was with friends a short distance away. Tomas, now seven years old, was in school.

Anna missed the warmth of the sun on her back, but the dismal day could not darken her mood. She had placed Stefan's hand on her belly the night before, and he felt the baby kick for the first time. *My baby, my sweet baby,* she was thinking when she heard the shouts of a young boy: "Soldiers!"

A boy ran through the fields toward them. "Magyars!" he shouted. "The king's men are coming." He had seen the red-and-green flags of the Kingdom of Hungary and the Baron's banner. The soldiers were coming over the crest of the road from the mountains in the north headed for the village.

Women rushed to gather their children. The horses could trample a curious child who got in their way. "Magyars!" A chorus of panicked voices echoed through the fields.

"Alex!" Katarina called for her son, expecting he would answer. "Alex!" Her voice was louder this time.

"He was over there!" Anna pointed in the direction where she had last seen the boy. "By the wagon, over there, on the side of the road. He might still be there.".

"Alex!" Anna joined her friend calling for Katarina's son. They reached the wagon, but he was not there.

"Alex!"

The cloud of dust from the pounding of the horse's hooves on the dirt road drew closer and the ground trembled.

"Alex!" Katarina's voice was frantic now and mingled with the shouts of other mothers calling their children.

"Alex!"

Tears filled Cecelia's eyes and her lips began to quiver. "It's all right, Ceci. The soldiers won't hurt you. We will find Alex." Katarina rocked the little girl, soothing her while her eyes scanned the fields looking for her son. It was too late. The soldiers were there. Katarina froze in place, holding Cecilia close to her chest. The peasants, who had been working in the fields, now stood motionless, their postures stooped, eyes lowered. Mothers gripped the hands of small children or clutched babies in their arms as the soldiers on their powerful steeds rode past them. This time the peasants were ignored by the Magyars, and the relief was palpable.

"There might be trouble in the village," a woman warned while rubbing the blisters on her hands.

"No, they are just passing through," another said hopefully.

"Maybe they are here to arrest the mayor," an old woman scoffed. The mayor, who had taken a Hungarian name and spoke only Hungarian, was scorned by the Slovaks.

Katarina ignored the women. She needed to find her son.

"Alex!"

An older woman who was leaning on her hoe pointed toward the mountains. "He was walking up the road that way."

"Alex," Katarina shouted. Now she was worried. Alex never went far. Was he hurt? Why didn't he answer? With Cecelia on her hip and Anna by her side, the women hurried up the road toward the mountain.

"Alex!"

Clang. Silence. *Clang. Clang. Clang. Clang.*

Katarina's heart pounded at the sound of the church bell. "Clang." There was trouble in the village. "In the name of the father," she prayed touching her forehead, "and of the son," her hand went to her heart, "and the Holy Spirit." She touched each shoulder finishing the short prayer. The women near her were doing the same, some holding Holy Rosaries.

"Alex!"

Clang, clang, clang. The call was more urgent now and the clanging of the bells echoed off the mountains.

"Alex!"

"Let me hold Ceci," Anna offered, taking the little girl from her mother's arms. "We will find him, Katarina. We will find Alex."

"Alex!" Katarina shouted again.

"Alex," Anna echoed.

Clang, clang, clang. The fields where the women had been working were now a cacophony of frantic, frightened voices intermingled with the clanging of the church bells.

Where was Alex? Where was her little boy?

Clang, clang, clang. "Fire!" someone shouted. Wooden rakes, scythes, shovels were abandoned as everyone ran toward the village, colliding with Katarina and Anna running in the opposite direction.

A wagon filled with peasants raced down the road, the occupants clinging to the sides as it sped around a curve.

"Alex!" Katarina's voice.

"Alex!"

"Have you seen my son? Have you seen Alex?" Katarina screamed in desperation, her voice shrill and loud, competing with the clanging of the church bells.

"Katarina!" It was a man's voice coming from the fields on her right. Katarina caught her breath. Jan was running toward her, and Alex was riding on his father's shoulders.

The boy was smiling, unfazed by the ringing of the bells or the commotion around him. He was with his father, getting the attention he wanted. Katarina controlled her anger at the boy. *Later,* she told herself. *Later, I will deal with him.*

Black billows of smoke rose over the rooftops of the village, and the air was heavy with the acrid smell of burning wood. All their homes were in peril. "Jan." Katarina reached for her husband's arm. "Tomas!"

"The schoolmaster will keep the children safe." Jan's voice was strong, reassuring, but there was anger in his eyes.

Anna tried to control her own emotion as her hands touched her womb and she felt the baby move. "Lord protect us. Where is Stefan?"

"Stay with us, Anna. Stefan will find us." It was Katarina's turn to comfort her friend.

The soldiers on horseback were coming up the ridge leaving the village. Their work in the village was done. There was a wagon behind them moving slowly, laboriously, up the steep slope of the road.

With trepidation the villagers moved to the side of the road, forming a ragged line. The soldiers were not here to help. They were leaving the village, unconcerned about the fire.

"The entire village will burn for all they care," an old woman uttered with contempt.

"Jesus, Mary, Joseph, help us," many were praying. The fear of a fire in the village was terrifying for these peasants who had so little.

There was a hush as the soldiers came closer, the only sounds the incessant peal of the church bells, the clatter of the horses' hooves, and the mournful creak of the wagon's wheels.

"Swine," a man with a large scar on his face mumbled as he spit on the ground. The soldiers did not notice, and the man's wife whispered a prayer of thanks.

There was a man in the wagon. His head and clothing were bloodied, his hands in shackles. The man did not look up, and it was obvious he did not want to see the faces of the villagers. He did not need or want, their pity.

"It is the teacher." Anna whispered.

"Why is he arrested?" Katarina responded, worry in her voice. "He is a kind, religious man."

"Don't know. He plays the organ at mass. That isn't a crime."

"Tomas told me he talks to the children in Slovak! I told him to be quiet."

"Who told the authorities?"

"There are spies everywhere."

"The authorities always find out."

The women watched as the soldiers disappeared around a bend in the road.

"The schoolhouse, the schoolhouse!" A child ran toward them, tears streaming down his face. "They burned the school and took the teacher."

"Swine," the man with the scar repeated with disgust.

"Anna! Anna!" Stefan ran across the field, his bare feet trampling the green leaves of the young potato plants. "Anna! Are you all right?" he asked reaching her.

"Soldiers, there were soldiers," she stammered.

"Yes, yes, I know, but are you all right? And the baby?"

"Yes, Stefan, we are fine."

Andrej, an experienced nine-year-old student, who had been in the school for two years and knew everything there was to know, was impatient. He was in a hurry to join his friends who had disappeared into the woods behind the school. Time was short. Soon the bell would ring, calling them to their classroom, where they would sit at their desks for what would seem an interminable time. The only permissible diversion was the walk to the water bucket at the back of the classroom, where a boy could linger while slowly sipping the cool water that had come from the village well.

Andrej took advantage of this small opportunity for freedom as often as possible. With strategic planning and a keen awareness of the teacher's routine, the walk to the water bucket gave him ample opportunities for mischief. Pulling Mary's hair was always an interesting diversion and punching Filip on the arm would be a prelude to the fistfight they would have after school.

This morning, Andrej had been given the responsibility of filling the water bucket. Usually, he could complete the task quickly and efficiently and still have time to join his friends. But this morning the teacher had told him to bring Tomas, a new student, with him. Tomas was shy, quiet, someone to be ignored, or tormented as the need dictated. *I do not need this baby following me to the well,* Andrej thought with ill-concealed contempt. *He will do nothing but slow me down.* Still, it was important to obey the teacher. The consequence of defiance was swift and painful.

"Let's go," Andrej commanded. Tomas had been waiting for him. He had arrived at the school early. This would be an enormous responsibility and he was ready.

"Bring the bucket."

"I have it."

"Good. Now hurry." Andrej watched as the younger boy lowered the bucket into the well.

"Don't spill it!" he admonished Tomas as they walked back to the school.

"I saw the teacher talking to you in Slovak yesterday." It was a statement of fact, and Andrej did not expect or want, an answer.

"He was helping me with numbers." Tomas's tone was almost apologetic. He knew it was forbidden to speak in Slovak at school.

"It's against the law, you know."

"I know," Tomas answered, concerned that Andrej knew his secret. *Could Andrej be trusted?* he wondered. On the way back, Tomas held the swaying bucket with two hands and prayed that not a drop would spill.

Andrej and Tomas were not the only ones who knew that the teacher would sometimes speak to his students in Slovak. A mother, meaning no harm, told a friend, and then another. The tale spread throughout the village—the teacher had broken the law.

"He is a kind man," the women gossiped, as they did their laundry at the spring or baked bread at the communal oven. "But foolish to disobey the law." *Very foolish,* thought an old woman who knew that the information would gain her favors with the mayor, who, everyone knew, enforced the laws of the Empire.

Tomas, his body squirming, his foot tapping nervously on the floor beneath his desk, wanted desperately to escape the endless frustration of the work in front of him. He glanced back at the bucket he had filled with water that morning. Andrej was there, glaring at him. A walk to the water bucket was out of the question.

The room was quiet except for the monotony of students reciting a poem in Hungarian. Most of the words were unrecognizable to Tomas. *Why do we need to study poetry? We only work in the fields.*

"Ouch!" It was a muffled complaint from the back of the room. Andrej was tormenting Filip again.

Glad it wasn't me, thought Tomas.

There were horses outside, men's voices, a distraction that many of the children welcomed. Perhaps they were here to talk with the teacher. Maybe they needed to speak to him alone. With a little luck, the teacher would tell them to go home for the rest of the day.

The door burst open, and soldiers stormed into the room. Tomas stopped squirming, his body tense, ready to run.

"Can I help you?" The teacher's voice was calm. "You are frightening the children."

The soldiers did not answer. They shoved the teacher against a wall and tightly bound his hands behind his back.

"Out, get out," another soldier shouted at the students, while he turned over desks and pushed frightened children out of his way. Andrej reached for Mary's hand and pulled her to the door. Tomas sat in his desk, too afraid to move until a soldier pointed a gun at him and shouted, "Get out!" Stumbling over a chair, the boy ran, his vision blurred by tears of fear and rage. They were hurting his teacher, the man who had helped him with his lessons. Somehow, he found his way out of the school and into the street.

The scene before her was ghostly, surreal. The wooden frame of the school, what was left of it, was black and charred. Dense clouds of gray smoke made their way through what had been the roof, while fine particles of black soot and glowing embers carried by the wind threatened every house in the village. The heat from the orange and yellow flames, consuming the desks, chairs, and books, flushed the cheeks of those who struggled to contain the blaze with buckets of water.

Anna, her clothing drenched from sweat, her arms aching, passed a bucket overflowing with water to the woman standing next to her. There was no time to stop, to allow her arms to rest, or to worry about the nausea that welled up into her throat. Her face burned from the heat of the flames, and tears streaked the soot on her cheeks. "Please, God, spare our village," she prayed. "Stefan, be careful." He was too close to the flames, and at times she could not see him through the smoke. "God help us."

It seemed like hours before the flames subsided, and nothing was left of the schoolhouse but smoldering ashes. The exhausted villagers put down their pails and watched the smoking embers of what had been their school.

"Make way. Make way."

"The mayor." There was disdain in their voices as the distraught peasants moved aside. A portly man, dressed in a black, cutaway morning coat with hickory striped trousers and top hat, was making his way through the crowd.

A man whose clothes had been scorched by the flames looked at those around him as he spit on the ground. "Traitor!" the man yelled, ignoring the panic in his wife's eyes. "What? Is he not a traitor?"

The mayor stood in front of what was left of the school. A pompous figure, he wore a large gold medallion, a symbol of his authority. A ribbon—bright red, green, and white—draped across his body from his shoulder to his waist, showed his allegiance to the Kingdom of Hungary. He puffed out his chest and scanned the crowd, looking for anyone who might challenge his authority. He raised his hand for silence.

"Mr. Hodermarszky, the teacher is a subversive," he announced. Pausing for effect he noted, with satisfaction, the dismay and shock on the faces of the peasants who stood before him. "He will receive just punishment." The mayor's eyes flashed with arrogance and defiance. Puffing his chest further, while pulling in his rotund belly, he continued, "his co-conspirators will be sought, and justice will be done. God bless Franz Josef, Emperor of Austria, King of Hungary, and his loyal subjects."

"God bless the emperor," the villagers mumbled. Submission meant survival.

That night, for the first time since Stefan had married Anna, the woman in black filled his dreams. Behind her was a wall of flames, and children were crying. "Why are they crying?" he asked, but she did not answer. "What can I do? How can I save them?" The specter drifted into the flames, and the crying stopped. In the morning he made plans to take his family to America.

Chapter 5 - 1889

The Journey Begins

Anna

It was agreed, just after our son was born, we would go to America. We would not be alone; Katarina and Jan would travel with us. Stefan's cousin Adriana would be there when we arrived. Well, if you must know the truth, when Stefan wasn't around, I cried, and I worried. I was about to be a mother, the thought of taking my child on such a treacherous journey seemed unwise. Could we not wait until the baby was older? I didn't ask the question. I could see that Stefan had made up his mind. He was unwavering in his determination to move his family to America.

We knew little about life in the small patch towns in the anthracite coal region of northeastern Pennsylvania. Heavens, I didn't even know where Pennsylvania was, and I knew less about coal. Adriana's letters assured me all would be well. Her husband promised to get Stefan a job in the mines, and the company would give us a house we could rent. I would have a home of my own. Perhaps going to America would be a good thing. At least, that is what I tried to convince myself.

Stephen, my little boy, was almost two when we were ready to begin the journey to our new home. Oh, I cannot begin to tell you how hard it was to leave our family, our friends, our home. But we were beginning a new life, and as it turned out, the day we were saying good-bye to our friends and family was the same day we met a young man who grew to be a very cherished part of our lives.

Emil

The green grass of the pasture was glistening with droplets of moisture, remnants of the afternoon shower that had banished the summer heat. The black stallion snorted and turned his head toward Emil. "The game must continue," the stallion seemed to say as he began to gallop. Emil, now a strong, agile sixteen-year-old, was ready for him. Together, the horse and the young man raced around the edges of the pasture, sharing a moment of friendly competition.

"Bence, I need to stop." Emil bent over, his hands on his knees, he was out of breath. But the stallion, not ready to rest, reared and stomped. "Shall we dance, then?" Emil said while hopping on one foot and then the other. The horse mimicked him, lifting his right leg in the air and then the left. The game continued until it was time for Emil to return to the stable. "I'm sorry, Bence, but the master needs his horse for his afternoon ride. I can't play any longer." Bence, understanding that the game was over, resumed grazing.

It had been six years since the stable master had hired ten-year-old Emil to muck the stables, sweep the tack room, wash buckets, and polish brass. The scrawny boy with the tangled hair and bare feet had grown into a strong, confident young man. He still mucked the stables, but now he groomed the horses, worked with the trainer, and, when needed, tacked the horses.

Emil did not resent the limits imposed on him by his station, and he no longer aspired to be a soldier in the cavalry. *Someday, I might be stable master,* he thought, but there was no hurry. For now, he would groom the horses, fulfill the requests of the family he served, and spend time with Bence.

"Good morning, Laci." The silver-gray mare lifted her head, her ears perked forward as Emil called out to her. "It is a beautiful day today." Emil leaned over the gate to her stall and offered Laci a carrot. "There is a guest at the manor who wants to go for a ride on the trails near the stream. You know the one." The mare nodded her head and neighed as though she understood. "You must behave today; the rider is a young lady. I do not know if she understands horses. It will be up to you to keep her safe." Emil's voice was soothing as he brushed her coat until it gleamed. He gathered the soft brown leather side saddle and the ladies' bridle. Laci patiently acquiesced as Emil placed the saddle on her back and tightened the girth.

"All right, my sweet girl, you are ready." Emil lead the horse to the courtyard and positioned her next to the mounting block. They waited, Emil held the reins, Laci stood at his side. There was laughter, loud and deep, the laughter of men enjoying each other's company. A woman spoke and Emil recognized the lady of the manor. "Suzanna, after your ride I would like to talk with you and your mother about plans for a small get-together with friends. Perhaps this Friday."

"Yes, Auntie, that will be very enjoyable." Emil tried not to listen. He was expected to stand, invisible, unnoticed until he was needed. Years ago, Emil had mastered the art of being the perfect servant, stable boy, and groom.

As the girl approached the horse, her blue satin dress softly, almost imperceptibly, touched his arm. The air smelled of roses. Laci moved, agitated, and Emil petted and soothed her with whispered encouragement.

"What is her name?" the girl asked as she stroked Laci's nose.

"Laci, Miss." For a moment, a very brief moment, Emil brazenly allowed his eyes to look at the girl. He inhaled. She was the most beautiful girl he had ever seen. Her royal blue satin riding habit shimmered in the afternoon sunlight, and there was a small hat with a blue silk ribbon perched precariously on ringlets of flaxen blonde hair.

Emil, regaining his composure, held the horse steady as Suzanna placed her left foot on the uppermost step of the stone block, put her right leg on the leg rest, and positioned herself on the back of the horse. *She knows how to ride.*

When she reached for the reins her fingers touched Emil's hand and lingered there. Her green eyes smiled down at him, and an unexpected shiver coursed through his body. No longer interested in him, she clicked, and turned Laci toward the gate. Emil watched, puzzled by the girl's actions and concerned about his body's response.

That night Emil was troubled as he struggled to push away images of shimmering blue satin, wisps of blonde curls flowing down a willowy neck, moisture that lingered on delicate pink lips. His body responded, and he could not resist the temptation. In the morning, he resolved his sin would not be repeated.

Suzanna nestled in the oversize canopy bed; her head rested on overstuffed down pillows. The room she occupied in her uncle's manor house was "satisfactory," she wrote in a letter to a friend. "The walls are a dark maroon. I prefer the airy blue and white colors of my room at home. The bed is comfortable and when the maid pulls back the drapes in the morning sunlight fills the room."

A knock on the door and Irene, Suzanna's lady's maid, entered with a glass of warm milk and a biscuit on a silver tray. "Good morning, my lady." Irene curtsied and closed the door.

"Good morning, Irene. Place the tray over there." Suzanna pointed to an elaborately carved table next to her bed. "I wish to stay in bed a while longer."

"Yes, my lady. Shall I open the curtains? It is a beautiful day."

"Please."

"Your aunt has inquired if you will join her and your mother for breakfast this morning."

"Irene, that would be such a bore. I would so much rather go to the stables to see the horses." Suzanna ignored the slight look of disapproval on the servant's face. "Please give my regrets to Mama and Auntie." There was no doubt her mother would speak to her about her rudeness, but this morning she could not listen to their talk of balls, weddings, babies, and scandals. She had been thinking of the groom who had seemed so taken with her yesterday. *I would like to see him again,* she thought, smiling at the memory of how he had looked at her. *Goodness knows how bored I am here, and how much I miss my friends.*

"I will wear my black boots today," Suzanna informed Irene. "And the green velvet vest with the black skirt."

"Yes, miss. And, should you want to go out, I will see that the bonnet with the emerald green ribbons is ready."

"That will be perfect, Irene. Thank you. The groom who assisted me yesterday, do you know his name?"

"Emil, I think. Yes, it must have been Emil."

"He is rather handsome, don't you think?"

"Yes, miss, he is handsome." Irene frowned ever so slightly. "Of course, he is just a stable boy."

Emil had a plan. He would avoid seeing Suzanna. If she needed a horse to ride, there were other grooms. When she came to the pasture he would politely bow and return to his work. Eventually, she would leave. Life would return to normal. With unusual intensity, he pulled the brush over Laci's rump, and she shook him away. "I am so sorry, my girl," he soothed the horse and tried to push thoughts of Suzanna from his mind.

"Good morning, Emil." Emil almost dropped the brush he was using to groom Laci. His body responded to the sound of Suzanna's voice in forbidden ways. *Why, why are you here?* He wanted to shout the words as he continued to stroke Laci refusing to look at Suzanna.

"Good morning, Miss." He glanced at her and his resolve vanished. She looked radiant, otherworldly, as the morning sun glowed around her and specks of sunlight shimmered in her flaxen hair.

"I brought some sugar for Laci." She lifted her skirt just enough to show the shape of her ankle and entered the stable. Suzanna walked up to Laci and the sleeve of her dress touched Emil's arm. She giggled as the horse took the sugar from her hand, and Emil felt his heart racing.

"Will you bring her to me this afternoon?" Suzanna looked at him with those eyes he found so captivating. The smell of roses surrounded her, and he wanted to reach out and touch her. He backed away from her, a temptress in the guise of an angel.

"Yes, miss." He bowed, hoping she did not see his discomfort.

Emil brought Laci to Suzanna that afternoon. He needed to see her.

It became a ritual, a visit to the pasture in the morning and a ride in the afternoon. Whenever their hands were close, Suzanna's fingers lingered on his, and he found it more and more difficult to pull away. She asked him questions, first about his horses, and then, more intimately, about himself.

"There isn't much to tell," was his usual reply, but on one afternoon, while they sat on the pasture fence, he told her the story of how he came to be at the manor.

"What a brave little boy you were."

"Y-you are the most beautiful girl I have ever s-seen," he stammered, appalled at his growing boldness.

"I need to go now," she said while gazing into his eyes. "Will you help me down?"

Emil, his hands on her waist, lowered her to the ground. Their eyes met, and her lips brushed his. With a smile, she turned and walked back to the manor house. *I will be banished in disgrace,* he thought as he watched her walk away. *My future here is over. There will be no forgiveness.*

Hastily, being careful not to take anything that belonged to the manor, he prepared to leave. He said his goodbyes to Laci and the stallion and felt the pain of loss. Without a glance toward the manor house, he began to walk down the dirt road. Like so many others, he would go to America and start a new life.

Departure

A soft red glow in the sky announced the arrival of a day free from rain, the smell of early spring flowers filled the air. Chickens clucked, pecking the ground, oblivious to the momentous events about to take place. A rooster crowed.

It was the year of our Lord 1889, and the village, like so many others in Eastern Europe, was preparing to send more of its young people on the long journey to America. Poverty, land shortages, conscription, and oppression drove them from their homes. The promise of jobs and the hope of a better future pulled them to America. Those left behind would anxiously await letters from their family and friends who made the journey. They knew that most would never return.

A weathered farm cart, designed for the transport of hay and grain, waited in front of the church. The driver of the cart appeared to be asleep as he loosely held the reins of the bony, sway-backed old mare who nibbled with her long teeth on the sparse vegetation. The driver was taking villagers over the mountains to the train that would take them to the Port of Bremen. This was not the first time he made this journey, and it would not be his last.

"Hello."

Emil startled the man, who looked up and frowned at the intruder who had interrupted his nap. "What ya want, boy? Can't ya see I'm busy restin'?"

"Are you going North?" Emil asked with his easy smile.

"Yup."

"Then I'm going with ya."

"Oh?"

"Yup." Emil mimicked the driver as he took an apple core from his pocket and offered it to the horse. The mare's wrinkled lips greedily took the apple, while her droopy eyes warily watched for any potential threat. Her ears twitched back and forth, discouraging an attack from an adventurous fly.

"Know your way around horses, do you?"

"Yup. Does your horse have a name?" The horse nibbled at Emil's hands, searching for another treat.

"Lenka."

"Hello, Lenka."

"So, you want to go North?"

"Yup. I'm going to America."

"It'll cost ya."

"I have money," Emil said with a confident smile.

"Show me."

"Here." Emil took a coin from his pocket.

"Got more than that?"

"Nope," Emil lied. Over the years he had stowed away the few coins that were given to him by guests of the manor.

"That will do, then." The man grabbed the coin before it could disappear back into the stranger's pocket. *Where did the boy come from? It's a wonder he had any money at all. Did he steal it? His clothes are decent. Not a peasant. Probably worked* at the manor house. *Was he a runaway? Does he need to sneak across the border? It's not my concern.*

"Do you have a name?"

"Emil, sir."

"Make yourself useful, Emil. Help with the trunks. You can sit on them."

"Yes, sir. Thank you, sir."

Doors creaked open, and the quiet of daybreak was banished with the laughter of children, the chatter of women, and the shouts of men who had work to do. They were there, at this early hour, to say goodbye to cherished members of their small community. The entire village would witness, with sorrow, the departure of the young people seeking a better life elsewhere.

Anna, with the help of her mother, had packed a suitcase with clothing for Stefan, a wicker basket with supplies for the journey, and a weathered pine trunk with everything else. Adriana had sent instructions. "For the journey, you will need bread, lard, sugar, and vinegar, as well as a spoon and a bowl for each of you. For your new home, take pictures out of their frames. Bring the pictures with you but leave the frames at home. Take the iron, but do not waste space on bedding."

Stefan, balancing the trunk on his shoulder, and his brother Marek, carrying a cardboard suitcase and a wicker basket, emerged from the house. Anna, holding Stephen on her hip, followed them. She carried a satchel containing steamship tickets, instructions from Adriana, and supplies for her toddler son. Women wailed at the sight of the young family ready to make the journey that would take them away.

An old woman with watery gray eyes, her wrinkled old hands trembling, held out a tiny package as Anna walked past her. "This will keep you safe, dear child," she said, pressing what appeared to be a piece of folded fabric into Anna's hands. Anna recognized the dingy yellow linen cloth edged with lace that was worn and frayed. Inside was a sealed prayer card containing a relic that had touched the clothing of Saint Stephen. Anna pressed the sacred cloth to her lips and closed her eyes. *Saint Stephen pray for us.*

"I will miss you, dear aunt," she said while cupping the woman's hand in her own. "Thank you for this precious gift."

Another woman handed her a jar of preserved pears. "Your little one will be hungry."

Anna, holding back tears, embraced the woman. "I will write, dear Barbela. You will always be in my prayers." Walking slowly to the wagon, Anna nodded and tried to smile at each villager who came to wish them a safe journey.

Who is that? A young man was helping Stefan with the trunk. *A stranger.* She watched him for a moment and wondered where he came from and where he was going. *Well, we are all in God's hands.*

"Ready?" Stefan asked when his wife and son reached the wagon. "Hand Stephen to me." The little boy giggled as his father lifted him into the wagon.

I'm ready. Anna reached for her husband's outstretched hands. She had prayed, cried, and spent long hours talking with her mother. *I am ready now.* She settled onto the bench and held her little boy in her lap. Anna glanced at Katarina, sitting on the other side of the wagon, and their eyes met in understanding. Even though it was time to leave, they were comforted by the fact that they had each other.

Katarina, a mother traveling with four young children, looked remarkably composed. Focused on her children she did not have time to be concerned about herself. Her infant son, Edward, was asleep in her arms, while Cecelia sat next to her clinging to her doll. Katarina had given Jan, her husband, clear instructions on the management of their boys. Tomas, now nine years old, and Alex, who was a precocious five-year-old, would need diligent supervision from their father.

"Sit them on either side of you," she had directed her husband. "They will get restless, and it will be up to you to prevent any disasters. I will look after Cecelia and the baby."

As Katarina anticipated, the boys, bursting with excitement, found ways to create minor disruptions.

"Matka, Tomas pushed me."

"I did not. I was trying to help you."

"No, you weren't!"

"Stop, sit here." Jan pushed Tomas down on the bench.

"You, sit here!" Alex found himself sitting next to his father, who was holding his hand firmly. Tomas was on the other side, a look of annoyance on his face.

The restless boys, sitting on the hard bench of the wagon, found it difficult to control their bodies. Their feet banged noisily against the side of the wagon until the driver turned to them with a look that filled their young souls with fear.

Tomas eventually settled down and began to think about the adventures ahead. He looked down the road curving like the body of a snake through the valley eventually being swallowed by the snow-covered mountains in the distance. He had never been as far as those mountains. *Would the flimsy wagon be able to make it through the mountain pass?* The boy pictured himself as a hero, single-handedly pushing the wagon up a steep incline. His father would shake his hand, and his mother would look at him with pride.

The daydreams continued, and there was the hint of a smile on the young boy's face. The train, the Port of Bremen, the steamship, the ocean, America, these wonders excited him. The boys in the village had spent hours perusing brochures and posters encouraging emigrants to come to America. His friends had looked at Tomas with envy. Someday, they hoped, they would ride a wagon through those mountains and go to America.

There was sadness in his mother's eyes, and he wondered why. They would be free from the confines of their village. The Magyars could no longer torment them. Perhaps he could even go to school, although he could not imagine why he would want to. He would go to work and give his mother the money he earned. Thinking of the hunger pangs that were so familiar, he imagined the feasts his mother would prepare with the funds that would supply a bounty for the family. He had been waiting for this moment for over a year.

Saying Goodbye

Stefan, looking down at his hands, sat next to his wife on the rough bench in the cart. He did not want his wife to know he still had doubts. But Anna knew and in a moment of intimacy and understanding, she placed her hand on his.

The moment of departure was near when Anna's father approached the cart.

"Take care of my daughter," he admonished Stefan, not for the first time.

"I will care for her, love her, and protect her," Stefan promised.

"And my grandson."

"I promise."

"Remember always that we love all of you."

"Father, we will remember." Anna touched her father's face as she spoke to him for the last time.

"Matka," Anna said while brushing a tear from her mother's face. "You will always be here in my heart."

One by one, members of Anna's family approached the cart, giving her small gifts of remembrance. Her little brother, Nathaniel, gave her a small wooden soldier. "For Stephen," he said almost shyly as he handed it to his sister.

"Stefan!" Lucia had been watching, waiting her turn to say goodbye.

"Lucia." Stefan reached over the edge of the cart to grasp his sister's outreached hand.

"Stefan, I will miss you and your family. You will not be here for my wedding." Her voice broke at the thought.

"Lucia, you and Karol will have a blessed life together. Take care of each other. You know that I love you and you will always be in my heart."

Karol put a protective arm around Lucia, pulling her gently away from the cart. *Karol will be a good husband for her.*

Stefan spotted his brother, Marek, with his halting gait, making his way through the crowd. *I made him a cripple, and now I am leaving him alone to care for the family,* Stefan thought, watching his brother. Guilt pierced his heart, and for a moment, he thought he saw the woman in black watching him from a distance.

"You will write," Marek ordered, his voice harsh when he reached the cart. He understood the forces that were pushing his brother and his family from their village, as well as the promises for a better life that were pulling them to America. "Terezia and I will look after Mother. You must not worry."

"Thank you, Marek, for all you do." Stefan struggled not to show any emotion as he said a final goodbye to his brother.

The parish priest, followed by a procession of altar boys, approached the wagon. Everyone bowed their heads as he began to pray.

"In the name of the Father, and of the Son, and of the Holy Ghost," he began. "O Almighty and Merciful Father, guide and protect these young families as they begin their arduous journey. Shield them from all evil, and from sin. May the blessings of Christ and his Blessed Mother be upon you forever." Gossamer clouds of smoky, pungent incense rose from the gold thurible, drifting to the heavens as the priest walked slowly around the cart, blessing the occupants and their belongings.

"Amen," all the villagers and travelers prayed in unison when the priest had finished the blessing.

The cart began to move, and the villagers backed away. A wail of grief from the elder women reflected the pain felt by the families being separated. Church bells began to ring. Children, caught up in the excitement, ran alongside the wagon, laughing and wishing the travelers a good journey. Anna looked at Katarina holding her infant. The women smiled bravely with their eyes.

The old horse strained to pull her heavy burden along the rutted dirt road, taking them toward the snow-covered mountains in the distance. Anna glanced at the wooden church with its linden trees out front, and she smiled with the memory of the day her Stefan had awkwardly watched her. *Will there be linden trees in America?* she wondered.

Her eyes lingered on the statue of the Virgin Mary that stood at the entrance to the church. The statue had been carved from a linden tree by her grandfather when she was still a little girl. The month of May, with its blue sky and fields of spring flowers, was Blessed Mary's month. For a moment, Anna pictured herself as a nine-year-old child participating in the crowning of the Virgin for the first time. Her mother had made her a new dress and had embroidered her apron with large yellow and blue flowers. "Blue, the Blessed Virgin's color," her mother reminded her daughter as she tied a large blue bow around Anna's waist. There were flowers everywhere. All the girls in the procession had flowers in their hair and carried a small bouquet to place at the feet of the Virgin. That year Katarina had the honor of leading the procession. She carried a wreath of spring flowers that would be placed on the head of the Virgin as the girls sang their tribute to Mary. The soprano voices of the young girls echoed through the village.

> *O, Mary, we crown thee with blossoms today!*
> *Queen of the Angels, Queen of the May.*

How happy I was, thought Anna. *How innocent.* The cart continued its journey, and the church with the precious statue, along with its memories, were left behind. The road meandered past lush fields and quiet valleys, places where they had labored for most of their lives. Hollyhocks and poppies lined the road.

"Stephen, my son, I will not let you forget where you come from." Stephen watched everything with wide eyes and the curiosity of a toddler, only smiling at the soft words he did not understand. "Look, Stephen!" Anna was pointing to a stork's nest in the chimney of a thatch-roofed cottage.

"*Vták*," her little boy replied, pointing as the stork stood in the nest.

"That's right, Vták."

There was a garden. It was filled with tender young shoots, reaching for the warm sun, promising a source of much-needed nourishment for the family that lived in the cottage.

"We will have a garden like that in America," she informed her husband.

"I am sure we will," he replied, hoping his voice held a confidence he did not feel.

The church bells were still ringing as the road took them over a hill and the village could no longer be seen. Before them were the mountains, and beyond, Poprad. From there a train would take them to Cracow, then to Berlin, and finally, to the port of Bremen. Anna had never ridden on a train, sailed on a ship, or ventured farther than ten miles from her village. She had never seen a body of water larger than the small stream near her home and could not imagine a city like Bremen or New York.

The stranger who was sitting on a trunk in the center of the cart, began to sing of longing and lost love. More tears were shed, and even the children were quiet as they listened to the boy's beautiful voice. But the melancholy songs soon ended, replaced with songs that caused laughter, lightening the spirits of the travelers.

Reaching Poprad the driver left them at the train station, taking with him their last link to home. The train rides from Poprad to Crakow, to Berlin, and finally to Bremen were tiring but uneventful. Sleeping on the trains and eating food the village women had packed in baskets helped to pass the time. Children, excited at first by the newness of everything, grew tired and restless, challenging their mothers' patience.

Jan and Stefan smoked their pipes and talked about the ship that would take them to America. They talked about the coal mines and the owners who lived like the aristocrats and landowners they knew so well. If there was concern about working in the darkness of the mines, deep inside the earth, it was never shared.

The women could not imagine the vastness of the ocean or the immense size of the ships.

"Katarina, they say there will be days, maybe weeks when we will not see land. There will be nothing around us except the ocean."

"Oh, Anna, we will have each other, and God will protect us."

"I dreamt that Stephan fell over the railing of the ship. His arms reached for me as he was swallowed by the dark waves that engulfed the ship. Katarina, I cannot tell Stefan, but I am afraid."

"The ocean will be beautiful, majestic," Katarina tried to reassure her friend. "We will see the sky reaching to the horizons. Imagine how beautiful the sunsets will be without mountains to hide its glory. Don't worry, Anna. The ship is large and the captain skilled." Anna was not reassured. Katarina was not sure she had faith in her own words.

The boy, who had been a stranger, now proved to be a welcome companion. They learned his name was Emil. His songs and stories of the horses he had trained provided entertainment in the long hours in the cart and on the trains. Anna decided she liked him and would watch over him. After all, he was traveling alone without his family. *Is there anyone who misses him?*

Anna

Somehow, we survived the wagon ride over the mountains, the hours on the train to Bremen, and the ocean voyage. But our ordeal was not yet over.

Castle Garden, have you heard of it? No, maybe not. Ellis Island was not yet open. So, where is Castle Garden? It's in New York City, a place called Battery Park. I'm sure I didn't know that at the time. It wasn't really a castle, you know, not like the castles in Europe, but it was very big. We slept in a boarding house that night, and the next morning a ferry took us to a place called Jersey City. From there, a train owned by the Pardee Mining Company took us to Ario.

The Voyage

The first part of their journey was over. The emigrants had arrived in the port of Bremerhaven and were ready to board the steamship that would take them to America. Anna, despite her resolve to be strong for her family, was nervous. The ship towered over her, its massive hulk dotted with tiny windows, and black smoke billowed from its stacks. She wondered how they would live inside the monstrous ship for a week or more. The young mother who had lived her whole life in a small, rural village had no way to know what a ship's deck would be like, or the tiny, cramped compartments where they would sleep. *How would she feed her family? Above all, how would she keep her son safe?* The fear of the unknown caused her stomach to churn.

People, strangers, were standing too close to her, pushing and shoving her as they moved closer to the ship's ramp. It was almost time to board. The noise around her was deafening, men from the ship were shouting orders, women were scolding their children, birds were screaming overhead. She closed her eyes and imagined she was back in the quiet fields of home. Only knowing that Stefan was close by reassured her. She heard his voice. He was talking to Katarina's husband, Jan.

"They say there is a storm on the Atlantic."

"It will be over before we get there."

"Hopefully."

Anna clutched her son, wrapping her shawl around him. For a moment, only his hair and hazel eyes were visible above her shawl. She was afraid he would be crushed by the people or lost somewhere on the wharf. "Lost," she said to no one, suppressing the tears that were forming in her eyes.

"Down!" Her son's command brought her back to the moment. The little boy was restless, wanting to run free. He wiggled and squirmed, attempting to leave the tight grip of his mother's arms. His chubby finger was pointing to the ground. "Down!" Anna held him tighter, not willing to let go.

"I'll take him," Stefan offered, reaching for his son and lifting him onto his shoulder.

Katarina was not too far away, struggling to manage an infant, a toddler, and two rambunctious boys.

"Tomas, come here, right now!" Katarina's oldest boy was wandering too close to the edge of the dock, and his younger brother Alex was not far behind.

"Jan, get Alex!" she called to her husband in frustration. Jan was leisurely lighting his pipe unaware of the antics of his sons.

"Alex! Stop! Jan!" Katarina called, exasperated. At least Cecelia was holding onto her mother's skirt and the baby was content in her arms.

"I've got him." It was Emil who grabbed Alex just as the boy looked over the edge of the dock.

"Thanks be to God!" Katarina said with relief as Emil took charge of the two boys.

The wait was over, steerage passengers, with their bags and boxes, trunks and suitcases, walked up the gangplank and onto the main deck of the ship that would take them to America. It took some time to get the families, which now included Emil, settled into the compartments reserved for steerage passengers. Children climbed on the bunks, making a game of their new surroundings. Hungry babies cried to be fed, hampering their mothers' determined attempts to maintain order. But when the ship's whistle blew, and the engines began to rumble, all games and efforts to unpack supplies ended in a rush to reach the steerage deck.

Music wafted down from the upper-class decks, and confetti spilled through the air as everyone waved to those waiting on the dock. Young men tossed their hats in the air, and older men slapped each other on the back in friendly camaraderie. But many of the women in the crowd were somber, clinging to their babies and wondering what the future would hold.

The families quickly settled into a comfortable routine, walking the deck, napping on their bunks, or spending time in the recreation room. Older boys explored the ship and amused themselves playing card games and flirting with the young girls who pretended to ignore them. Husbands and single men met in a room reserved for them. They gambled, drank whiskey, and smoked their cigars. The women tended to the children and talked quietly among themselves.

This brief respite of calm ended abruptly as the ship crossed the North Sea. The passengers watched as black, billowy clouds formed on the horizon, and the ocean waves turned dark and ominous with their white tips crashing against the side of the ship. Nausea and weakness spread throughout the steerage deck. Passengers crept into their bunks and prayed for the storm to pass.

Anna and Katarina came prepared. Mrs. Ciernik gave them potions, herbs, and creams and instructions on how to use them. "To prevent sickness caused by the rocking ship make a tea from these herbs. For pain use these soothing creams. One spoonful of this potion can be used to reduce fever." Anna and Katarina felt confident in Mrs. Ciernik's remedies.

Rosaries, blessed by the priest were ever ready, and the women had faith that God would protect them. But it was not enough. One by one, the rocking ship sent nearly everyone to their berths.

When the storm subsided, sickness was replaced with boredom. Jan and Stefan left the care of the children to the women, while they occupied themselves with games of poker in the smoke-filled room reserved for men. Anna and Katarina played with their babies on the steerage deck. They laughed at Stephen, as a sudden tilt of the deck caused him to fall on his well-padded bottom. His tears of surprise were wiped away by his mother's kisses. Katarina's little girl, Cecilia, made a friend, and they engaged in a quiet game of make-believe.

Emil took charge of Tomas and Alex, and the three explored the ship, or at least, the places open to steerage passengers. "I want to be a sea captain," Tomas proclaimed, watching the waves hit the side of their ship. "I will see the world."

"A chef," Alex declared as they explored the huge kitchens. "If I am a chef, I will never be hungry." When the three adventurers attempted to invade the boiler room they were summarily returned to their cabin.

Three days into the voyage, sickness of another sort began to spread among the children in the steerage compartments. Fevers racked their tiny bodies, and there was no way to relieve their distress or reassure the frightened mothers. The sounds of crying babies who could not be comforted prevented parents from sleeping, while other children were listless and quiet, except for a moan or a whimper in their feverish sleep.

"We have Mrs. Ciernik's creams, herbs and potions. Our children will be safe."

"Let's pray the rosary." Gathering their husbands and children the families knelt together and prayed.

Tomas was the first of Katarina's children to come down with the sickness. He was flushed and hot with fever and complained of a headache. Katarina put him in his bunk and rubbed Mrs. Ciernik's cream on his neck and chest. He drank the tea offered, followed by one spoonful of the potion. Tomas was too sick to complain.

Alex, still healthy, accepted the tea but protested when he was confined to his bunk. By morning, he too was consumed with fever.

Cecelia, Edward, and Stephen seemed to be safe from the fever and the mothers thanked the Lord for the protection He had given them.

While Katarina nursed her sons, Anna took the other children to the steerage deck, hoping the fresh air would keep the sickness away. She held Katarina's baby in her arms as she watched Stephen and Cecelia play. "Please keep them safe," she whispered while fingering her rosary.

Finally, after seven days at sea, they entered New York Harbor. The two families stood at the railing of the ship. Katarina held Edward in her arms, while Cecelia clung to her skirts. Jan held the hands of his two rambunctious boys. Anna and Stefan stood close together with Stephen on his father's shoulders.

"Lady," Stephen said, pointing to the Statue of Liberty.

"Yes, Stephen, Lady. She is welcoming us to our new home." Anna said a prayer of gratitude as she saw Castle Garden, the circular sandstone building that served as an immigrant processing center. For now, her little family was safe.

A Coal Train

The twelfth of April 1889 was a dismal and dreary day. A thick veil of gray clouds covered the sky, while the sun struggled to make an appearance. The ordeal of Castle Garden was behind them, and now, droplets of saltwater stung the cheeks of the immigrants huddled on the deck of the ferry crossing New

York Harbor. They were going to a town called Jersey City, where they would board trains that would take them on the next leg of their journey.

Women pulled their shawls tighter around their shoulders and were thankful for the babushkas that covered their hair. Hope and anticipation, mixed with anxiety and fear, were present on their weather-beaten faces. The men pulled their caps farther over their eyes, their pipes and cigars clenched between their teeth. Young children huddled behind their mothers' skirts, while the older children watched from vantage points near the railings.

Anna listened to the voices around her. She recognized some of the words and dialects—Russian, German, Slovak, and Hungarian were familiar, but others were a mystery to her. Still, there was a common language shared by all. Unspoken words, a knowing gesture connected these strangers who had left everything behind to start a new life in America. The women smiled at each other with empathy as one rocked an infant and another struggled to contain a restless four-year-old. The men shared the names of their destinations. They were here to work in the coal mines, steel mills, and factories in America. There was no need to say more.

Katarina and her family were not with them. They were detained at Castle Garden. Cecelia had a fever. "She will need to stay for observation," her frantic parents were informed. Anna watched the family being taken away by nurses. There was no explanation, no time for goodbyes, just a final pleading expression on Katarina's face as she looked back to where Anna and Stefan were waiting.

Emil leaned on the railing of the ferry and pointed to the train terminal in front of him. As always, he made friends quickly, and the gang of young men who stood next to him had already formed a bond. Free of the worries that plagued men with families, they were all on a grand adventure. *He will do well in America,* Anna thought, not for the first time.

The ferry slowed as it approached their destination, the terminal for the Lehigh Valley Railroad. The air was thick with smoke from the nearby coal-burning factories, and Anna coughed. Her eyes burned from the smoke, and her anxiety caused a tightness to grow in her chest. "Holy Mary, help us," she prayed as they prepared to disembark the ferry.

Rough-looking men with weathered faces guided the ferry to the dock, yelling commands in a language Anna did not understand. A child began to cry as the men and women gathered their belongings.

An agent from A. Pardee Brothers Coal Company stood near the dock, looking bored. Another group of Hunkies were headed to the coal mines near Hazleton, Pennsylvania. He would take them to the coal train as arranged by the company. The train would take them to their destinations, the coal patch towns around Hazleton. He often remarked to friends about the efficiency of the arrangement. The trains carried coal from the coal fields to the city. A passenger car was attached to the empty train which carried the workers to the patch towns.

As usual, he expected the people in his charge to not understand anything he told them. Blank stares, perhaps a shake of the head "yes" or "no" would be the only responses to his verbal instructions. He relied on gestures to show them where to go. Checking his pocket watch, he thought of the warm beer and pastrami sandwich that awaited him.

"Quickly! Move quickly!" he shouted as his charges disembarked from the ferry. Perhaps if he shouted louder, they would understand. "Over there." With a stern, almost angry voice he gestured for them to stand near a sign that read <u>A. Pardee Brothers Coal Company.</u>

The agent watched the motley assemblage make their way to the sign. *Stupid, they are so stupid. Why bring them here? Too many already. Jews, Italians, Poles and now the Hunkies. Look where they live, those filthy slums in the city. The smell, sickness, the noise. You can't even understand what they are saying. Enough!*

Yet, here they were, and it was his job to get them to those cars. Checking a list of names, satisfied that all were accounted for, the agent pointed to a door of the terminal and signaled the immigrants to follow him. Stefan rebalanced the weight of the trunk on his shoulders and picked up the suitcase with his right hand. Anna positioned Stephen on her hip and carried her satchel and wicker basket with her right hand.

With a mixture of excited anticipation and fearful trepidation, the men, women, and children made their way to the door.

The agent of the coal company led them through the terminal and outside, past the passenger trains, and toward the tracks that held the freight trains. It was a coal train that would take them to Hazleton. The train that had brought coal from the mines of Pennsylvania to New York City now would make a loop back to the mines with a passenger car attached.

Stefan frowned, and Anna looked anxious as the passenger trains were left behind and only freight trains were before them. Trains made of empty cubes on wheels covered with dingy, black soot formed bleak, depressing chains as far as the eye could see. On other trains, the cubes contained uncovered mounds of glistening black coal. *Surely, we will not be riding in an open box.* Anna could not speak her fear as she held Stephen against her bosom.

Everything was covered with coal dust, the ground, the rails, even the faces and clothing of the men who were unloading the coal cars. All that remained of vegetation looked dark, miserable, smothered. Thin patches of grass struggled to survive on the barren landscape. A single white flower on a tall stem held its head high, defiantly challenging anyone not to notice its majesty. Barren, dark, the drab landscape was very different from the villages they had left behind. For a moment Anna closed her eyes and pictured the blue sky and endless fields of home. *I will find strength in the memories.* She struggled to keep up with the man who was leading the little assemblage over the tracks and around the coal cars.

They were ignored by the laborers unloading coal from the trains, and the immigrants did not understand the coarse language of the workers as they passed. In time, they would recognize the derogatory word, "Hunkies." To some, these new immigrants were inferior to others who had come before. The way they dressed, their broken English, the poor, crowded homes where they lived, all attested to their inferior status. They were not Americans. They were not welcome.

The noise was deafening. Men were shouting unrecognizable commands, while train engines rumbled, and train brakes squealed. A loud blast from a train farther down the tracks announced its arrival.

Anna covered the ears of her now-frightened son, sheltering him with her shawl. She was tired. She wanted to sit and feed her baby, to close her eyes and imagine, for a moment, that she was safe in her mother's home.

Two men, walking with authority, met them. They spoke to the agent who had overseen them, and, satisfied, the men waved to the immigrants to follow.

They walked, the small assemblage of men, women, and children, over train tracks, around a steam locomotive, and past cars filled with coal. Anna's arms ached. She wanted to rest, to put Stephen down for just a moment. The handle of the suitcase cut into her hand.

"Let me help you," offered Emil. He had been occupied with a young girl he had met on the ferry when he noticed how tired Anna looked.

"Thank you." Anna smiled, handing the suitcase to Emil.

"We are almost there, Anna."

"Yes, almost there."

Reaching the train, Anna juggled Stephen on her hip and nearly tripped on her skirts, as she climbed the stairs to the platform. Stefan, adjusting the trunk on his shoulder, followed her. The family found two seats near the back of the car. Like all the others, they were covered with coal dust. Stefan reached for his son and, smiling at the now sleepy boy, placed him on his lap and stroked his hair. "My good boy," he said as the child rested his head on his father's shoulder. Anna settled into the seat near the window. *Is this how it is to be?* she wondered as she used her hands to wipe away some of the grime on the window.

A whistle sounded and with a jolt the train started to move. Couplings rattled, steam and smoke erupted from the engine, as the train picked up speed. Fearing the unknown, yet anxious to get to her new home, Anna watched the changing landscape. The city was left behind, replaced with farms and small villages. The countryside was not much different from the home she had left behind. The train passed a small hamlet with a church towering over the houses. Anna thought with a sigh of relief, *Maybe I can live here.*

She glanced at her husband and son. *They look so alike with their sandy-colored hair and hazel eyes.* Exhausted, lulled by the clickety-clack of the train wheels on the railroad track, she lowered her head onto Stefan's shoulder. The musty smell of his wool coat mixed with the smell of tobacco was familiar and comforting. Stefan placed his arm around her and drew her closer. Feeling the strength of her husband's body close to hers, lulled by the rhythm of the train, Anna fell asleep.

**1889-1897
America**

Chapter 6 - 1889

Ario - A Coal Patch Town

Anna

Ario was our home. We raised our family there. Ario was what they called a "patch" town. Coal companies built them. They owned the towns, and they owned us.

When we arrived that April in 1889, there was one main road and a few alleys branching off here and there. The town boasted a school, a church, and a Company Store. Was I happy in Ario? We raised seven children there and buried four. Life was hard, but there were many moments of joy that I will always cherish.

I was lonely those first few months. I missed my family, my mother's voice calling for the children and Stefan's sister-in-law singing to her baby. They were all so far away. The house was silent when Stefan was at work and Stephen was asleep.

Katarina and her family were eventually released from Castle Garden and joined us in Ario. We met at the church or at the well, but Katarina was busy with her children and chores. There was little time to visit.

So how did I manage in those early days? Adriana! She was family, Stefan's cousin, and always willing to help. There was so much to learn about life in a coal town. Remember, I could not speak or understand the language. I could not read or write in English. Adriana showed me how to buy on credit at the company store, and how to sign my name in the ledger. In later years, when times were good, she helped me open a savings account at the Pardee, Markle & Grier Bank in Hazleton. Imagine, a woman with a bank account! How important, how American! Without Adriana, life would have been very bleak indeed. But I was young and strong, and the work needed to be done.

Our home was in the Slovak section of Ario. In its way, that was a comfort, since the sounds and the smells reminded us of *home. The Hungarians lived farther down the street, not far from the Lithuanians. We didn't much care for the Hungarians, the Magyars, and they didn't like us much either. The Italians, well, they lived in an alley farther up the hill. They ate strange foods—lots of tomatoes. We preferred cabbage. The Americans, those who spoke English and were born here, mostly Irish, I think, did not bother with any of us. We were all "foreigners" to them.*

What was it like to work in the mines? I only know what I saw. The men came home covered in mud, blood, and coal dust. They coughed and spit bloody phlegm tinged with black soot. Strong, brave men they were to enter the dark caverns deep inside the earth. The mines robbed them of their health, but not their pride.

Home

Snow-capped mountains were in the distance, the radiant blue sky stretched above her. She could feel cool, damp grass beneath her feet. "Matka, I'm home." Her voice was not her own. It was the voice of a stranger, the voice of someone lost. The little white cottage with its thatched roof was there. Was that her father waving to her? She could not see his face. A woman was standing in the doorway of the cottage. "Matka, it is me, Anna. I'm home, Matka. I'm home." A train whistle blew. She tried to push the sound away. "Matka, I'm home." The train whistle blew again, and the dream began to fade. She felt Stefan's hand resting on her shoulder.

"Anna, Anna, wake up." The brakes screeched and complained as they pushed against the wheels of the train. "Anna, wake up. We are here, Anna. We are home." With a jolt, the train came to a stop.

Anna rubbed the sleep from her eyes, and her hand moved slowly across the window, pushing the dust aside. The train stopped alongside a black mountain of coal. The sun had been vanquished, leaving a shadowy light that cast gloom over the landscape. She could not see the sky. *Nothing will grow here,* Anna thought. *It will be barren for all eternity.*

"Anna, everything will be all right," Stefan reassured his wife. "We are together." Stefan placed his hand on her shoulder. "That is all that matters."

She took his hand and cradled it against her cheek. "We are together."

During the long hours of the ride from Jersey City, the steady rhythm of the train and the monotony of the landscape had caused many of the passengers to close their eyes, and many had fallen asleep. Others, gazing at the passing farms and villages, reflected on their new circumstances and thought of the homes and families they had left behind. Even the children were subdued, and, with a few exceptions, the ride had been quiet, almost peaceful.

The train jolted to a stop. Mothers called to their children, hungry babies began to cry, and men shouted orders.

"Let's go." Stefan balanced the trunk on his shoulder and led the way to the front of the car. Anna held her sleepy child on her hip, and the suitcase in her other hand, as she followed her husband. When she reached the landing, she looked out at the main street of Ario with its rows of uniformly gray two-story wood-frame houses that stretched endlessly, monotonously, down a wide dirt road. Here, there were a few trees with tender young leaves beginning to appear. Behind fences, she could see grape arbors and bean poles. *Well, maybe things grow here after all,* she thought, relieved.

"Name?" asked an official from the coal company as Stefan reached the last stair of the train's platform. Without a smile or word of welcome, the official looked at Stefan and back to the ledger he was holding. "Name?" he repeated.

"Dusick," Stefan answered, adjusting the trunk on his shoulder.

"Back Street." The man, holding a rough sketch of a shanty, pointed down the street and made a gesture to turn left. "House ten."

The picture of the shanty had two doors, and the man pointed to the door on the right. Stefan nodded and repeated the words: "Back Street, house ten."

"Wait, Stefan. Emil. I want to be sure Emil has a place to stay."

"Emil," Stefan called to the boy, who was standing with a group of young men who had been among the first to get off the train.

"Wasn't that an amazing ride?" Emil pronounced as he walked over to Stefan and Anna. "Did you see all those factories, the farms, the villages? What a place this is! I can't wait to see the mines. Did you see the pile of coal?" The questions were rhetorical, no answer expected. How could it be otherwise?

"Where will you be staying?" Anna asked. "You can stay with us."

"There is a boarding house at the end of the street. A Mrs. Nagy owns it. They say she is a very good cook."

"All right, then," Anna said, adjusting Stephen on her hip.

"I will see you in the mines." Emil laughed, running to join the young men headed for the boarding house.

Anna and Stefan followed others walking down the main street of Ario. They passed the blacksmith shop, carpenter shop, mule stables, and what they would later learn were the boiler houses. Anna juggled Stephen and her suitcase to make the sign of the cross as they walked past the church.

Towering over the patch was a hulking wooden building with an odd shape nestled on a bare hill behind the houses. Each floor was lined with windows and narrower than the one below. Five rows of windows, Anna counted. Rickety stairs wound their way on the outside of the building. A long, covered ramp, like an elephant's trunk, extended from the top of the building to the ground below. The building seemed to be alive. Chains rattled. Men were shouting. Then there was the sound of rocks tumbling, crashing onto a solid surface, followed by the grinding roar of machinery. A dingy cloud of black dust poured from broken windows. It was as though the building was possessed by the devil.

Children, playing with marbles in the street, gave them a cursory glance and then resumed their game. A boy, perhaps thirteen years of age, stood leaning against a building. He had a wooden crutch under one arm, and his right leg was

The Road to Lattimer · 73

missing. Vacant eyes looked out of a face covered with coal dust. Anna turned away. There were children in her village who had been trampled by horses, disfigured by disease, or died of starvation. She held her son a little tighter. "I will protect you," she whispered, but, in her heart, she knew that might not be possible.

When Anna thought she could go no farther, they reached the alley where the man had pointed. Instead of the two-story houses she had seen on the main road, there were only unpainted shacks hidden behind fences made of branches and sticks. She followed Stefan down the narrow, rutted road, the hem of her skirt turning black from the coal dust that seemed to cover everything, even the road.

An old woman struggling with a rusty water pump looked suspiciously at the strangers as they walked by. *Not unlike some of the women back home,* Anna thought, noting the woman's gray hair was hidden by a black babushka. *I will say a prayer for her tonight. When I am settled, I will bake her some bread.*

A man, with wrinkled skin and gray, watery eyes, was sitting on a three-legged stool, a clay pipe in his mouth. He coughed a deep, painful cough, and spit black phlegm onto the ground.

"Back Street, house ten?" Stefan asked the words with a heavy accent, but the old man understood. With gnarled fingers, the man pointed down the street. These were not the first immigrants to ask him directions.

"*Dakujem.*"

The man nodded and coughed again.

The tenth house on Back Street was a wooden shack with a rusted tin roof. There were two wooden doors hung precariously on rusted hinges. Two families would occupy the shanty. Broken windowpanes were covered with oilcloth. Remnants of an untended garden was visible along the side of the house.

Stefan opened the door on the right, it appeared to be unoccupied. Anna followed him into a small, dark room. There was a rope bed, a chair, a kerosene lamp on a wooden box that had once held blasting powder. Frayed brown curtains hung on the single window. *I will make this place our home,* Anna thought, while lowering Stephen to the floor.

"It is ours, Stefan," Anna said, taking her husband's hand. "We are home. Together, we will build a life in this place."

The tender moment was interrupted by the booming voice of a large woman standing in the doorway.

"Stefan. Welcome! Welcome!"

Anna and Stefan stared at the apparition. Stephen hid behind his mother's skirts.

"Are you going to invite us in?"

The woman, not waiting for an invitation, floated into the room. Her massive body barely navigated the door, her muscular arms were filled with baskets and blankets. A large man and four noisy children followed her. The quiet, dismal room was instantly transformed into a place of laughter and warmth.

"Anna, this is my cousin Adriana." Stefan laughed as he recognized his cousin Adriana and introduced her to his wife. Before Anna could respond, Adriana dropped her bundles and drew Anna into her ample bosom. "Welcome, Anna. Welcome to Ario." Adriana was laughing and crying and squeezing Anna with such exuberance that Anna could hardly breathe.

Adriana's children did not wait for introductions. Like their mother, they had taken ownership of the small room, running in circles, giggling. Adriana's booming voice filled the room, while the men slapped each other on the back. Everyone forgot little Stephen, standing next to his mother, thumb securely planted in his mouth, looking as though he would cry.

"Oh, my little boy, I am here." Anna released herself from Adriana's arms and picked up her son.

"This is our son, Stephen."

"Hello!" A thunderous voice shook the room and even rattled the windows. Anna turned in surprise to see a large man carrying a heavy wooden box into the room. "You will need this," he said to her without introduction. The box was filled with coal.

"Johan put it by the stove in the kitchen," his wife ordered, as he dodged children and stepped over boxes. "Don't just hand it to the lady."

"Oh, yah," the man said, vanishing into the kitchen where the men were gathering.

"Elsa, welcome." Adriana had wrapped her strong, thick arms around the tiny, fragile-looking young woman who had followed the man into the house. "Anna, this is Elsa," she announced. "That bull of a man is her husband."

"Hello, Elsa. Thank you for the coal," Anna said, as one of Adriana's boys pushed past her. Adriana ignored her high-spirited sons, as she reached for Anna's arm to steady her.

"From my garden. Welcome to Ario." Another woman's voice was soft and sweet as she held out a basket filled with potatoes.

"Th-thank you," Anna stammered, struggling to gain control of the situation. She was about to suggest that they bring the basket into the kitchen, but the coarse laughter of the men and the smell of tobacco smoke made her hesitate. "We can put them in here for now."

"I made these for you," a little girl, her voice timid and shy, looked up at Anna and proudly presented a plate with tiny pastries filled with cheese. "Mama showed me how. She said you would like them."

"I like them very much. We can put them on the little table over there."

More neighbors arrived, most speaking Slovak, or heavily accented English. People were laughing and talking all at once. Children were banished to the yard to continue their games. Someone placed a miner's cap on Stefan's head, and canteens filled with beer magically appeared.

"Ivan brought his fiddle," someone shouted, and they could hear a polka being played in the street.

"Come, dance," Adriana insisted, pulling Anna with her. "Elsa's daughter will watch Stephen."

Finally, the house was quiet. Stephen was asleep, bundled in blankets on the floor next to his parents' bed. Stefan reached for his wife's hand and guided her first to the door and then into the dark night. Tall trees cast their shadowy silhouettes against the night sky, and a dim yellow light flickered from a window in a neighbor's house. A baby cried. Stefan pointed to the North Star and said the names of familiar constellations. "They are the same," he whispered, still holding his wife's hand.

In the distance, a hill with a sharp peak glowed with blue, orange, and red light. It was a smoldering man-made mountain of coal dust and rock. The air smelled of sulfur fumes. Rumbling sounds from the breaker that never slept muffled the sounds of the night creatures that roamed through the streets and narrow alleys of the village. *This is our home now.* The thought was shared but left unspoken.

Day 1

A rooster crowed, and for a moment Anna thought she was in her mother's house. She listened for the familiar sounds of her childhood; her mother singing to the baby, her father coughing while he lit his pipe, her brothers mumbling in their sleep. But there was nothing, no sound, except the persistent crowing of the rooster and Stefan's soft breathing.

Stefan stirred in his sleep. He had been restless during the night, and she had felt his body stiffen. *Are you afraid of the mine?* He would not share his apprehension with her. His trepidation would not show on his face. Yet she knew, she was his wife.

"I love you, Stefan," she whispered. Slowly, so as not to disturb him, she moved away from her husband and put her feet on the rough planks of the floor. Her little boy was there, next to the bed, bundled in blankets, still asleep. "My sweet baby," she whispered, bending down to stroke his cheek.

The room was dark, and still unfamiliar, but she waited until she reached the kitchen to light the kerosene lamp. "There," she said to no one as she lit the lamp and surveyed her kitchen. There was a coal cook stove with a coffeepot and a cast iron skillet. Cracked plates, cups, and cutlery rested on a shelf next to the stove. A lunch pail and canteen supplied by Adriana, or perhaps left by a previous occupant, hung from a hook waiting to be filled. A bare plank table with a wooden bench supplied by the coal company completed the meager furnishings.

With an effort she started a fire in the cook stove and slowly added small pieces of coal. *Thank you, Johan for the coal.* Satisfied that there was enough heat, she began to make the coffee and placed slices of kielbasa in the cast iron pan. It smelled like home. She smiled at the thought. *I will make a home here for my husband and our children.*

She felt strong hands caress her shoulders and lips kiss her neck. The smell of him, the strength of his body as he pushed against her, banished all thoughts except for the love she felt. Her body melted into his, while her hand stroked his rumpled hair and worked its way down his face and neck until it reached his shirtless chest. She felt the heat rising through her body. It dissipated when a little voice said, "*Tatá, Tatá.*"

Laughing, Anna turned to her husband. "Go, Tata. Go play with your son. I have work to do."

"Up you go." Stefan lifted his son onto his shoulders. "We need to attend to manly chores."

Anna smiled at them as they headed for the door. Father and son walked together to the outhouse, where there were lessons a little boy needed to learn.

Eggs crackled in a generous dollop of bacon grease, the warm smell of coffee permeated the air, and a lunch pail sat on the table waiting. The little family sat together and prayed that the Lord would bless them. If Stefan was afraid, it did not show. For the moment Anna's loneliness was replaced by the joy at seeing her little family together. The first day in Ario, the beginning of their new life had begun.

A Coal Miner's Wife

Anna, standing barefoot, holding her son on her hip, watched from the doorway as the man she loved walked away from her. For the first time, she felt the ever-present fear of a miner's wife. Would he return to her at the end of the day, or would he be buried deep inside the earth, crushed beneath a mound of falling rocks? Acceptance of this risk was part of the unwritten contract between a coal miner and his wife. Tightness gripped her chest. Blessed Mother keep him safe.

"Down," Stephen said, squirming in his mother's arms, his child's hands pointing toward the ground. "Down," he persisted, intensifying his efforts to be released as he squirmed and twisted, pushing against his mother's chest.

"All right, down." His mother laughed, marveling at her son's strength. It was not so long ago that he was a helpless infant content to sleep in her arms. She watched as he began to explore the tiny room, toddling from the bed, to the suitcase, to the trunk, turning to check that his mother was still there.

"I'm here, Stephen," she reassured her son. "I will always be here for you."

Anna's eyes lingered on the trunk and the small suitcase that stood next to the bed. Silently they stood there, a reminder of home, of the distance they had traveled. "We are so far from everyone," she lamented. Her son would not understand the loss she felt thinking of the family she had left behind. She imagined her mother pounding the dough that became the warm bread that would sit on the table, the smell tantalizing and inviting. She remembered her father on a dark winter evening, sitting near the stove with his beer and his pipe, looking tired but content. A moment, just for a moment, if she could be back in her village surrounded by her family, it would be a respite from the fear and the loneliness she felt. Her hand glided over the trunk, and she thought of its contents. There were family treasures to be inspected, photographs of those left behind, a scarf she had embroidered, and a handkerchief with a crochet border she carried on her wedding day.

She watched her son crawling under the bed, exploring the new space. *The suitcase, I'll begin with the suitcase. The trunk can wait.* The suitcase wasn't heavy, it only held necessities for Stephen. Placing it on the bed, Anna removed the belt that held it shut, opened the suitcase, and began to inspect the contents.

Clink, clink, clink. Stephen reached for the end of the strap and dragged it across the room. *Clink, clink, clink.* The buckle hit the floor with a rhythmic sound that fascinated the toddler. *Clink, clink, clink.* He looked at his mother for approval, but Anna was busy inspecting the contents of the suitcase.

A child-sized, wide-brimmed, charcoal-colored, felt hat sat atop a pile of children's clothes. Removing the hat from the suitcase, delighting in the miniature details, she tickled her son with the white feather stuck in its band, and they both giggled. "This belonged to your father when he was a boy." She placed the hat on Stephen's head, but the little boy pulled the hat off his head, threw it on the floor, and resumed his exploration of the dark but inviting cavern under the bed.

"You will need to grow a little to fit into some of these," Anna realized, placing linen trousers and a miniature white shirt on the bed. She held up a child's vest for closer inspection. The vest was made of russet brown wool with an intricate pattern of red and yellow flowers embroidered around the edges.

"Your godmother made this for you." Stephen, still uninterested in the contents of the suitcase, had renewed his fascination with the belt. *Clink, clink, clink.*

A fur cap for the winter, cloth slippers, and a pair of leather boots were placed next to the child's clothing on the bed. Anna put her hands on her hips while she surveyed the apparel on the bed and assessed future needs. "It will be enough," she said, returning everything except the hat, to the suitcase. "You can wear the hat to church on Sunday," she said to her son, who was again crawling under the bed.

Anna opened the trunk and removed a crucifix wrapped in a piece of richly embroidered linen. *It is so very beautiful.* Her fingers touched the rough surface of the cross made of inlaid ceramic tile chips. White daisies with green leaves, also made of inlaid tile, were interspersed with other religious images, their meaning unknown to Anna. Her eyes rested on the suffering crucified Christ, "Keep my family safe," she prayed.

"I want you to have this," her mother had told her as she reverently took the crucifix down from the wall and handed it to her daughter. "It belonged to your grandmother." Anna knew the story. Her grandmother's brother, a priest, had been sent to Rome when he was in the seminary. The cross had been purchased from a vendor outside the Vatican and given to Anna's mother.

Now the crucifix would hang on a nail in Anna's home. *Bless this house, bless our bed,* Anna prayed as she hung the precious cross. The piece of linen with its red and yellow flowers was draped over the wooden box that served as an end table.

Squares of thin cardboard protected photographs of her family. There was a picture of her mother and father on their wedding day. *They were so young.* Her mother was sixteen when she was married, her father was only a few years older. Anna placed the photographs on the wooden box next to the bed.

An iron was packed among linens in a corner of the trunk reminding Anna of chores that were waiting. She sighed, but it was not one of sadness, just acknowledgment of her responsibilities. She placed the iron on a shelf in the kitchen.

There was a dress for her and a suit for Stefan that they would wear to church on Sundays. Smoothing them out, satisfied that they would do, she hung them on the hooks next to the bed. The scarf, the embroidered handkerchief, and a few mementos were returned to the trunk. "There, we are ready to begin our new life," she said, lifting her son and cradling him in her arms. Stephen giggled with the innocent joy of a child delighting in his mother's love.

Stephen was asleep on the bed with his mother close beside him. There would be time later to scrub the coal dust from the floors and make a soup from the potatoes, green beans, and kielbasa the neighbors left the night before. Perhaps she could find an onion or some garlic in the abandoned garden near the house. She studied Stephen's little round face, the shape of his nose, marveled at the length of his beautiful eyelashes. *My son!* Her body relaxed and she closed her eyes.

She heard them outside, the laughter of children, a woman's loud voice giving commands. When the door burst open, Anna sat up with a jolt, ready to protect her son from the trespassers.

"Anna, are you there?" Before Anna could respond, Adriana entered the room trailed by her three youngest children.

"Adriana! What's the matter?"

"Nothing, nothing, dear. It's time to go to the store."

"Oh! But" Anna's response drifted away as Adriana's boys knocked over the suitcase as they rolled around on the floor, testing their strength in childish combat. Adriana did not seem to notice. Stephen, startled awake, by the commotion, stared wide-eyed at the intruders.

"You need supplies, and I was on my way to the store, so here we are."

"Oh!" Anna watched the woman who had now taken control of her life and her home. "I, I think I should wait until Stefan gets home.

"Hmm, and what will you feed your family until then?"

"We have the food you brought last night."

"And when that is gone?"

"I don't know." Anna paused for a moment. "We have been hungry before." Anna was not unskilled in making do with very little. There were sure to be mushrooms in the woods, and perhaps some onions or garlic in the garden behind the shed. "We will be all right," she stated with confidence and pride.

Adriana, hands on her hips studied the young woman. *She is determined and proud. Nevertheless, it is my duty to help her.* "We will go to the company store," she commanded. "No need to go hungry." It was clear to Anna that there would be no recourse. The formidable woman had taken control.

"Come along. You can buy food and other supplies on credit and pay for it when you can. Boys! Outside. Now!"

"Are you sure? It doesn't seem right." Anna still had doubts as she picked up Stephen and followed Adriana and her boys out of the house.

"It is the way it is done. You are in America now."

As always, Adriana had taken charge of the situation. They were going to the company store. Stephen was placed in a pushcart, a makeshift affair that was just a wooden box on wheels.

"He will be all right," Adriana reassured the toddler's mother. "The boys will take care of him." Anna was not at all comfortable with the situation as she watched her son disappear around the bend in the road.

The smell of cabbage being fried and bread baking, mingled with the smoke from the boilers in the colliery and the coal-burning stoves in the homes. Ario was a noisy place, children playing, dogs barking, women's voices calling greetings, and in the distance, the workings of the mine. The alley was bordered by unpainted shanties fronted by jagged picket fences. Black dust was everywhere.

Adriana walked with a steady, powerful gait, and Anna struggled to keep up. Adriana did not seem to notice. She wanted to talk, and Anna was expected to listen.

"We came here twelve years ago, you know. Lived on Back Street in a shanty like yours. Now we live in a two-story double on Main Street. So much better. It isn't easy for an immigrant to get a good job inside the mine, even harder to get a miner's certificate. When we first got here Cyril hauled rock and slate to the slag heap and fed coal into the boilers. I needed to take in boarders to make ends meet in those years. Cyril needed contacts and paid bribes before he got a job working as a laborer in the mine. Even more bribes were needed to get the miner's certificate."

"But Stefan will work with Cyril in the mine?" Anna was stunned. *Had Cyril paid a bribe to get Stefan into the mine as his laborer?*

"Yes, Cyril needed a laborer to work with him. The inside boss agreed."

They had turned onto Main Street, a dirt road lined with straight rows of identical double houses. Sheds, privies, and vegetable gardens stuck into any available space filled the backyards.

"That's where we live," Adriana changed the subject, pointing to an unpainted two-story double-frame house. "We have two rooms upstairs and two down. For now, the boys have the two bedrooms to themselves. Cyril planted the plum tree and grapevines for me, and I insisted on sunflowers and poppies.

They remind me of my mother's garden. We even have a smokehouse in the back, where Cyril cures kielbasa. Now, Cyril wants to buy a pig, but I'm not sure we have the money."

"A pig! How wonderful." Anna had decided she would talk to Stefan later about Cyril. If he had paid a bribe to get Stefan work in the mine, they would pay him back.

"Hurry along now, we have shopping to do." Anna made the sign of the cross when they walked past the small church. She touched her forehead, her heart, her left shoulder, and then her right. It was a Catholic custom that was often done out of habit. But today Anna was comforted by the simple gesture of faith. The Lord was here, even in this dark, strange place.

Anna stopped, frozen in place, her eyes wide with fear, wishing she had not allowed the boys to take Stephen away from her. Three men on horseback were riding down the center of the street. Identical gray helmets, with straps fitting tightly under their chins, and shiny badges in the center of their helmets left no doubt about their authority. The ammunition belts across their chests and the guns at their sides made it clear they were in charge. "Police!" Anna whispered, pulling her shawl tighter around her shoulders.

"The Coal and Iron Police," Adriana uttered with disdain and hatred in her voice. "The Pardee brothers pay them to keep order in the town. Come on, keep walking. We have every right to be here."

"Shouldn't we stop?" Anna implored, still haunted by memories of the police beating the schoolteacher and burning the school.

"No."

"I need to find Stephen." The color had drained from Anna's face, and she could hardly breathe.

"Stupid, dirty Hunkies," Anna heard one policeman say as he spit on the ground. Although she did not understand the phrase, it was clear the contemptuous words were meant for her. With relief, Anna watched the police move away from them.

"Come on, let's find the boys." Adriana took Anna's arm, and they continued walking.

Adriana stopped in front of an unimpressive gray building that reminded Anna of an oversized crate. Wooden steps lead to a rickety porch A faded crimson door marked the entrance to the store.

Adriana's boys were already there, kicking a ball that appeared to be made of old socks. Stephen was watching them intently from the pushcart.

"You can get everything you need here," Adriana asserted, guiding her friend into the store. The space was dark and gloomy, the floor black with coal dust. It smelled musty and old, a mixture of kerosene, pickles, leather, and wool.

Every available space was filled with merchandise. Shelving containing neat displays of canned goods, boxes of cigars, dishes, and other household goods covered every available wall, reaching from floor to ceiling. A stack of kitchen chairs placed on their sides were precariously perched on a top shelf. Miner's tools, picks, shovels, blasting powder, caps, boots, and lunch pails filled one section of the cavernous space. Racks of clothing for men, women, and children were next to tables with bolts of fabric and sewing supplies. Seven large sacks of flour were stacked next to a pickle barrel, and near the front counter was a coffee grinder, strings of garlic, and scales for weighing merchandise.

A young man was standing on a ladder behind the counter. He was arranging canisters of tobacco and was oblivious to the women watching him. The ladder nearly touched the ceiling, and Anna worried for the man's safety. A clerk, a crisp white apron tied around his waist, stood behind the counter watching the customers who had just entered the store. He knew one of the women but the other looked like an immigrant just off the boat. He hid his scorn, behind a practiced professional demeanor.

"Good morning, Mr. Kelly," Adriana addressed the clerk with her most beguiling smile.

"Good morning, Mrs. Banik.".

"This is my friend and cousin, Mrs. Dusick. She will be opening an account today." *Another immigrant who will not pay her bills.* He nodded as he recorded Anna's name in his ledger.

"What do you need today, Mrs. Dusick?" he asked, though he suspected she did not speak English.

"We need some muslin for curtains and some coffee," Adriana spoke for her.

"Muslin for curtains," she said to Anna in Slovak. "You can dye them with the used coffee grounds."

"But—" Anna started to object, but Adriana continued to make her requests, not listening to her.

"Thread." The clerk placed a spool of yellowed thread on the counter.

"Seed packets, please, Mr. Kelly." Colorful packets of corn, beans, and sunflower seeds appeared. "You will need to start a garden."

"It will take work to clear it." Anna sighed, thinking of the weeds and tangles of brush that filled the area behind her house next to the outhouse.

"Cyril will help. We can do it on Sunday."

"You are good friends."

"We are family."

"Yes, family."

"Soap."

The pile of supplies was growing, and Anna began to worry. "How will I pay for all of this?" she asked Adriana, but the question was ignored.

Adriana inspected the merchandise that was accumulating on the counter, seemingly unworried about the cost. "Flour, salt, and yeast, that should do it." The clerk produced the items, but his expression was not kind or deferential. The woman who could not speak English would be in debt to the company store for a long time.

"Will that be all for today, Mrs. Dusick?" There was mockery in the clerk's voice as he placed a sack of flour on the counter. Anna did not understand the words, but she heard the scorn in his voice.

"Sign here," the clerk grumbled, pushing the ledger to Anna. With shaky hands, Anna scratched out her name in the ledger.

Adriana purchased three pieces of hard-black licorice called coal candy, to give to the children.

"We will settle the bill on payday," Adriana said to the clerk, as she signed her name in the ledger. But they both knew there would not be enough money and the debt would continue to grow.

The small kitchen was now ready for Anna to welcome her husband home. There was an egg and flour, bacon grease, cabbage, and an onion, necessities all given to the young family by generous neighbors or purchased at the company store. "Halushki." Anna beamed, satisfied that her family would eat well tonight. The soup can wait till tomorrow. She sprinkled flour on the table, a familiar ritual that reminded her of home. An egg, flour, a little water, and the dough for the noodles began to take shape. When Stefan came home, the house would smell of cabbage and onion simmering in bacon grease.

The young mother touched her abdomen as she admired the flowers on the table. She had picked them that morning with her son. Soon it would be time to tell Stefan that they would be bringing a new life into this world. *Bless us, sweet Jesus. Bless my growing family.*

A laborer in a mine

The alley was quiet in the hours between dawn and sunrise, and the morning sky was a hazy yellow, the sun still hidden behind the mountains. Scraps of food near a wooden gate occupied a snorting pig, while a goat nibbled on a dandelion that had taken root near the well. The door to an outhouse opened, and a man, still pulling up his trousers, returned to the dismal dwelling he called home.

At the communal well, the squeak of a pump handle, followed by a gush of water, startled a feral cat. A woman wearing a scarf and a drab-colored dress covered with a stained and yellowed apron was filling a wooden bucket with water. The woman liked to come to the pump before her neighbors, as their gossip did not interest her. "Better to get there before the others," she would tell her husband. "No need to waste time waiting in line." Her husband would have preferred she served him breakfast before going to the well, but he did not have much say in the matter.

It was not long before the breaker whistle sounded, disrupting the morning routines of the families who lived in Ario. Doors opened, and men dressed in oil-soaked overalls, jackets, and gumboots kissed their wives and children goodbye and entered the alley. Cloth miners' hats with leather brims and oil-wick lamps identified the men as miners headed for the underground pits. Boys, wearing shabby, ill-fitting clothing black with coal dust, raced from their homes, enjoying their last few minutes of freedom before sitting on the wooden benches where they would spend most of the daylight hours. The men and boys were headed to the mine, the breaker, the mule barn, and the boilers, all part of the Ario colliery. Greetings in many languages filled the air, accompanied by the crunch of the gravel under the men's heavy footsteps as they walked toward the main street of the town.

Most of the inhabitants of Back Street were Slovak or Polish. Italians lived on South Street, English and Irish, who were born in Pennsylvania, lived in the frame houses on Main Street. As Stefan made his way down the alley, the greetings he heard reminded him of home.

Over a hundred men and boys were now walking down the narrow dirt road, past the rough wooden fences that protected the meager gardens of the shanties. Stefan looked at the faces of the men around him. There were older men, with gray-streaked mustaches, faces creased with age and worry, their skin permanently blackened with particles of coal dust that could not be washed away. Some had visible wounds attesting to the hazards of work in the mines, a scar across a face, a missing finger, a limp from an old injury. Still, there was determination in their stride. They were proud, these old miners, proud of the work they did.

Younger men, with jaunty steps, laughed and joked, betting on the outcome of a poker game and planning to meet for a beer when their shift was done. Beer flowed freely in the patches. The miners said that beer would wash the coal dust from their bodies. "I will need traveling money," the men would tell their wives on payday. Everyone knew it would be used to buy a beer on the way home from the mines.

Stefan saw a woman holding the hand of a small boy whose face and clothing were covered with coal dust. She was taking her son to the breaker, where the little boy would pick slate until it was time for his mother to walk him home. *Not so different from our village,* Stefan thought, thinking of the children who worked in the fields at home. *It is right that everyone helps when the family is in need. That is the way of things.*

"Stefan! Hey, Stefan!" Cyril waved to the man who would now be working for him. Cyril had been leaning against a fence waiting for Stefan. Adriana, her skirts billowing in the wind, was on the porch behind him. Louis and John wrestled in the dusty patch of the front yard, and four-year-old Patrik sat next to her, preoccupied with the slate board and chalk his father had given him. Jacob, her oldest, was not there. He had joined the other breaker boys earlier that morning.

"Good morning, Cyril," Stefan called back.

This would be Stefan's first day in the mine, and Adriana wanted to wish him well. It was also her habit to stand on her porch each morning and watch her Cyril leave for the mine. Cyril—she looked at her husband leaning against the fence, smoking his clay pipe. *He is a good man. Please, Lord, keep him safe.* A miner's wife never knew what the day would bring. *Would her husband come home to her or would she watch them carry his shattered body from the mine?* She pushed the thought away.

"Mornin', Stefan," Adriana called to him. "How is our Anna this morning, and your little Stephen?"

"Both are well."

"Now you take care of my Cyril today," she chided, although they all knew it was Cyril who would be watching out for Stefan.

Stefan smiled and tipped his hat.

"Let's go," Cyril said, handing Stefan a short-handled shovel and a pick.

At the base of the mountain was a black hole framed by wooden beams. To Stefan, it was like the doorway to hell. A wooden coal car attached to heavy coupling chains waited on what looked like a small railroad track. *That car will carry me into the darkness,* Stefan thought, feeling a tightness in his chest.

"We'll wait over there." Cyril walked to a small lean-to shed open in the front. "It will protect us from the rain."

Stefan did not see any threatening clouds in the sky, but he followed Cyril anyway. The men already in the shed moved aside, making room for Cyril and Stefan, greeting them with silent nods. Their grimy faces, with their large mustaches, bore the inscrutable expressions common among immigrants.

"Mornin'," Cyril said, his face as unreadable as the others.

"Mornin'," a few responded with mumbled acknowledgment.

Laughter erupted from a group of Americans standing near the shed. It was the ribald laughter that one sometimes hears when men are gathered together away from family. Stefan had the uncomfortable feeling they were laughing at him.

There were over two hundred men smoking pipes and cigars assembled on the road or waiting in the shed. Some began to board the mantrip car, and Stefan noticed there were boys among them. *Not more than eleven or twelve years old,* he thought. *Are those boys strong enough to lift the coal?*

"Nippers, spraggers, mule drivers. You'll get to know them soon enough. Your life will depend on them." One of the boys positioned himself precariously on the edge of the car, his feet resting on the coupling chain. "A dangerous thing to do," Cyril shrugged. "The young take unnecessary chances."

"All aboard for the bottom," the top-man yelled. The car was filled with miners, laborers, and young boys, all sitting with stoic faces and their backs to the mine entrance. A warning bell sounded, the cables holding the car in place started to grind, and the wheels turned grudgingly as the car began to slide down the slope. As though from an unheard command, the men lowered their heads in unison as the car passed through the low opening of the mine entrance. For them, it was a routine part of their morning, and their expressions were devoid of emotion.

"We're next," Cyril said, as the clanging of the cables and the grinding of the wheels announced the approach of the now-empty car.

"All aboard for the bottom," the top-man yelled again. Stefan followed Cyril to the car.

"Sit by me. Always sit in the same seat, bad luck if you don't." The dangers of the job made miners superstitious. It was not wise to change your seat in the mantrip car, eat in a different spot, or begin a new job on a Friday. If a woman entered the mine, the miners were known to leave.

Stefan hoisted himself into the car and sat next to Cyril. He did not know that Cyril's last laborer, the unfortunate Jarik, had sat there less than a week ago. There had been an accident. A coal car was coming down the slope and gaining speed. Jarik did not hear it until it was too late. His screams had reverberated off the walls of the mine as his leg was crushed under the heavy wheels of the car. His days working in the mine were over. Without a leg, his choices were limited; join the boys in the breaker, move away, or starve. Cyril could not help him. It was often the case that a miner who was injured or old could no longer work in the mine. "Once a man, twice a boy," the miners would say. As boys, they worked in the breaker, and when they were old or injured, the breaker claimed them back again. Cyril later learned that Jarik had boarded a train and headed west. "No partic'lar destination," he was told.

The smell of dust and fumes from the depths below, the knowledge he would be swallowed by the dreary, sooty darkness of the mine, caused Stefan's stomach to tighten. *I am entering hell.* His body tensed with apprehension. He could not help but wonder if he would ever see daylight again.

"All aboard for the bottom," the top-man yelled again, then a warning bell sounded, and the hoisting engineer lowered the car into the yawning abyss. Stefan's eyes were riveted on the small patch of sunlight at the entrance as the car jerked and slid slowly down the slope of the mine. Fearfully, he watched as the window of light grew smaller until it completely disappeared. Darkness enveloped him. He sensed the presence of the men around him, but all he could see was black. The car stopped with a jolt. In unison, as though on signal, the men lit the lamps attached to their caps and scrambled out of the car.

"That's the inside boss over there," Cyril informed Stefan, pointing to a man leaning out of a small window of an office made of rough wooden planks. Light from pit lamps flickered, casting shadows on the white-washed walls behind him.

"Mornin', Mr. Ahern," Cyril barked. "This is Stefan, my new laborer." Neither man mentioned the bribe that had been paid to get around the law that would have prevented Stefan from working inside the mine.

"Sorry about Jarik," replied the inside boss. But he did not look sorry; accidents happened all the time. "Bad luck," he said, while absently using his shirt sleeve to polish his spectacles.

"Hmm," Cyril mumbled, ignoring the reference to Jarik. "We will be working the Rose Garden." Cyril glanced at the slate board next to the office. "Seems to be all clear." There were no notes on the board from the fire boss who had made his inspection during the night. No gas had been detected, so it was safe to work in the area.

"Yup." The inside boss grunted. "All checked out fine."

Cyril took a brass tag with a number from his pocket and hung it on a pegboard on the wall next to the boss's office. The tag would let the mine operators know where he was working if there was an explosion or cave-in.

The inside boss handed a tag to Stefan while nodding his head toward the board. "Here's yours. The number is on the tag."

"So, I am number 26984." Stefan studied the tag for a moment and then placed it on the pegboard next to Cyril's. Cyril was walking with a deliberate and thoughtful pace down the gangway. Stefan grabbed the pick and the shovel and followed Cyril into the sunless tunnel before him.

Stefan, accustomed to the cool air from the mountains and the sweet smell of endless meadows, found it difficult to breathe in the damp, dark tunnel. Stale air heavy with coal dust smelled of mold and mildew growing on the old timbers. The sounds of the mine surrounded him—the snap, crackle, pop of the walls, the crunch of the gravel beneath his boots, a man's rough voice in the distance, the clank of picks, and the scraping of shovels. Rushing water beyond the walls reminded him he was deep inside a mountain. His hands touched the wall and felt the water trickling down, filling the ditches on either side of the gangway. The light from his lamp illuminated the slick of violet oil covering the water beneath his feet and rust on the rocks. His lunch pail banged against his knee. *I love you, Anna.*

They were in a maze of endless tunnels that narrowed as they moved deeper into the mountain. They turned to the right at the first fork in the gangway, and then to the left. Stefan was disoriented with only the light flickering from his lamp to pierce the darkness. He wondered how he would find his way back if something happened to Cyril.

"Welcome to the Rose Garden," Cyril announced, crawling on his belly as he entered a tunnel. "We will work in this chamber and take the coal from the face over there."

Stefan followed the light from Cyril's lamp into a room that was darker than a moonless night. He touched the jagged rock above his head. There was not enough room to stand. He listened to the creaks and groans of the mountain and shivered when loose pebbles fell to the ground. The air in the room was cool, but fear warmed his body, and he felt moisture beneath his miner's cap. His body stiffened as he fought the urge to run from this place.

"Any movement or bulging of the timber could be a warning of an unstable roof," Cyril was saying as he inspected the timbers. Satisfied, he hit the ceiling with the blunt end of his pick. "Looking for loose rock," he explained. For an instant Stefan imagined tons of coal and rock falling from the ceiling, crushing them, burying them in this place.

"Need to buy me a new pick before I'm killed," Cyril said, examining the wear on the pick that had served him for many years. It was a common saying among miners, reflecting acceptance of their fate.

"Start loading the coal over there into the coal cart. We need to load four tons of coal into that car, and six more like it before the end of the day."

A large pot, called a boiler, was on the stove ready with hot water for Stefan's bath. A wooden tub, Anna found in the shed, waited outside the back door.

"Your father will be home soon," Anna informed her little boy, who was currently amusing himself by climbing on and off the bed.

"Anna, Stephen." The door opened, and a tall, frightening apparition appeared in the doorway, white eyes rimmed in red, staring out of a face covered with soot.

Stephen ran to his mother and hid behind her skirts.

"Stephen, it is me, Táta."

A tiny head with large eyes and a thumb securely tucked in his mouth, guardedly appeared from behind his mother's skirts. He stared at the frightening creature standing in the doorway. The face broke into a wide grin, exposing white teeth, which alarmed the child even more.

"Stephen, it's me, Táta." But the child would not move from the safety of his hiding place.

"Am I that frightening, Anna?" Stefan laughed, moving into the room and closing the door.

"He will be fine. Just let me take your clothes." Anna was eyeing the black, wet, footprints on her clean floor.

Black hands reached for the soft miner's cap on Stefan's head. Stephen, eyes wide, still clutching his mother's skirts, watched, transfixed, eyeing the light-colored hair that appeared as the cap was removed. Stefan handed his jacket and then his shirt to Anna. The specter in the doorway began to look familiar to the little boy. Finally, when Anna took a cloth and wiped the coal dust from her husband's face, the boy recognized his father.

"Táta." With giggles and hugs, father and son were reunited.

"Stefan, I have a bath waiting for you." Anna had the damp, dirty clothes in her arms and smiled as she watched her husband and their son.

"Good."

"I'll hang these behind the stove to dry," she offered, taking her husband's sodden, mud-covered coat.

"The mine was damp," he explained, watching her hang his clothes behind the stove. "Where the ceiling was low, we needed to crawl." Anna could not visualize what this dark, damp tunnel must have been like.

"Go on the porch and wait for me," the wife commanded her husband. Stefan was too tired to question and obeyed the command. When she appeared at the door carrying a bucket with hot water, he smiled in appreciation.

Kneeling over the wood tub, Stefan felt the warm water trickle over his head, neck, and shoulders. With gentle hands, Anna washed away the dirt that covered his body, and Stefan sighed with contentment. When she reached his hands, she found cuts and blisters beneath caked blood covered with coal dust. Gently, she caressed each finger in turn, soothing the hands that had worked with the pick and shovel for ten hours in the mine.

Stefan did not question where the tub or soap had come from. He was too exhausted. With a sigh of gratitude, he accepted Anna's attention, ate the Halushki she had prepared for their meal, and fell asleep as soon as he reached his bed. "We will talk another day," Anna whispered to her husband.

Dark piercing eyes stared at him above the veil that covered her face. The woman was silent, eerily silent. What he could see of her olive skin was almost translucent. Stefan shivered in the cold, damp mist that engulfed them. He wanted to leave this place, but he could not move. If only the woman would go away.

"What do you want?" he asked. She did not answer.

"What do you want? "He struggled to move, but his body was not his own. Still, her black eyes watched him, unwavering. Was there a warning, an accusation in her eyes, or just sorrow?

"Tell me, tell me now. What do you want me to do?" His body seemed to be floating effortlessly. He was moving through the mist toward the woman. But still, he could not reach her.

"What do you want from me?" His voice was louder now, more desperate. He knew she had the answer. The answer to what? What was she trying to tell him?

The woman's gaze turned away from him. Another woman was standing in the mist, her arms reaching for him, her face filled with love.

"Matka." Sorrow and regret filled his soul as he reached for his mother. "Matka." He woke missing his mother.

Three weeks later the letter arrived. His dear mother had gone to the Lord.

Chapter 7 - 1891

Breaker Boys, Nippers, and Mule Drivers

Anna

In the summer of 1891 Rose was a year old and learning to walk. She had my hair, the color of the earth. I looked forward to the day when I could weave it into long braids as my mother had done for me.

Stephen was three that year. He had hair the color of wheat, the same as his father at that age. His eyes were hazel, large, and almond shaped. He was shy and did not readily go with strangers but watching him play with his father on Sunday afternoons filled me with joy. With two young children and a coal miner husband, there was no time for me to be concerned about myself. I forgot, momentarily, about the pain in my back and the morning sickness that became the cause of much distress.

Stefan was learning to speak English, a necessity for passing the miner's exam. I had no such incentive. Rarely did I meet anyone who spoke English; even the sermons in St. Joseph's church were in Slovak. The clerk in the company store was often annoyed with me, but eventually, I learned enough to make my needs known.

Cyril and Adriana were so good to us. Adriana was always there to help me when needed, Stefan worked with Cyril until he moved to Lattimer.

By the summer of 1891, Cyril and Adriana had two more children. Girls! The sweetest little girls a mother could ask for. Elizabeth was born in 1889 not long after we had arrived in Ario. Helena arrived a year later. Adriana's four boys doted on their little sisters.

Stefan rarely talked about his work in the mine, but I knew the dangers. I heard stories about accidents, rock falls, fires, explosions and I could see the scars on my husband's body. I could imagine what it must have been like so deep inside the earth.

Emil—you remember, I told you about the young man, boy really, who had traveled with us across mountains and an ocean. He had become a member of our family, and I loved him and cared for him as though he were my little brother. We were so proud of him when he became a mule driver in the mines. "He loves those mules," Stefan would tell me.

Jan and Katarina were eventually released from Castle Garden, and I was glad to have my childhood friends near me again. They lived in a shanty not too far from us, and we would meet at the well and talk about our lives. I worried about her and her family. Jan could only get a job as an ash wheeler at the boilers, and the pay was barely enough to keep the family from starving. Katarina took in boarders. Jan needed to send their oldest son, Tomas, to the breakers when he was only eleven years of age. Katarina and I prayed together the first morning Jan took Tomas to the breaker.

Breaker Boys

It was two years since we arrived in Ario. Jan and Katarina lived not far from us. The meager pay he earned as an ash wheeler was barely enough to feed his growing family. In the summer of 1891, the demand for coal was down and Jan was working three days a week instead of six. Like all of us, he owed more to the company store than he could ever hope to repay.

Tomas, Jan and Katarina's oldest boy, had just turned eleven when he decided he was old enough to help his family. "School is for sissies. I wanna work in the breakers," he had informed his father. "I can bring home money, help the family." Tomas never cared much for school, and, in his estimation, if you asked him, he knew all the reading, writing, and arithmetic that was necessary. He could read a newspaper headline, sign his name, and he knew how to count change at the store. What more did a boy need to know?

Jan had agreed with his son—it was time, and there was no choice. Tomas would leave school and work in the breakers.

"How old is the boy?" the mine inspector asked. The law required that a boy be at least twelve years of age before working in the breaker.

"Twelve," Jan lied. Tomas was eleven.

"Small for his age."

"Yup." Jan signed his name to the forms. The mine inspector, sure the father was lying, only shrugged. It was not his concern. For a few cents, the form was notarized, and Tomas was approved for work in the breakers.

Katarina filled two lunch pails that dreary morning in the fall of 1891. Her little boy would go to work in the breakers for the first time, and her heart was filled with sadness. She knew the dangers—little bodies crushed in unforgiving machinery, missing arms and legs the result of a moment of carelessness.

She tried to smile as she pushed back his hair and placed his cap snugly on his head. "You make me proud, Tomas," she said, kissing him as she had done every morning before sending him off to school. But this morning, her little boy was not going to school learning to read and write. Today would be spent picking slate and rocks from piles of coal. He would return to her with his clothing and face dark with coal dust, his tiny fingers red, cut, bleeding. Like the other mothers in Ario, and across the anthracite region of Pennsylvania, she would apply goose grease to his hands to ease the pain until calluses formed and the bleeding stopped.

Mimicking his father, Tomas walked with a steady, confident gait as they joined the other men walking down Back Street.

"*Zadar Boh*, Stefan."

"Zadar Boh, Jan. So, Tomas, you are working in the breaker now."

"Yes, Mr. Dusick. Time for me to help my family."

There was a thunderous crash, the sound of rocks tumbling, chains grinding, and men shouting. They were approaching the breaker, a straggling hulk of a building that dominated the landscape. The courage and determination Tomas had felt earlier, drained from his body. Soon he would be trapped in that place of horrors. He had seen the breaker boys, with their grimy faces and hardened hands, swearing, chewing tobacco, often bullying the younger boys. Many bore scars from their work. He knew a boy who had lost a leg, and others who had lost fingers. Tomas had seen the still, white body of little Harry, who had been smothered in coal dust when he fell through the coal chute. He had heard the women wailing and the men looking somber. As with all fatal accidents in the colliery, the death of this young boy affected all of them, and a sense of sadness had descended on the households of Ario for weeks.

"Tom." It was Jacob Banik, Adriana's son.

"Hiya, Jake." Even though Jacob was three years older than Tomas, the boys were friends.

"Goin' to the breaker?"

"Yup." Tomas was glad to see Jacob. Tomas knew Jacob was respected by the boys in the breaker; he had a reputation.

Jacob's reputation as a troublemaker began on a July day a few months after he had started working in the breaker. The air in the breaker was stifling and filled with coal dust, making it difficult to breathe. Jacob's back and shoulders ached from bending over the coal chute for interminable hours. There were cramps in his legs. Without thought, he uncurled his throbbing legs and straightened his back. Instantly, he felt the painful impact of a boot pushing him back down. Rage consumed him as he stifled a cry of pain. The boot lingered on his back until Jacob wanted to scream in anguish, adding to his humiliation. The pressure on his back was released and he heard the breaker boss move away. With shaking hands Jacob picked up a piece of slate, and then another. Without thought of the inevitable punishment, he threw one piece of slate into the conveyor belt and another at the breaker boss.

"What?" the breaker boss called out, his face red, his stick raised above his head, ready to administer discipline. A rock hit him from behind, and then another. In seconds, boys were on their feet, and pieces of slate were being thrown at the helpless breaker boss and into the conveyor belt until it ground to a halt.

"I'm goin' swimmin' upda crick," Jacob shouted, ducking as a piece of slate flew over his head. "Can't work now. The conveyor belt is broke."

"I'm going wit' you," a boy answered, scrambling from his bench and jumping across the breaker chutes.

"Ain't no work until they fix the conveyors."

"I'm outta here." Shouts of rebellion filled the air, and no one listened to the threats of the breaker boss, who had lost control of the boys.

"Run, before the boss gits ya." A boy pulled at the jacket of his brother, a child of perhaps seven years of age.

Laughter and shouts of jubilation echoed through the building as the boys climbed over the stalled machinery and ran out of the breaker before anyone could stop them. When they reached the swimming hole, the boys dived into the water, splashing, laughing, and describing the breaker boss in the most unflattering terms.

Jacob was a constant challenge for the bosses but, he was admired by the breaker boys for his daring. "Oh, he's a devil, he is," the bosses would say among themselves. They watched him closely. The breaker boss often singled him out for punishments, but Jacob never cringed or called out. He was kicked and hit with a stick, but his face was always rigid, his lips tightly closed. However, once, when the boss, wearing hobnailed boots, stomped on Jacob's fingers, he plotted his revenge. "We will strike," Jacob vowed to himself. But for now, all he could do was whip pieces of slate or rock at the boss when his back was turned.

Jacob helped little Tomas learn the ways of the breaker. He understood the boy's trepidation as he watched the ponderous machinery pulling a coal car slowly, steadily up the ramp to the top of the breaker; a second car was not far behind. Thunderous, rolling crashes were heard as the coal was dumped into the tipple at the top of the breaker. An empty car appeared, making its way down the opposite ramp. Another crash rang out as coal poured from the second car. Machinery, with sharp teeth, ground the large chunks of coal into smaller pieces with a deafening roar. Tomas shivered, and his stomach churned. His father's face gave an almost imperceptible grimace, and his lips tightened. But Jacob watched with the practiced expression of a man with experience.

"It's nuttin'. Just the coal gettin' ready for us," Jacob tried to reassure Tomas.

"Yah, I know," Tomas answered, trying to look unfazed.

"Don't worry, Mr. Chuba. I'll be wit' him." Jacob looked at Jan, man to man. He was letting Tomas's father know his son would be looked after. "Come on, Tommy, we'll be late." For a moment Jan watched as his son walked with Jacob toward the noisy, dirty breaker.

It's time, he thought as Tomas disappeared among the crowd of boys. *It's time for Tomas to contribute to the family.*

"A fight!" someone shouted. "A fight." The rallying cry reverberated through the air. Maybe there would be blood!

"Yer ignernt!" a boy with a black eye and a scar on his face was taunting a scrawny boy half his size.

"Yer pa is ignernt!" the boy countered, bravely standing his ground. He looked close to tears.

"Shut yer mout' or I'll shut it for ya!"

Jacob watched them for a moment, assessing the potential seriousness of the confrontation. When fists were raised, he decided to intervene.

"Gotnee tabacca?" Jacob's voice was calm, quiet as he positioned himself between the boys. With his enemy momentarily distracted, the smaller boy bolted up the stairs to safety. Tomas watched in admiration.

"Git yer own." The boy gave Jacob a shove and followed the younger boy up the stairs of the breaker.

"Come on, Tom," Jake said, giving Tomas an American name. "Ever' ting will be aw right. Jus stay away from dat one. He tinks he's tuff."

The breaker whistle blew, summoning the boys to work. They bounded up the stairs, pushing each other, shouting insults, and making heated comments about lunchtime rivalries. The wooden stairs groaned their objection beneath the pounding of the heavy shoes. When they reached the door of the breaker, the breaker boss was waiting, his stick pounding in a forceful rhythm against the door, reminding the boys he was in charge, and that no shirking would be tolerated.

"Sit a'side a me, Tom," Jacob commanded. Tomas lowered himself onto the pine board that was lying astride a long iron trough. The floor slanted in front of him, and he could see the conveyor belts that would carry the coal to him. He knew that his job would be to separate the pieces of slate from the gleaming anthracite coal. "It will be easy," he told himself.

Four boys were in front of him, four boys behind him, sitting on their own boards. Jacob and two other boys were to his left. Hundreds of boys and men filled the room, and their voices grew louder and echoed from the walls.

"Yo, Ant'ny," one called out. "I tink Rudy is afta me. He wants a beat me up."

"Don' worry 'bout it."

"I'm gonna get kilt."

"Nah, you'll be aw right."

Tomas was too nervous to worry about Ant'ny, or Rudy, or the boy who might kill him. He wanted to cry for his mother, to hide in her embrace, to sink into her chest, engulfed by warmth and love. Even school seemed preferable to what was about to happen in this place of misery. He thought of his teacher, Miss Simmons, her smile, her gentle encouragement as he tried to make sense of the words in his reader. She was always kind to the children, giving them candy at Christmas and colored eggs at Easter, even when forced to use the paddle on a misbehaving youth. She never used the ones with holes drilled in them. "Those holes make the punishment unnecessarily cruel," she would say.

The breaker boss stood off to the side, ignoring the boys. He held a broom handle in his right hand and tapped it idly into the palm of his left hand. A noise distracted the breaker boss and he turned. At that moment, a strategically thrown object hit him hard in the back. He turned around and, with a snarl, prepared to find and punish the culprit. His first thought was Jacob. A rumble, a crash, the entire building began to shake as the machinery started to whirl. He would get the boy later.

"Tom! Here," Jacob shouted, throwing Tomas a wad of tobacco and a handkerchief. "Like this." Jacob demonstrated how to chew the tobacco and tie the handkerchief over his mouth. Tomas looked around. All the boys were doing the same thing. "It will keep the coal dust out of your throat.

"When the coal comes, slow it down like this." Jacob moved his legs rapidly back and forth, pretending to slow down the coal. A thunderous roar sounded, and Tomas saw an avalanche of black coal pouring into the coal chute. A cloud of coal dust engulfed the breaker. Dust entered Tomas's lungs, and he started to choke. He pulled the handkerchief farther up his face, covering his nose, so only his eyes were visible. The boys at the top of the shoot kicked the coal slowing its advance as they picked out pieces of slate. Tomas held his breath as he watched. The coal was relentlessly pouring down the chute toward him. There was no escape.

Tomas's body trembled as the coal reached the boy in front of him. Pressing his lips together he fought the urge to cry and struggled to control his bladder. *I can't fail my responsibility and disgrace my family?*

Coal reached his feet and he began to kick. The force of the rocks was more than his frail child's legs could handle and his efforts did little to slow the flow of the black river of coal. He struggled to keep his balance. The breaker boss was watching him. "Pick out the slate," Jacob said nudging his charge. Tomas bent over the coal and began to pick out the pieces of slate. His hands began to bleed as he reached past the coal that was as sharp as broken glass.

I'm a slate picker now. He tried to smile as he threw a piece of slate into the trough next to him and sat up straight for just a moment to ease his back that had begun to ache. A stick poked his back and he stifled the urge to cry out in protest. Hunched over, his eyes fixed on the black stream of coal, his legs moving rhythmically, he began again to pick out pieces of slate and rock from the coal. He would remain like that for the next five hours. Bloodstains began to cover the coal that flowed past him. His fingers were cut and bruised, but the man with the stick was never far away. The tears streaked down his dust-covered face, but no one noticed or cared.

At home, Katarina prayed to the Blessed Mary to take care of her little boy. *Jan is doing the right thing,* she prayed. *Tomas is such a little boy, so innocent. Dear Holy Mother, I cannot protect him. I cannot protect my family.*

Emil the Mule Driver

Perched precariously on the edge of the coal car, Emil guided his mule through the darkness of the mine. "Gee," he shouted. A long, braided, black leather snake whipped through the air. The mule responded by pulling the car toward the tunnel on the right. "Way–haw." Emil cracked the whip again, and the car was pulled to the left.

"That's my good girl," Emil's voice was softer now as he reassured his mule that all was well. "Soon you'll get a rest." At the sound of his voice, the mule's ears flicked in understanding as she continued to plod along the gangway. Molly and Emil, who had worked together for almost a year now, were a team. They were partners in the mining business. Molly trusted Emil, as he had rescued her from her previous driver, an impatient and cruel boy who did not respect Molly's intelligence.

Emil's first job in Ario was the thankless, tedious job in the breakers. When he turned seventeen, a friend found him a job on a timber gang, hauling wood beams that would shore up the roof of the gangway. He was young and strong and did not mind the work—at least he did not have to sit all day picking coal. The pay was better, and he was able to save some money. *Someday I'll own my own horses, or maybe a mule.*

On Sunday afternoons he visited the mule barn, and over time he developed a friendship with a champagne-colored mule of exceptional intelligence named Molly. He brought her treats of alfalfa and oats, and she devoured the gifts as though she had not been fed in weeks. When he stroked her back, he searched for tender spots and rubbed them with ointments.

It was a Monday morning, the sun was just above the horizon, the air was crisp, and the men of the timber gang were engaged in raucous laughter as they waited for the wagon that brought the timbers they would haul into the mine. A chamber just off the gangway needed more props to support the roof, and the men would be inside the mine most of the day. They were enjoying the short respite the tardy wagon was affording them.

There was a commotion inside the mine, nothing unusual, just an ornery mule that was not responding to the commands of his driver.

"Molly!" Emil recognized her cry. "I know the mule. I can help," he said to the man standing next to him. "Shouldn't take long."

"Damn fool," Emil shouted when he saw the driver standing next to the agitated mule, beating her with his whip. Emil grabbed the boy's wrist just as the whip was about to land on Molly's back. Without warning, Molly raised her hind legs and knocked the driver to the ground.

"What the hell!" the driver screamed at the mule while scrambling to get back on his feet. "Goddamn mule could have killed me."

"But she didn't," Emil said while stroking Molly's neck. "It's all right, girl," he soothed. "It's all right, my precious." Molly seemed quite satisfied with herself as she accepted the attention of her friend. After all, she could have killed the driver, but had shown, in her opinion, incredible restraint.

The recalcitrant mule and the ensuing commotion did not miss the attention of the inside boss, who was speeding down the gangway in a trip car.

"Go! Pick up your pay on Saturday, and then pack your things." Beating a mule was an offense not to be tolerated. Losing a mule cost the company money. A mule driver could be replaced.

"See if you can do something with her," he ordered Emil, handing him the whip as he walked away.

Months later, Emil and his mule "Molly" were approaching the closed ventilation doors near the end of the gangway.

"Hey, Lazlo," Emil called out to the nipper he knew was sitting in the darkness.

"Hey, Emil," twelve-year-old Lazlo called back. He had heard the shouts of "Way-haw," followed by a crack of a whip. He recognized Emil's voice. Far off in the distance, a pinpoint of yellow light appeared in the cavernous blackness of the gangway. The nipper knew it would be the miner's lamp attached to Molly's harness. As he squinted his eyes to better see through the darkness, large ears appeared like an apparition. Lazlo opened the door and pushed his small body against the wall. There was always the risk of injury, or even death when the mules passed through the narrow opening.

Emil could not see Lazlo, the nipper, whose clothes and face were black with coal dust. He knew, from experience, that Lazlo spent the day sitting on his bench listening to water trickling down the walls and to the creaking of the mountain above him as it settled. Only the light from the lamp on his cap and the red eyes of the rats pierced the darkness.

Lazlo had been working as a nipper since he was eleven. Before that, he had been in the breakers. Now, he sat for endless hours on his crate, surrounded by the black walls of the mine. Regulating the ventilation doors was an important and dangerous job. It was necessary for the doors to be closed to control air flow through the tunnels. When the brakeless coal cars were approaching, the nipper opened the doors to avoid a collision. It was a dangerous job; if he was too slow to open them, or worse, fell asleep, he would be crushed when the mules and the coal cars crashed through the heavy doors.

"Hiya," Emil called to the boy as he got closer to the doors and he could see the light from Lazlo's little lamp.

"Hiya," Lazlo called back. He liked Emil and was always glad to see him.

"Named the rats yet?" Emil called to the boy; his tone lighthearted. The large rats in the mine often proved a welcome distraction from the boredom. Lazlo would feed them crusts of bread, and when he was careless, they would steal food from his dinner pail. Lazlo had named the largest and most vicious rat Franz Joseph, Emperor of Austria.

"No, I hain't," he lied.

"Don't let 'em steal yur sangwich," Emil shouted from his perch on the coal car. Molly slowly moved past the boy, ignoring him. She knew she was pulling the last load of the day and was anxious to return to the comfort of the stall and a wad of tobacca.

When the coal car had disappeared around the bend in the gangway, Lazlo pushed the door shut and sat back down on his crate. The heavy blackness surrounded him again. He listened to the scratching of the rats and the creaking of the mountain above him. Before too long, his eyelids grew heavy, and the boy fell asleep.

Chapter 8 - 1895

No Guarantees in the Patches

Anna

By 1895 our lives had settled into a routine. The friendship between Adriana, Katarina, and me strengthened as we shared the difficult, as well as the joyous, moments of our lives. We prayed, laughed, and cried together. Our families were growing, and there was seldom a year when one of us was not expecting the arrival of a new baby. We rejoiced at the birth of each child and mourned together whenever one of the little angels went to the Lord. In 1895, my youngest were still home with me, and Stephen had just started school. Adriana and Katarina had children working in the breakers and the mines. It was the way of things, you see. We accepted this without question. Starvation was the alternative.

There were no guarantees in the patches. When the breaker whistle sounded an alarm in the middle of the day, our hearts would stop as we ran toward the mine shaft. Our husbands, our sons, were they injured? Were they buried in the mine? Was there hope, or were some of us already widows?

Even our homes did not offer a safe refuge from discomfort and fear. Oh, we were used to the bitter cold in winter, the stifling heat of summer, but in our home-country, a house could be relied upon to stay where it was built. Not so, in the patches. Abandoned mine tunnels beneath our homes, empty, cavernous spaces waited, silent. Without warning, a rumble, and a home would crumble into the pit. It happened to my neighbor. God and the angels were with the family that day. No one was in the house when it fell into the earth.

Sometimes the men drank too much, but who could blame them? They spent their days in the darkness beneath the earth, and the stop at the saloon after their shift offered a respite from the hardships they endured. Adriana confided in me that she was worried about Cyril.

"When he drinks too much, he bellows and shouts and curses," she told me.

"Does he hurt you?" I asked.

"No, never," she would reply. "His anger is at the company men who care nothing about fairness, or the men who work for them."

Adriana's Family

It was cold that morning when Adriana left her warm bed and walked barefoot to the kitchen. Fresh snow had fallen during the night, and frost covered the windows. The house was quiet and dark in the hour before dawn. Adriana shivered as she drew her shawl tighter around her shoulders.

The dim light from the kerosene lamp she carried cast specter-like shadows on the floor and walls. The gray-speckled enamel coffeepot and a slightly rusted cast iron kettle sat atop the hulking black mass of the coal-burning stove. On a shelf next to the stove was a chipped ceramic pitcher and heavy plates with delicate indigo blue edgings. Each plate was slightly different, she never had enough money to buy a complete set.

An unpainted wooden table was pushed against the wall opposite the stove. In the summer, Adriana would pick wildflowers with her children and place them on the table. This morning there was only a large loaf of rye bread covered with a yellowed cloth and a ham purchased from the butcher last payday.

Five dented and slightly rusted tin lunch buckets hung in a neat row from pegs on the wall by the door. They smelled of the coal mines. Twenty years ago, when they arrived in Ario, there had only been one lunch bucket. But over the years, each boy, in turn, had been sent to the breaker, and eventually into the mine. The buckets waited to be filled with tea and sandwiches. Adriana was proud of her boys. They were strong, sometimes willful, but they understood their responsibility to the family.

Fast and agile, fourteen-year-old John worked as a spragger in the Ario mine. It was important but dangerous work.

Spraggers used sticks called "sprags" to control the speed of coal cars as they rolled down the slope of the mine. Running alongside the cars, dodging low ceilings and navigating narrow passageways, the boys jabbed the sticks into the wheels of the cars to slow them down.

John loved the work with its challenges and dangers, and he was not averse to breaking rules in the name of fun. More than once, he had stood on the bumper of a car, whooping and hollering as he rode it down the slope. Adriana, knowing her son's recklessness, feared for his safety. "He will be too quick to take risks," she told his father.

"John will be fine," Cyril reassured his wife. Cyril knew of their son's antics, but he did not share them with Adriana.

Twelve-year-old Louis worked as a nipper in the mine. He spent his days opening and closing ventilation doors as the mule-driven coal cars approached. Boredom filled his day, and he often drifted off to sleep. The only light was from the flickering flame in the kerosene lamp on his cap. As Louis watched the shadows dance on the walls his mind drifted, his body relaxed, and his eyes closed. The crack of the mule drivers whip alerted him, and he snapped to attention and opened the doors. There was a moment of noise and life and calls of greeting. The doors closed again and all that was left was darkness. "You'll be killed if you're sleeping when the mules come through," the inside boss warned him. Louis understood the risk, he knew the stories, boys crushed by the doors.

At the end of the shift, the breaker whistle blew, and it was time to leave his post. His spirit revived, and he was ready for adventure. Joining his brother and their friends for a smoke, the gang of boys walked through the patch, looking for mischief.

Adriana's middle boys, John and Louis, were a constant challenge. "So, like me. Rules or punishments don't seem to matter," she confided to Anna and Katarina when they met at the water pump or after church on Sundays. Her friends nodded in understanding. Everyone knew of the antics of the Banik brothers.

When Mrs. O'Hara's undergarments disappeared from her clothesline there were whispers that the Banik boys were responsible. Old Mr. Toth's goat was found tied to a tree behind the company store, where it feasted on boxes of produce that had just been delivered. The Banik boys were suspected of the crime. And then there was the incident that became a family legend.

"You shoulda heard Mrs. Johnson scream when she saw the snake slithering through her window," Louis bragged to his siblings.

"Well done!" John and Louis declared, slapping each other on the back. Patrik was silent and could not understand why his brother would do such a thing. Elizabeth, now a very grown up six-year-old, turned away in disgust. Little Helena had a nightmare of black, glistening snakes entering her room and crawling into her bed.

Their father had not been so understanding when the boys and their gang were caught by the Coal and Iron Police. The punishment had fit the crime, but Louis was not remorseful. "It was well worth the beatin' I got from Pa," he bragged.

Patrik, just eleven, was a sensitive, intelligent child, who, unlike the other boys, loved school. In the evenings, he sat with his mother at the table and read to her from *The Hazleton Sentinel.*

"Mr. and Mrs. Abrams of Hazleton are announcing the engagement of their daughter Agatha to Lieutenant John McCarthy of Wilkes-Barre." Patrik read the words as though they announced an event of urgent importance, and Adriana pretended to be interested.

"I want to write for the newspaper," he informed his mother. "I need to stay in school. That's what Miss Simmons told me."

"I will speak to your father. I am sure we can keep you in school a little longer." But Cyril did not see the value of too much schooling. When Patrik was ten he was sent to the breaker. Patrik never complained, yet Adriana saw the sadness in his eyes.

"You can go to school in the evenings," she told her son. "You will be a fine journalist someday."

Now, on this cold January morning, Adriana waited to hear her boys running down the stairs.

"Mornin', Ma! Smells good." Thick slices of ham sizzled in bacon grease on the stove when Jacob, Adriana's oldest son, entered the kitchen.

"Mornin', Jake." Her son had insisted on being called Jake ever since he went to work in the mine. *How handsome he is.* Jacob, eighteen now, was taller than his father, but with the same massive build, black hair, and blue eyes. Jake worked with his father in the mine. He was learning the skills he would need to be a certified miner.

"Hungry?" She did not need an answer. Her boys were always hungry. "Toast will be ready soon."

"Ma!"

"Ma!"

John and Louis were running, pushing, shoving, skipping down the stairs with youthful energy. Patrik, ignoring the antics of his brothers, chose a more dignified pace.

"My angels," Adriana greeted her daughters, Elizabeth and Helena, as they entered the kitchen and buried their faces in their mother's skirt. Their tiny feet, in thick, patched socks, had muffled their footsteps as they came down the stairs.

"Mama, I had a bad dream," Elizabeth's voice was muffled by her mother's skirts.

"I did too," mimicked four-year-old Helena. "Daddy was angry."

"Hush. Daddy isn't angry at you." Adriana and Cyril had been arguing the night before. Cyril had been drinking.

"But, Mama..."

"Hush. I have some milk and bread for you. Go sit by your brothers. Jake, go get William."

William was Jake's favorite sibling, and it did not take long for him to return to the kitchen with the three-year-old on his shoulders.

After the girls and William settled, Adriana took the five lunch pails down from their hooks, poured water from the kettle into the pitcher for tea, and began to assemble ham sandwiches. Soon Iva, just three months old, whimpered in her cradle, waiting to be fed. Cyril still slept in the room next to the kitchen.

That Sonofabitch Murphy

The house was dark except for the flickering light from the kerosene lamp on the kitchen table. It was cold in the room; the only heat was from the dying embers from the coal stove. Adriana sat in a rocking chair wrapped in a quilt. She was worried. It was getting late and her husband was not home. Murphy! She knew he was cheating the miners. The men who worked in the mine were angry, but her concern was with her husband. He was drinking too much and would not be silent about the contempt he felt for the man who was cheating him.

Murphy, an Irish American mine boss, despised the immigrants, and they returned the sentiment. He was a company man and making money for the owners by cheating the miners served his purpose. His profit-making shenanigans would be noted, and he would get favored treatment.

Miners were paid by the weight of the coal in their coal car. Murphy was the mine boss who weighed the coal. Yesterday, when Murphy accused Cyril of mixing dirt and slate with the coal, a fight had ensued.

"There's dirt and slate mixed with the coal. It will be deducted from the weight." Murphy didn't bother to look at Cyril while he recorded the adjusted measurements in his ledger. Cyril would not get paid what he was owed.

"You bastard! There ain't no dirt or slate in there!" Murphy ignored him until Cyril's punch bloodied his nose and knocked him to the ground. Cyril, accompanied by cheers, left Murphy there and headed for the tavern.

The evening was uneventful. The girls entertained William with a game of hide and seek while she fed Iva. When it was time for bed, Adriana told her youngest children an ancient tale about the beautiful princess Biela and the wicked elf. Prayers were followed by a lullaby and the children went to asleep.

It had been snowing most of the day and Louis and John spent their few hours of freedom using cardboard sleds to slide down the culm bank. Exhausted when they returned home, they barely acknowledged their mother before they went up to bed. Patrik, was content to sit near the lamp in the kitchen reading an old copy of *National Geographic* his teacher had given him. Reluctantly, he returned the magazine to the shelf when Adriana ordered him to bed. If only Cyril and Jake were home, all would be well.

She heard them in the street. Angry voices, soothing voices, a thud, a swear, and then the door opened. A blast of cold air preceded three men, a dusting of snow on their hats and jackets. Cyril, supported by Stefan and Jake, staggered into the room. His face was red with drink, his eyes glazed and unfocused.

"Help me with his coat and hat."

Cyril swayed while his friends pulled off his hat and coat. "Murphy," he spit out the name with contempt.

"Later Cyril, we'll talk later." Jake tried to calm his father.

"Put him on the bed," Adriana commanded.

"Murphy cheated him again. I was there," Stefan told her. "Cyril punched Murphy in the face, but we pulled him away."

"Shouda been four tons, not three." Cyril's words faded, replaced with a loud snore. Adriana pulled off his mud-covered shoes, and Jake covered his father with a blanket. Iva, who had been asleep in the cradle by the bed, began to whimper. Jake and Stefan, looking uncomfortable, backed away as Adriana picked up the baby and rocked her.

"I should go," Stefan whispered.

"Thank you for bringing him home, Stefan," Adriana spoke softly while attempting an unconvincing smile.

Stefan hesitated as he reached the door. "He needs to keep his mouth shut, Adriana. No good will come of complaining. The Irish boys were in the saloon tonight. You know, Shawn and Jim O'Shea, friends of Murphy. Murphy's cousin Jimmy Donegan works with the Coal and Iron Police. The O'Shea boys heard Cyril threatening Murphy."

"Don't worry, Ma," Jake said, but he was not at all sure that his mother should not worry. He knew the reputation of the O'Shea boys and Murphy, and the Coal and Iron Police. They detested the immigrants. They hated the way the immigrants looked and the way they talked, but mostly they hated that they took away the American jobs.

The next morning, Jacob filled a mug with coffee and settled himself at the table. "How is Pa?"

"His head will hurt, but it will serve him right." A cloud passed over Adriana's face as she arranged the thick slices of bread on the flat surface of the stove. "You saw how all the noise and commotion frightened the girls."

"I'll speak to him, Ma."

Adriana did not answer or look at her son. She just tended to the toast. The jagged edges were turning black, and the smell of burnt bread mingled with the aroma of coffee on the stove. Eggs in a dollop of bacon grease sizzled in the cast-iron pan. The smells and sounds of home that would be comforting on an ordinary morning did not do anything to relieve the tension in the house. This morning Adriana was in no mood for the foolishness of her sons as they clattered and banged down the stairs. She barely gave her little girls a hug when they entered the kitchen and she left Jacob to tend to William.

Eviction

Adriana could not sleep. It was a week after the Murphy incident, Cyril was still defiant and angry. He was drinking heavily. The smell of whiskey and beer on Cyril's breath and his loud snoring kept her awake. She wanted to talk to Cyril. She would tell him she understood why he was angry with Murphy. Together, they could discuss what was best for the family. The drinking and fighting could not continue. The entire family was at risk of being the victims of Murphy's ire. Perhaps tomorrow they could talk. *Cyril's a good man,* she told herself over and over. *Murphy is responsible for this.* Frustration at her helplessness made her body tense, and it seemed like hours before she drifted into a restless sleep.

"Quiet. You'll wake your father and the baby." Adriana's tone was harsher than she had intended. She was angry with Cyril, worried about her family, and frustrated that she could not give Murphy a piece of her mind. "Just sit and eat your breakfast."

"Sorry, Ma," the boys said in unison as Adriana placed a platter of ham, toast and eggs on the table. "Sorry Ma," little William mimicked his brothers. The girls, sensitive to their mother's mood, sat with concerned faces and drank their milk. The usual rambunctious behavior of the children was subdued but not totally under control. Adriana was sure she saw Louis kick John under the table. John scowled at Louis while he inhaled a slice of ham. The look clearly indicated the score would be settled.

Cyril, his head pounding, listened to the clink of tin lunch pails being placed on the kitchen table, the giggles of his little girls, and dogs barking in the street. His stomach churned as he smelled coffee and burnt toast. The room at the front of the house where he slept with Adriana and baby Iva was right next to the kitchen. There was no avoiding the sounds and smells of his family beginning their day. *Murphy*, he thought with a deep sigh as his arm covered his eyes, and he tried to will away the throbbing in his head.

There was a commotion in the street, horses, loud angry voices that Cyril tried to ignore. He sat up; waves of nausea filled his throat.

Lord have mercy. The ruckus was in front of his house. *Mother of God, what is the trouble?*

"Open the door, Banick!" A hard loud, knock on the door and then a thud as a heavy boot kicked it open. Iva, in her cradle next to Cyril's bed, screamed.

Startled by the noise, Adriana dropped the pitcher of tea. It shattered on the wood floor. "Cyril!" she shouted as she ran from the room. Jacob stood so quickly he knocked over his chair.

"Stay here!" Jacob commanded, glaring at his younger siblings. "Stay here!" None of them listened.

Everything was chaos. Adriana watched in horror as a man in uniform punched Cyril in the stomach. Stunned, Cyril braced himself against the wall. "A message from Murphy," the policeman said with disdain. "We don't want troublemakers here."

"Clear the place out," the policeman, who appeared to be in charge, commanded. With a smirk, the man who had punched Cyril picked up a chair and threw it into the street.

"Shut her up, or I'll do it for you!" Another policeman was moving to the cradle, where Iva was wailing. Adriana pounced on him and scratched his face, drawing blood. Stunned by her ferocity, the man backed away from the cradle. Adriana, panting, her eyes blazing, picked up her baby and moved next to her husband.

"We will be all right." Cyril's voice was cold, and there was defiance in his eyes as he took Iva from his wife.

"Noooo," Adriana protested as a man tore down the picture of the Holy Family from the wall.

"Let it be, Adriana." There was anger in his eyes as he touched Adriana's arm, trying to calm her.

"Leave that alone!" Adriana kicked and screamed as her sewing machine, a prized possession, was being lifted by two burly men. In seconds, she was on top of one of them, scratching and kicking until Jacob pulled her away.

"Let me go!" Adriana, overcome with anger, struggled to free herself from her son's strong arms. "Let me go!"

The men ignored her as they threw rope beds, clothing, and blankets into the street. When they were done, the family's meager possessions were in a haphazard pile in front of their home. The man Adriana had scratched and kicked was standing in the street holding a bloody handkerchief to his cheek, and he was now walking with a limp. Cyril knew there would be consequences, and the thought of his wife in jail made his stomach churn.

"We won't press charges against your wife this time," Murphy's cousin Donegan informed Cyril. "You need to teach your wife respect," the policeman continued. Despite his anger, Cyril had to suppress a smile at the thought of teaching Adriana anything.

Standing in the street, stunned by the events of the morning, the family huddled together. The little girls clung to their mother's skirts. Baby Iva was in her arms. Jacob held wide-eyed William, and Cyril had his arms protectively around his wife's shoulders. The boys, John, Louis, and Patrik, stood in front of the family, their fists tightly clenched.

Slowly, doors opened, and neighbors joined in solidarity with the family. There was a common bond among these families forged by shared difficulties. They all knew the sadness, the sense of loss, the fear of an uncertain future. Eviction could happen to any of them. Survival in the patches was only possible because of the bond that developed among the people who lived and worked there. Standing in the snow with the homeless family, it did not take long for assistance to be offered. Beds were carried to Anna's home, where the family would sleep. Pots, pans, dishes, and furniture were brought to already overflowing storage sheds. The family would be cared for until Cyril could find a new job.

"We will start again, Cyril," Adriana said, taking Cyril's arm as they walked to Anna's home.

"Yes, we will start again."

Husband and wife, their shared indomitable spirit giving them strength, walked through the snow, homeless for now, but not defeated.

"We don't want agitators here!" The Welsh mine supervisor in Lattimer scowled. He knew all about Cyril's problems with Murphy at Ario.

"I have skills and experience."

"So do a lot of men who don't cause trouble."

"Here." Cyril handed the supervisor an envelope.

"I see you are willing to work." The supervisor smiled, opening the envelope. It contained most of Cyril's savings. "All right. You can start tomorrow. Just an ash wheeler for now."

"I understand."

"There is an available house in Lattimer II." Cyril knew the Italians lived on Scotch Hill in the hills above Lattimer I, while the Slavs lived near Lattimer II. *We will be living in a shanty again.* He knew the place well, as he had friends there. It was a drab place with a narrow, rutted dirt road. Fences made from branches hid the shabby houses and their gardens. Each house had a rain barrel. It was a long walk to the only well.

"Thanks." Cyril's voice and face were expressionless as he turned and left the supervisor's office.

A week later Cyril and his sons loaded hand carts with pillows, blankets, the cradle for the baby, and Adriana's sewing machine. When everything was ready and goodbyes had been said, the family made their way to the dirt road that snaked through the strippings between Lattimer and Ario.

"I am so sorry, Adriana," Cyril said to his wife when they reached the shanties in Lattimer II.

"We are starting over, Cyril. Just starting over."

Chapter 9 - 1896

Love in the Patches

Anna

Emil, you remember, the young man who traveled with us to America. I was very fond of him. He was here without his family, so we made him part of ours. When our little Rudi was born Stefan and I agreed that Emil, and his lovely wife, Edita, would be his godparents.

Emil and Edita—we were delighted when they found each other. I remember their wedding. As in the old country, the celebration lasted for days. There were music and dancing and plenty of beer and food. Holubky—you may know it as stuffed cabbage—pierogi, kielbasa, all were in abundance. My specialty was the poppy seed cake and nut bread made the way my mother had taught me. It brought back so many wonderful memories of my own wedding. Oh, and then the dancing! How I loved it when Stefan took me in his arms and swung me around the dance floor.

Emil bought Edita a lovely blue dress for the wedding. It had lace around the bodice and neck, which was an extravagance not often seen in the patches. She treasured it for years, saving it for special occasions.

We missed Emil when he moved to Harwood to live with Edita's family, but her family needed him. It was the way things were done back then.

Emil and Edita

Emil stood at the batter's plate swinging his bat, watching the pitches, planning his play. The team from Harwood was a formidable rival, but expectations were high that Ario would break the tie and win the game.

While walking to the batter's plate, holding the bat loosely at his side, Emil noticed a girl intently watching him. She seemed to be analyzing his movements, assessing the likelihood that his swing would hit its mark. Emil thought he had seen her before, perhaps at another game or maybe in church; he was not sure.

There was nothing unusual about the girl; indeed, she was rather plain and not his type at all. She was flat-chested, her cheeks were pale, and her hair was thin; he preferred girls with ample bosoms, pink cheeks, and thick, curly hair. It was the disconcerting intensity of her scrutiny that caused him to look back at her in the seconds before he swung his bat. The bat hit the ball with a snap, sending it high over the trees in left field. The spectators roared. With a confident jog, Emil moved from base to base. When he passed the girl, who was now standing but not cheering, he tipped his hat.

He saw her again, this time at Sunday Mass at Saint Joseph's in Hazleton. She was sitting with her family a few rows in front of him. When she stood, he noticed that she was tiny, perhaps slightly less than five feet tall, and her waist was so small he imagined he could place both hands around it. She was wearing a straw hat with a blue band and a blue dress festooned with tiny yellow flowers. *She looks lovely,* he thought, no longer noticing her straight hair and tiny bosom. As she left the church, she smiled at him, and he noticed there was a cute dimple in her left cheek.

That afternoon, when Ario was playing the team from Crystal Ridge, he looked for the girl, but she was not there. The disappointment he felt was strangely unsettling. She was not at church the following Sunday. He was not sure why he cared.

A week later Ario was playing Harwood, and Emil could think of nothing but the girl. Would she be there? He was at bat when he saw her sitting on the hill next to the field. Was she smiling at him? Distracted, he heard the call, "Strike two." He turned his attention back to the game. When the game was over, he watched her walk away with the pitcher from Harwood. "Why am I jealous?"

"Her name is Edita. That's her brother, plays for Harwood. I think his name is Samuel." A friend had noticed the look on Emil's face as he watched the girl.

"Oh."

"She likes you. I can tell."

"Who?"

"Edita."

"Maybe."

"Come on, let's get a beer."

"How about a game of horseshoes?" A few of the young men from the Ario team had gathered outside the church. No game was scheduled, so a different distraction was needed.

"Poker and a beer?"

"Nah, horseshoes."

"What about you, Emil?"

"No, but thanks anyway. I'll walk to Hazle Mines. I want to watch their pitcher, Samuel. He's good." That was the truth. Samuel was a formidable opponent.

"Edita might be there," his friend teased.

"Maybe."

The game had already started when he arrived. *Edita, where are you?* he thought as he wandered through the crowd of spectators. It seemed that all of Harwood and Hazle Mines were there. A straw hat with a blue ribbon caught his attention. Edita. Casually, with his eyes seemingly intent on the game, he walked in her direction. Still watching the game, he sat on the grass next to her. For a few minutes, they sat in tortured silence, watching the game and seeming not to notice each other.

"Well!" she said, still looking at the field.

"What?" He was not sure she was even speaking to him.

"Well, you are here! Finally!"

"What?" he said again, astonished at her boldness.

"I've been waiting for you." Her eyes teasing him. "Ever since you smiled at me in church, I have been waiting for you."

Just then her brother pitched the ball, and the umpire shouted, "Batter out!"

Harwood won the game! Edita, seemed to have forgotten Emil, she ran toward the field where the Harwood players and their elated fans were gathering. "Samuel!" She was laughing as she held onto her hat, the blue ribbon trailing behind. "Samuel!"

Emil just stood where he was, unsure what to do. Should he leave, or follow her to the field? He felt like an outsider as he watched Samuel lift Edita off the ground and she kicked her heels back, her face beaming with excitement and pride. Her brother lowered her to the ground. Something was said, and then Emil saw them looking at him. Edita waved to him, reached for her brother's arm, and together, they walked to the place where Emil was standing.

"Samuel, this is Emil from Ario."

"Emil. Saw you at the game we played in Ario. Good game." Samuel's voice was congenial as he reached for Emil's hand.

"Thanks. Congratulations on your win today."

Emil began attending Sunday mass with more regularity than he had in the past. Perhaps Edita would be there. She was not. He watched for her when Ario was playing Crystal Ridge. He took a chance she might be at Beaver Brook when they were playing Harwood. She was not in church or at the games. Was she ill? Was she avoiding him? The thought was more upsetting than he cared to admit.

It was Palm Sunday, a beautiful April day, and Emil had gone to mass with Anna and her family. He looked for Edita but did not see her. As is the Catholic custom, he knelt in the pew and made the sign of the cross, preparing himself to participate in the Holy Mass. But his prayer was a wish, that Edita would be there.

"Emil." He heard her voice and his heart melted. She was standing there in the aisle, watching him. "Can you walk me home after church?" she whispered. Her tone was inviting and a little conspiratorial. "Samuel wants to go off with his friends. My parents could not come today."

He nodded and thought his voice would fail him. "Of course," he heard himself say.

Edita took Emil's arm as they walked down the stairs of the church. When they reached Laurel Street, he asked about her brother and her family. They talked about Easter and the traditions that the families shared, but after a while, they were silent, content to walk together. Somehow neither felt uncomfortable with the silence. It seemed so natural for them to be together.

The young couple approached Broad Street. There were carriages and trolleys and shops that spoke of wealth and a way of life very different from the coal patch villages where they lived. Beyond the trees, lining the sidewalk on the opposite side of the boulevard, they glimpsed the white Pardee Mansion with its spacious lawns and gardens.

"Imagine living there!"

"I can't imagine," Emil answered. "What do they do with all those rooms?" Emil did not care about the mansion or those rooms; he was marveling at the delicate way Edita was holding his arm. *As light as a feather, she is.* He imagined for a brief instant lifting and lowering her gently onto a bed. His face felt hot at the thought, but fortunately, Edita was looking at the mansion and not at him.

"My cousin worked there as a servant."

"Was she happy working there?"

"Yes, I think she was. She likes being around beautiful things. She told me about a burgundy sofa with cushions so soft they cradled your body when you sat in it." Emil was not sure what burgundy was, some type of red he supposed. "Flowers and birds and dolphins were carved into the wood," she continued.

"Oh," was all Emil could think of to say. "Come. Let's go." Emil took her hand, and together, they ran across the wide avenue, laughing as they dodged carriages and horses.

Throughout the summer Emil found opportunities to walk Edita home after the games or after mass on Sundays. He became friends with her brother Samuel and was invited to their home for Sunday dinner.

It was a hot July day, and they sat on a hill watching a ball game, her tiny fingers intertwined with his. He thought he saw love in her eyes when she turned and looked at him. He knew then he wanted to be with her for the rest of his life.

Emil had just checked on his mules, who were fed, stalled, and tucked in for the night. The mule boys left for the day, and he walked home for dinner. His thoughts were on the chicken soup he knew would be in the pot tonight. It was Monday, and Ida always made chicken soup for her boarders on Monday.

"Emil." Stefan was walking toward him, a deep frown on his face. "There was a rock fall in the Harwood mine."

"Who?" A rock fall would mean injuries.

"Mark Kolar." Emil froze. Mark Kolar was Edita's father. Emil had found Mark to be an amiable man who welcomed Emil into his home. They talked about baseball, and he told Emil he played when he was young. "I was a star player," he asserted proudly, and no one challenged him.

"Is he…?"

"Yes. They pulled him out alive, but…"

"What happened?"

"Mark and his laborer were robbing the pillars again." If you worked in the mine, you knew pillars of coal held up the roof of the mine as gangways were expanded. "Dangerous work removing them pillars. The owners want every bit of coal they can get. If you're told to rob the pillars, you robbed the pillars. Took your chances. Mark ran out of luck."

"Was there a warning?"

"Larry told me the miners heard the mine 'working' right before the roof collapsed, but Mark didn't listen. He wanted to finish the job. Get his full weight of coal."

"I need to go to Harwood. Edita needs me."

"Yes, go."

"Tell Mrs. Nagy not to expect me tonight." Harwood was ten miles away. Emil would not return before dawn.

Yellow light from a kerosene lamp flickered, casting shadows on the tear-streaked faces of those who had gathered in the dark room. Edita, shock, and grief on her face, sat next to her mother, while Samuel stood behind them, his hands resting on their shoulders. Their sister, Emma, a flaxen-haired ten-year-old, was sitting with a neighbor, who was trying to comfort the distraught child.

The body, cleaned and packed in ice, rested on a table in the center of the room. Edita's mother had dressed her husband in the one suit he owned, and Samuel had placed a baseball cap in his father's hands. There were other women in the shadows of the room, arranging flowers, preparing food, cleaning away blood-stained clothing, and comforting bewildered children. The ritual had been repeated many times in the coal towns. Death was a frequent visitor to their homes. Accidents in the mines killed many men and boys; babies and children died of diseases; women lost their lives in childbirth.

When Emil arrived in Harwood, it seemed the entire patch was at Edita's home. Outside, people formed a line waiting to get into the house. The kitchen and downstairs front room were crowded. Women, carrying platters of food squirmed through the throng to find room to place their dishes. Everyone shared the family's anguish and were ready to offer support. The door was open, so Emil squeezed through the crowd and entered the room where Edita and her family had assembled. His heart broke when he saw the woman he loved in such anguish.

"Edita, I am so sorry, my love."

"My father," Edita sobbed, as she unsteadily rose from the chair.

"Yes, I know," he said, wrapping his arms around her.

"I heard the breaker whistle," she stammered. "We all ran to the colliery. Somehow, my mother knew it would be Father. "Mark!" she called over and over as we got closer to the mine. They carried him out on a wooden board, his crushed arms and legs dangling over the side. Not Father, I thought, it could not be Father. His body was broken, Emil. His clothes were covered with blood, but he was still alive. 'Mark,' Mama kept calling to him, willing him to live. She fell on him, her body covering his wounds." Edita stopped for a moment, unable to go on, as she was crying again. "Her apron, her dress, her hands, Father's blood was all over her. He died there, in her arms." Edita could not say more.

Emil wrapped his arms around her, and they stood there in silence for a long time. Eventually, he took her outside, and with his arms around her, they walked under the stars.

"My dear Edita," he whispered. "I will take care of you."

A few months later they were married, and Emil moved to Harwood.

Chapter 10 - 1897

Family Traditions

Anna

On Easter Sunday 1897, we had been in Ario for eight years. Yes, eight years. By that time, I had given birth to four more children: Rose, Lucia, Robert, and Rudolph. We called him Rudi. He was just six months old that Easter. My family, my children, meant everything to me. Sometimes, I look back on those years when the children were young, and those memories, even now, make me smile.

There were days when a walk in the woods with my children provided an escape from the coal dust, the noise from the breaker, and our endless toils. Even now, I can still imagine the feel of soft earth, covered with leaves and pine needles, beneath my bare feet. We would listen to the rustle of the leaves as an unseen animal scurried away. When we were thirsty, we would take big gulps of the cool water from the mountain spring, and Rose would complain when her brothers deliberately splashed her face. I let the children work these things out for themselves. Along the way, Rose would pick wildflowers for the table in the kitchen, and, depending on the season, we would either gather mushrooms or pick blueberries.

Stephen was ten that summer. Next summer he would be working in the breaker. I remember watching him running with his friends, laughing as they played children's games. He was so sweet, so innocent, but I knew the breaker would steal that from him. We had no choice, you understand, our family was growing, and the money Stefan earned wasn't enough to cover our bills. Starvation wages! That is what they paid him for his backbreaking work. Starvation wages!

Rose was seven years old in 1897, a beautiful little girl with abundant brown tresses and green eyes just like mine. She was such a help to me as she learned the skills she would need to manage her own home someday. My friend Adriana had four boys before she gave birth to a girl. I don't know how she managed.

I remember the first time Rose cut the noodles for the Halushki. She was only three, or thereabouts, barely able to hold the large knife steady as she pulled the blade through the dough. But she was determined, her face serious as she obeyed my order to keep her fingers out of the way. The noodles were jagged, and of every imaginable shape, but in her mind, and mine, they were perfect. She did not notice, or care, that flour was everywhere, on her face, hands, the floor. We cleaned up the mess, and I sent her to play with her little brother. That night, Stefan commented on the wonderful noodles and all their interesting shapes. "I made them," Rose told her father. "I did it myself."

Lucia, my third child, was named after Stefan's sister. She was a good baby, quiet, but she was never strong. When she was just a year old, there was an outbreak of measles in Ario. Stephen proved to be immune to the disease, and Rose recovered quickly. But poor Lucia was not able to fight the evil that had invaded her tiny body. We called the doctor, and then the priest. She went to the Lord while I cradled her in my arms. Stefan made a tiny casket for her, and we buried our baby girl in Saint Joseph's Cemetery in Hazleton. We marked her grave with a wooden cross. There was no money for more.

How proud I was of my children when they, each in their turn, knelt at the communion rail for the first time. I made Rose's dress. It was just white muslin, but we bought a satin ribbon for her waist, and Adriana, her godmother, made her a veil that reached to the hem of her skirt.

Often, a professional photographer from Hazleton would come to the church and take a photograph of all the children for the newspaper. How angelic they looked, how innocent. I kept the newspaper clippings and put them in the trunk next to my bed. Perhaps my grandchildren will find them.

There was a little church in Ario. It wasn't a very big church, you understand. The bishop would arrange for a priest to visit the church at least once a week to say mass, and we would receive the Holy Sacrament. That little church was a place *where we found peace and comfort, easing the trials of our daily lives. Katarina and I would go there to say our rosaries and to meet with other Catholic women. We had formed a little sodality devoted to the Blessed Virgin Mary, and our mission was to help those in the community with the greatest need.*

There were many Sundays when we would walk to Saint Joseph's Slovak Roman Catholic Church in Hazleton. There, unlike in Europe, we could pray and sing in our native language. "Vitajte," Father Jaskovic, the pastor, would say, greeting us in Slovak as we entered the vestibule of the church. We felt at home there, with others whom we shared memories of a faraway place and time.

Easter Sunday – April 18, 1897

The smell of kielbasa boiling on the stove permeated the small kitchen. Eggs, absorbing the flavor from the meat, clanked together in the same pot as bubbles of water floated to the surface. Sweetbreads were baking in the oven, warming the small kitchen, and the Hrudka, an egg cheese ball made only at Easter, drained in a cheesecloth over a bowl. A crock of fresh sauerkraut had appeared from the storage space beneath the house, and a small ham had been procured after much bargaining with the butcher. Anna had planned for this day, saving coins in an old battered tin cup kept above the stove.

Three-year-old Robert watched, mesmerized, as the water boiled, and the eggs bounced merrily among the plump chains of kielbasa. The smell of the Easter foods caused his mouth to water and his stomach to make bubbling noises. He was hungry, so very hungry, but neither the contents of the pot nor the breads baking in the oven, could be touched until after Mass on Easter Sunday morning.

It was Holy Saturday, the day before Easter. The Lentin fast had been observed, the crucifixion of our Lord Jesus had been commemorated the day before, and now the preparations for the celebration of Easter had begun.

Anna was preparing the food for the Easter basket to be blessed by the priest that afternoon. Blessing of the food to be eaten on Easter Sunday was an ancient and cherished tradition. For Anna, the ritual reminded her of home and her childhood. Like her son, she too had smelled the kielbasa and watched the eggs boiling in the big pot on the stove in her mother's kitchen.

"The kielbasa is ready," Anna called to her children, as she removed the fat, juicy links of meat from the boiling water and placed them on a large white chipped platter to cool. "Rose, you are old enough now to manage the eggs." With great care, the little girl scooped the eggs from the pot and placed them on the platter next to the kielbasa. Everyone stood back and hungrily admired the moist eggs and glistening skin of the meat. "A little taste, please, Matka?" little Robert asked hopefully.

"This is still a fast day, Robert. We must remember our Lord Jesus sacrificed for us. We will feast in celebration tomorrow, after Mass." Robert was still not sure he understood why he needed to wait. Perhaps later Matka would see how hungry he was and make an exception. Surely Jesus would understand.

Later, when the contents of the platter had cooled, and the breads were removed from the oven, Anna summoned her children again. "Rose, we are ready for the embroidered towel that will line the basket. It is in the trunk by the bed." Rose knew where the cloth was stored, waiting for this special occasion. With long, irregular childish stitches, she had decorated the edges of the towel with remnants of blue and yellow thread. Now, she would have the honor of lining the basket with the cloth.

"Stephen, put the bread in the center of the basket.

"Robert, put the eggs over here."

"Be careful not to drop them," his sister warned. Since the day he was born, Robert had been her responsibility.

"Rose, put the kielbasa here, and the horseradish there."

"What is missing?" Anna scrutinized the basket, scratching her head.

"The Hrudka, Matka," the children shouted in unison.

"Oh, yes. I forgot." With a smile, she walked over to the shelf where the egg mixture wrapped in cheesecloth was draining into a big bowl. "Yes, I think it is ready," she said, squeezing any last bit of moisture from the ball of eggs.

"We will put a few slices of the Hrudka here, and the ham in this corner." The family stood back and admired the basket they had prepared. What a feast they would have.

"Matka, can I have an egg now?" Robert asked hopefully. "I am so hungry, and one egg will not be missed."

Anna smiled at her impatient son and shook her head. "No."

The basket was covered with a second towel. This towel, also richly embroidered, was yellowed with age. Anna's mother had given it to her daughter when she married Stefan. "With this cloth you will start your family's Easter traditions," Anna's mother said hugging her daughter. Covering the basket with the towel her mother had given her she handed it to Stephen. Holding Rudi in her arms, Anna watched from her porch as the children walked to the church, where the priest blessed the food to be eaten on Easter morning.

Anna took extra care to prepare her family for the Easter celebration. She had aired and brushed Stefan's wool suit. It was the same one he had brought from Slovakia years ago, and there were patches of cloth sewn into places that had worn thin. *But he will still be the handsomest man in the church,* she thought, as her hand brushed away a few strands of hair that had fallen on the collar.

Their son Stephen wore the suit Anna had bought for his first communion a year ago. She had taken down the hem of the trousers, which were still too short. "It will do for another year." She sighed, tugging at the hem of the trousers in a vain attempt to make them reach the top of her son's shoes. "You are growing so fast," she said, giving him a hug.

Robert wore the hat with the feather that had belonged to his father when he was a little boy, and baby Rudolph had a new sweater Edita had knitted for him.

Anna tied jade green ribbons on Rose's long braids, and a matching ribbon adorned the waist of her dress. Stefan bought white carnations for Anna and Rose.

It was a chilly Easter Sunday morning. Winter had not fully made its exit from the coal fields of Pennsylvania. But the cloudless sky promised a beautiful early spring day as the family walked the two miles to Saint Joseph's Slovak Church in Hazleton.

Like many of the patch towns around Ario, there was a small park where families gathered. Wooden tables with rough-hewn benches were strategically positioned under ancient oak and maple trees. A shallow pond, with a green layer of duckweed covering its surface, offered little boys a place to search for tadpoles and crayfish. There was a baseball diamond for older boys and a horseshoe pit for the men. The fields overflowed with clusters of wildflowers for girls to gather as gifts for their mothers. Only the presence of a dark and barren culm bank that towered above the park, a reminder that this was a coal town, marred the bucolic setting.

It was here that the families of Ario gathered on Easter Sunday 1897.

Jackets off, sleeves rolled up, the men, overheated and excited, waited for Stefan to pitch his horseshoe. Stefan and Jan needed one more point to reach the agreed upon forty points to win the game. Cyril had just made a ringer; his second shoe lay in the pit a few inches from the stake. Everyone was quiet as Stefan picked up his first horseshoe.

The men focused on the game; the pain in their backs, the suffocating coal dust that filled their lungs, and their growing debt to the company store, were forgotten. All that mattered was the horseshoe, the pit, and the score. There was a hushed silence as Stefan swung the horseshoe, feeling its weight, judging the distance to the stake. A loud clang. Stefan's horseshoe hit the stake, spun, and landed on top of Cyril's.

Jan cheered, Cyril frowned, while his son Jacob just took a big gulp of his beer. Stefan allowed himself a rare smile of self-satisfaction. Cyril's three points had been canceled. The tension in the air was palpable as Stefan picked up his second horseshoe and prepared to pitch it toward the stake. He swung his arm, and, with a clank, it landed leaning on the stake; the game was over. Pats on backs ended the friendly competition. The sweet, tangy smell of stuffed cabbage and the knowledge that the women had spent the week baking poppyseed cake and nut bread drew the men away from the horseshoe pit to the tables where the families were gathering.

Stomachs were full, the little ones tired as the sun reached the horizon. Women gathered the children and prepared to return to their homes. The men sat at a table with their beer, cigarettes, and pipes, playing a last game of poker. Five chips were in the pot. Cyril was shuffling the cards, as smoke from his pipe swirled past his eyes.

"The mine in Lattimer was closed again last week." Cyril began to deal the cards.

"Same in Ario." Stefan took a puff from his pipe, intently watching the deal.

"Can't survive like this." Cyril finished the deal. "Can't pay down my debt, can't feed my family."

"It's just the way it is." Stefan shrugged.

"Pardee and Markle, greedy bastards."

"And Coxe, he ain't no better."

"The union... Cyril's voice trailed off. He was holding what he was sure was a winning hand.

"The union only cares about the Americans. They want the likes of us out of here."

"Don't trust Fahy, anyway." Stefan was echoing the sentiments of most of the men in Ario and Lattimer. John Fahy of the United Mine Workers had tried to persuade them to join the union but had given up and left. "Besides, it's all been tried before," Stefan asserted, clenching his pipe in his teeth. He was watching Cyril, the unmistakable glow in Cyril's eyes, his flushed cheeks, the self-satisfied smile on his face.

"I'm not joining any union," Jan declared while curling the end of his handlebar mustache. He was holding a pair of aces and was also watching Cyril.

"I fold," Stefan said, putting down his cards. His two clubs would not match whatever was in Cyril's hand.

"All they want is my money," Jan complained. "Thirty cents they want. Thirty cents. If I had thirty cents, I'd buy a new dress for my Katarina." He looked around the table. Stefan had folded and was relighting his pipe. Cyril was still looking pleased with his hand. He was never good at bluffing. It was impossible to tell what cards Jacob was holding. "I fold." Jan laid down his cards.

"I'll raise a chip." Cyril grinned, looking at his son. He was holding three kings.

"I'll call you." Jacob put down his cards while watching his father. The glow in Cyril's eyes faded when he saw his son's cards. Jacob had a full house.

"Time to go home," Stefan announced, getting up from the hard bench and stretching his back. "Good game."

Walking alone Stefan reflected on the events of the day. It was a day to worship the risen Christ, but it was also a day filled with the warmth of family and friends. It reminded him of his childhood and his family. America! Was life any better here?

Chapter 11 - 1897

Trouble in the Patches

Anna

People don't like to talk about what happened the summer of 1897. Even after all this time the memory is still too painful. Most just want to forget. But now, I don't think that is the right thing. People need to know what happened—it is our story, our history. There are lessons to be learned.

The Americans did not understand us. "They live in squalor," they would say. "They are different from us." We had trouble with the language. With our heavy accents, we could see on their faces they did not understand what we were saying. They thought we were stupid. The American miners resented us because our men were willing to do the worst, most dangerous work, and paid the lowest wages.

But, despite all the hardships, we had our dreams. We worked hard and, when times were good, saved our money. Some of us bought land, others sent money home to families still in Europe. But when there was no work, we watched our savings dwindle and our debt grew. That's what it was like the summer of 1897. The men were working only two, maybe three days a week. It was harder to pay our bills and feed our families.

We needed coal for cooking and warmth, so we picked what we could from the culm bank. You may have seen these large mountains of rejected slate, mud, and pieces of coal from the breaker. I stayed near the bottom of the bank, but some women would risk climbing higher in search of larger pieces of coal. We knew the dangers. Women had died climbing the culm banks, crushed by falling rock. The Coal and Iron Police, paid by the company, would chase us away from the bank. "Stealing," the bosses called it. Our men dug it, and the way we saw it, it was ours. We needed that coal. Why should we buy back what our men had dug from the mine? But Pardee, the owner of the mine, did not see it that way. Jesus have mercy on his selfish soul.

The tragedy of 1897 began in Honey Brook, a patch town south of Hazleton. A man named Gomer Jones was responsible.

August 11-20

Emil was in the Harwood mule barn nursing a wound on a hapless mule who had suffered an unfortunate accident that morning.

"Honey Brook! Gomer Jones!" A boy stood in the doorway of the barn. His message sounded urgent and startled both Emil and the mule.

"What is it?"

"The company store!" The boy did not stay to explain.

"I'll be back soon," Emil comforted the distraught mule, handing her a wad of tobacco. "Gotta see what's happenin'."

A crowd was gathering outside the company store. "Gomer Jones." The despised name permeated the air, amidst grumbling and angry shouts.

"What happened?" Emil asked a rough-looking miner, who he knew worked at Honey Brook.

"The mule drivers in Honey Brook walked out."

"Why?"

"Jones moved their mules to Audenreid." Emil understood. Keeping all the company mules in a central location would save money for the company. Gomer Jones was the division superintendent for The Lehigh and Wilkes-Barre Coal Company that owned collieries near McAdoo. His job was to make money for the company and to return discipline to the mines. Jones cut back wages, laid off workers, and enforced strict discipline. "Slave driver," the newspapers called him for his tyrannical treatment of the workers he supervised. Jones despised the Irish workers and had a special disdain for the immigrant miners, calling them lazy, compliant, and stupid. The workers hated him just as much, and maybe more.

"It will take my boy an extra hour to get his mules each mornin', and another to return them at night," the man grumbled. His son was a mule driver at Honey Brook. "Pay doesn't start till they get the mules to the mine."

"Bastard."

"My boy said they tried to reason with Jones, but he wouldn't listen, so they walked out."

"Good for them."

"The next mornin' they lined the road, preventin' the mules from returnin' to the mine. Jones didn't like it one bit. He hit one of 'em with a crowbar."

"That sonofabitch."

"Boy's name was Boden, John Boden. Tough kid. Boden fought back, and the others attacked Jones. Mighta killed him if he wasn't rescued by another supervisor."

"Jones got what he deserved."

"Yeah."

"It didn't stop there. The boys ran to the whistle tower and blew the whistle, callin' on everyone to stop work. Over eight hun'ert of us went on strike today, supportin' the boys."

Word of Jones and the crowbar spread throughout the region, and by Monday, over three thousand workers from The Lehigh and Wilkes-Barre Coal Company went on strike. They'd had enough of Jones, enough of the disrespect, the discrimination, the lack of work, and meager wages that could not support a family.

The company retaliated by firing employees sympathetic to the strike and sent well-armed Coal and Iron Police to patrol the patches.

A boy, perhaps eight years old, sat in the middle of the blueberry patch, a bucket in his lap. His clothing was muddy and covered with leaves. He had spent the morning searching for the last of the precious fruit that still clung to the bushes. It was a sweltering late summer day, and sweat was visible on his tattered shirt, but for today, he was free, free to feel the sun on his face and smell the earth below his feet. The breaker, towering over the landscape, was silent, the mine closed. They were on strike.

The Road to Lattimer · 139

With his mouth full of blueberries, the boy stopped his work to watch a hawk being tormented by a gaggle of crows. He was the first to see them, the Coal and Iron Police.

"Billy! Look," the little boy called to his brother, who was a short distance away. Six men on horseback, their rifles resting across their arms, were headed toward them. "Coal and Iron Police."

"Quiet," Billy whispered, crawling to his brother. "They haven't seen us yet."

"Are they here for the strikers?"

"Maybe. Can't be good."

"We need to warn them," the older boy whispered, pulling his brother farther from the road. The younger boy nodded understanding. The boys sneaked back up the hill and ran toward home, stumbling on the tangle of weeds and underbrush, ignoring the thorns that cut their bare legs and arms, the blueberries forgotten.

"Coal and Iron Police!" they yelled, running down the main street of the patch.

When the police reached the main street, the miners were ready for them. The men stood along the road, silent, eyes glaring defiance. The police had hoped to instigate violence, but this time, it did not happen. They passed through the patch without incident, and the strike continued.

The meeting at Michalchik's Hall

By August 16 tensions were running high among the southern and eastern European miners in the patches south of Hazleton. Gomer Jones, and his confrontation with the mule drivers was now a symbol of the oppression and cruelty of the mine owners. The once-docile immigrants were enraged by the new Alien Tax that singled them out as foreigners. Many had been in America for over ten years. Their children were being raised as Americans. Despite their willingness to work hard and accept the most dangerous jobs, the men were unable to support their families. Now, the men who had once been so docile were united in their determination to reclaim their dignity. On

August 16 hundreds of miners gathered in Michalchik's Hall in McAdoo.

The room was dank and filled with smoke as angry men shouted in Slovak, Italian, German, and Hungarian and called for violence and continuation of the strike. With a calm, authoritative voice, Jozef Kincila, a Slovak miner, brought order to the room. After heated discussion, the men settled on two demands: a wage increase and the removal of Gomer Jones. Demands were telegraphed to the Lehigh and Wilkes-Barre supervisor.

The strike against The Lehigh and Wilkes-Barre Coal Company continued for four more days. On August 20, a ten-cent raise went into effect, and the conduct of Gomer Jones was to be investigated. The miners who worked for The Lehigh and Wilkes-Barre Coal Company went back to work. The strike was over, for now.

Anna

We read about it in the papers, the troubles in Coleraine and McAdoo. It all felt far away, the strikes, the violence. I had my family to care for. I talked with Adriana and Katarina when we met at the Women's Catholic Guild on Sunday afternoons.

"My Jan wants nothing to do with the union or the strikes," I remember Katarina saying, and I understood how she felt.

"We need to join them," Adriana thundered in reply. "Cyril agrees with me." I listened. We had heard that our Emil was becoming an active member of the Union. We prayed for him, his wife, Edita, and their new baby.

In August 1897 we felt, for the first time, the effects of the Alien Tax. Oh, I can see from your puzzled faces you never heard of such a tax. Praise the Lord it no longer exists. The companies were being taxed for each immigrant they hired, deducting the tax from the workers' already meager wages. I didn't understand it all, the politics, but it was clear the American workers resented us. We were a threat to their jobs, to their way of life. The Alien Tax was meant to discourage the owners from hiring our men.

It was a Saturday in August, as I remember, payday. I can still see my Stefan wearing the black suit we brought from Europe. He always wore that suit on payday. I placed my head on his shoulder and felt the coarse wool against my cheek. The smell of tobacco and coal dust that lingered in the wool was familiar and comforting. There were worry lines on his face that morning. "We will be all right," he assured me. "We will be all right."

But it would not be all right. He looked defeated when he came home and placed the few coins on the table. The company had deducted the rent, the doctor, the company store, and now, the Alien Tax. Most of what was left would be needed for the bribe Stefan paid for an extra day of work. There would not be enough to feed our family, and our debt to the company store would grow. Katarina later told me that Jan had not brought home even that meager amount. Adriana showed us the big red **X** *on Cyril's pay slip next to "store." She had gone to Hazleton to buy sugar and flour. "Why not?" she scoffed, always defiant, always rebellious. "It is cheaper there." But there were consequences for not using the company store. The* **X** *was a warning. It told her to be careful.*

"They are always watching," I remember telling her.

"They own us," Katarina said, her voice meek as always.

"No one owns me," Adriana had scowled, her face red with anger. But we all knew we belonged to the company.

August 27-28

It was noon on what should have been a workday. CLOSED the large black letters were printed on a wooden sign. The men were sullen as they stared at the sign. It was the third day that week that the mines in Lattimer and Ario were shut down, the breakers silent. Grumbling, they picked up their shovels and picks and headed home or to the tavern.

The house was unusually quiet as Stefan sat at the small table in the kitchen with the newspaper on the table in front of him. Anna, Rose, and three-year-old Robert were in the garden. Stephen was in school, and baby Rudi was asleep.

Staring at the newspaper, Stefan absently rubbed the hard, jagged scar on his shoulder. The memory of the pick digging into his flesh years ago was long forgotten, but the wound had been deep, and his shoulder was now stiff with arthritis.

A picture of striking miners carrying pistols, clubs, iron bars, and sticks marching down Broad Street in Hazleton dominated the front page of the newspaper. Some of the demonstrators were wearing street clothes, others were still in dusty, coal-covered work clothes, but anger and determination were on every face, unifying the demonstrators in solidarity. They intended to arouse the miners of the entire Lehigh coal region. Five hundred men had joined the march that had begun in Coleraine and Beaver Brook. They were headed to Milnesville.

He searched for faces of men he knew. Emil was there, right in front, holding a red flag, a symbol of their solidarity and fortitude. Stefan was surprised to see Emil, since the miners of Harwood, like those in Ario and Latimer, had not joined the strikes flaring up around the region. Stefan, like others he knew, was reluctant to inflict on his family the suffering that would be the inevitable result of a strike.

Stefan read the article slowly, struggling with the words. Some were easily recognized— strike; Alien Tax; foreigners. He read the names of patch towns south of Hazleton—Evans; Beaver Brook; Honey Brook; Coleraine; McAdoo.

According to the newspaper, public sentiment favored the miners. Small businesses would benefit if the miners were no longer required to purchase goods at the company stores or buy meat from the company butchers. But there was fear as well, as the residents of Hazleton watched the loud, boisterous mob march through their city on their way to Milnesville. Would there be trouble? Would there be damage to private property or an assault on innocent bystanders?

The newspaper reported that the mine operators believed that the foreigners, usually compliant, would eventually go back to work. There was no mention of the eight hundred Winchester rifles being secretly acquired and stored by the Coxe and Pardee coal companies. Unknown to the miners, Calvin

The Road to Lattimer · 143

Pardee, the owner of Harwood, Lattimer, and Ario collieries was determined that his mines would not be shut down.

Anna, a basket of vegetables on her arm, came into the house. She was surprised to see her husband still sitting at the table with the paper in front of him and frowned when she saw how sad and dejected he looked.

"There will be trouble, Anna," he told her without explanation as he stood and walked to the door. Staring at the picture of the striking miners, she was afraid, afraid for her family.

When Jan and Stefan entered the saloon, the air was stifling and smelled of tobacco and stale beer. There was a profound tension in the room, as suppressed anger that had amassed for so long was released in animated discussions about the unrest in Coleraine and McAdoo.

"They broke the windows in Jones' house." The voice of the tough-looking kid who shoveled coal in the strippings was louder than the others. "We should do the same to Murphy and all the rest." The men around him agreed with grunts of approval. At one time or another, all the men had been cheated of wages or forced to pay a bribe. *Like vengeful children,* Stefan thought, listening to the younger men who did not have families to provide for.

"If we all walked out, what could they do to us?" Jerome, a boy who worked in the breaker, had joined the men at the bar. "The boys in Coleraine walked out!" A cap covered in coal dust sat on the back of Jerome's head, and his face was still smooth and hairless, but his eyes were those of a much older man. It was five years ago when he had watched his younger brother killed in the breaker. "He slipped, Mama. He fell into the coal shoot. I could not save him," he had tried to explain to his distraught mother as they carried the little boy from the breaker. Jerome still had nightmares reliving that horrible day.

"Deputies, Coal and Iron Police, Pinkerton detectives, all have guns," an older man interjected, while he touched a scar on his face that was partially hidden by his mustache. Years ago, he had tripped and fallen on a jagged rock in the mine. The gash had become infected. He was lucky to be alive.

"They shut down Silver Brook, Hazle Mines, and Ebervale. At Milnesville they got Van Wickle to listen to their demands."

"Nothin' will make Pardee listen."

"D'hell wit' Pardee," an Italian yelled. "We gotta strike."

"I want none of it." Jan scowled pushing back his chair. Without another word he left the saloon. Stefan quietly finished his beer and did the same.

Anna

It seems strange to me now, in the middle of our troubles, Hazleton was celebrating the new American holiday, Labor Day. The holiday marked the end of summer and acknowledged the contributions of the working classes. Still, I doubt that immigrants were among the workers being celebrated.

I have such wonderful memories of the parades on Broad Street. American flags flew on every street corner, and a profusion of red, white, and blue bunting was draped over all the buildings. The air always smelled of sausages, pretzels, and beer sold by street vendors. Our children sat on the curb and waved miniature flags at the dignitaries riding in carriages or the extravagantly decorated floats with large signs advertising the organization they represented. Marching bands, with their drums and trumpets, always heightened our festive mood. Bright red firetrucks with their bells clanging were a favorite of the children. The firemen would always throw treats for the children, who laughed and cheered as they scrambled to catch each small treasure. And then, there were the companies of soldiers, who would spin their rifles and return them to their shoulders with military precision. Middle aged men who had fought in the Civil War marched in groups proudly displaying the union flag. Oh, what a sight it was! How proud we were to be Americans.

Labor Day 1897 we took the children to see the parade in Hazleton. We tried to forget, at least for a day, the talk of unions and strikes. Edita and Emil did not join us that year. They had a new baby, and Edita decided they would stay in Harwood and watch the Harwood parade.

September 6, Labor Day

Edita rocked her baby in her arms as she watched the Harwood Labor Day Parade. Emil left her standing there as he walked among the spectators, reminding the men of the meeting that night at the schoolhouse. "Tonight, there will be a vote. We need you there. Should we shut down our colliery?" Emil made it his responsibility to see that every man and every boy working in the Harwood mines attended that meeting.

Since he moved to Harwood, Emil had earned the friendship and respect of the Harwood miners with his honesty, openness, and his skill with the mules.

"He's the best damn mule driver in the Leigh Valley," Samuel, Emil's brother-in-law, would tell anyone who would listen. Even though he was an immigrant, it did not take long for his skill with mules to be recognized, and he was now the supervisor of the Harwood mule drivers.

Emil's anger at the treatment of the mule drivers in Honey Brook was well known. Whenever groups of miners were together, he reminded them of the cruel and arbitrary actions of Gomer Jones and the bravery of the mule drivers who confronted him. "They started a strike, presented their demands, and they got a ten-cent raise," he reminded them. "We have been passive too long."

Now, as he walked along the parade route, he shook hands, patted backs, and reminded the men to come to the meeting. "Come and state your grievances. It is time to act," he repeated over and over until his voice was hoarse.

That night, the miners of Harwood crowded into the small schoolhouse. After much loud, and sometimes unruly, discussion, they settled on three grievances to be taken to the superintendent of the Harwood mines. They demanded a pay raise of ten cents a day and a reduction in the price of blasting powder. There would no longer be a requirement to shop in the company store and use the company doctor.

They met again at the schoolhouse the next day where John Fahy, a representative of the United Mine Workers, spoke with them.

"You are not alone," Fahy told them. Eight thousand miners were already enrolled in the union. "You have a right to peaceful protest, and you will not be arrested as long as there is no violence."

The miners believed him.

That night, while the miners of Harwood were meeting, the mine operators and owners of the region had a secret meeting of their own. The impact of the economic depression of the 1890s was still affecting their profits. They agreed not to give in to the miners' demands. Sheriff Martin was told to call a posse to supplement the Coal and Iron Police. Peace and order would be maintained with force, if necessary. "This lawlessness must end."

Anna

The day after Labor Day a small group of striking miners marched through Ario on their way to Lattimer.

I was at the well, Rose was playing with Robert and Rudolph, and Stephen was in school. Other women were there, gossiping while they waited for their turn at the well.

The sounds that filled the air were what you would expect—women's voices, children laughing, a baby crying. These sounds were a part of our daily existence. And then, everything changed.

"Strikers!" A boy was running down our alley, his face flushed with excitement. "Strikers!" he called over and over until he reached his mother. "Strikers headed for Lattimer!" The boy was breathless and animated. "I saw them. I saw them myself."

Many of us were frightened as the strikers marched through the village. They were an angry, shouting, club-wielding mob.

"I could not sleep for days after I saw those horrible men. They were so angry." Mrs. Kroger, the wife of the butcher, told everyone who would listen. "I collapsed, you know, when one of them shook his club at me."

It was the first time we had seen the strikers. It would not be the last.

September 7

It was Tuesday, and in Ario, Anna and Katarina were ironing. It was a ritual observed by women in the patches. Clothes washed on Monday, ironed on Tuesday. Adriana, in neighboring Lattimer, not for the first time had decided it was not how she wanted to spend her morning.

"William, Helena, come along." Without explanation, Adriana took the hands of her two youngest children and left the house, the pile of clothing still waiting for her attention.

"Keep the children close to home today," Cyril had warned her. "There is a possibility some strikers might be in the area."

"Pish," she had responded, dismissing him with her hand. "Strikers! Just men." He knew better than to challenge her. She would do what she wanted anyway. Her intention, on this sunny morning, was to visit her friend Mary Septak. With her three youngest children in tow, she ignored her husband's warning and left the house.

"Mama, look." Little William was pointing at a group of men standing in the dirt road, rifles held carelessly in their hands.

"Deputies." Adriana spit out the word while adjusting one-year-old Iva on her hip. Cyril had warned her they might come to stop the strikers.

"Mama, who are they?" asked six year old Helena, her lower lip beginning to quiver. She had never seen so many men carrying rifles. "They look angry, Mama."

"It's all right, sweetheart. They are deputies. See the badges on their coats?" Adriana was watching with growing apprehension as the Coal and Iron Police formed a line blocking the road. *They are waiting for the strikers,* she thought. *Pardee doesn't want them reaching his mine. God help them if there is gunfire.*

"William, put that down this instant." Three-year-old William had picked up a stick and, pretending it was a rifle, aimed it at the deputies. She heard them before she saw them. Strikers, with sticks and clubs, were walking menacingly toward the deputies.

"Mrs. Septak is waiting for us. Hurry now!" Adriana's voice was stern as she picked up William, grabbed Helena's hand, and hastily made her way to Mary's house.

Safe inside Mary Septak's house, Adriana watched the terrifying events from the small window at the front of the house. The miners shouting threats and waving their sticks and clubs had confronted the police. Adriana held her breath. The deputies lifted their rifles and were ready to fire. *Lord have mercy,* she prayed. To her relief, the strikers slowly drifted away. For now, a violent confrontation had been avoided.

"It is time to fight, not run away." It was Mary, angry and ready to fight who had also watched the confrontation. "I'll show them how." Mary Septak—sometimes called Big Mary-was well known as a force to be reckoned with. When Big Mary spoke, people listened. Even the trolley conductor was said to be afraid of her. If Mary felt like paying for a ride she paid, if not she simply took her seat. Mary ran a boarding house and had seen the suffering caused by the inhumane conditions in the mines. Now she was ready to stand beside the striking miners offering encouragement and hope.

That night, the saloon in Lattimer was filled with thick, eye-watering smoke from cigars and pipes mingled with the smell of beer and whiskey. Loud male voices, the clang of glasses, the scraping of a chair, created a cacophony of sounds. Coal dust covered the floor and darkened the faces and clothing of the men. Tensions escalated.

"The superintendent at Eberville drew his revolver on marchers." There was grumbling among the men as they acknowledged the event.

"The windows of his office were broken in retaliation." The men cheered their approval clanking their beer mugs in unison.

"Gunfire in Beaver Meadows and now deputies in Lattimer." Many of the men were now ready to join the strikers, but a few still hesitated. Nevertheless, it was agreed, they would a message to the strikers in Harwood. "If you will support us, we will join you." A loud outspoken Italian was delegated as the messenger.

Anna

Stefan did not come home until late the night of September eighth. The memory of that night lingers in my soul, and I cannot forget how I felt. It was past dark, the evening stars lit the heavens, and I had said my prayers. The children were asleep, and I had gone to bed but was unable to quiet my mind. Knowing the men of Ario and Lattimer were talking about joining the strike that had spread through the region prevented sleep. My brows were creased in a frown and my body was tense as I thought of the consequences of a strike. We would be evicted from our home. Starvation would surely follow. My children... I worried so about my children.

Stefan's warm body smelled of beer and tobacco, when he joined me in our bed. He pulled me toward him, and, as always, we drew strength from each other. Then he spoke the words I had feared. "If the men from Harwood will support us, the men of Ario and Lattimer will strike." He did not see the fear in my eyes as I nestled my head into his chest, and he stroked my hair. I did not sleep much that night.

The woman in black

The woman, the woman in black floated out of the gray, ethereal fog that engulfed him. He was dreaming, he knew he was dreaming, but his body and his mind were frozen there, riveted on the image of the woman. As always, her face was expressionless, her dark eyes focused on him.

Stefan thought of his brother. "It is my fault, Marek. You are crippled because of me." There was now a sadness in the woman's eyes. "Matka, I was not there for you, when father died. I left you when you were sick." A little gypsy boy walked out of the mist and silently stood by the woman. "I sinned when I called you swine and thief. You were like dirt to me." But that was not all that tormented his soul. "I killed a man and felt no remorse. I did not protect my friend. Josef, I am so very sorry." But Stefan felt no relief. He was not forgiven for his sins.

In the distance, their voices smothered by the fog, he heard children crying, women weeping. The mist moistened his face. *Like tears,* he thought. The crying stopped, replaced by the sound of guns, the metallic smell of blood. Blood—red, thick—darkened his shirt, covered his hands. Men were screaming. Stefan wanted to run, to leave this place, but he could not move. "What do you want from me?" Stefan shouted at the apparition. "What do you want me to do?" The woman did not answer.

September 9

With the help and encouragement of the handsome, soft-spoken, and persuasive John Fahy of the United Mine Workers, the miners of Harwood formed the Harwood Local of the UMW. "We must build a strong union," Fahy had told them. "Only then can we talk to the owners as equals and demand concessions."

By September 9, 1897, elections had taken place. The miners had chosen Joseph Michalko, John Eagler, and Andrej Sivar to be the officers of their Local. Also, despite reservations, most of the Harwood miners had paid the thirty cents union dues required for membership. Now, the miners were holding a meeting at the schoolhouse to decide the next course of action.

Sitting at a student desk that was far too small for a grown man, Emil looked around the room with pride. Michalko was sitting at the teacher's desk at the front of the room, Sivar was standing next to the American flag, and behind Eagler, someone had written, Harwood Chapter of the United Mine Workers on the chalkboard. Emil was proud of what they had accomplished. The men in the room were ready to take control of their destiny.

"We'a ready to strike. We'a need'a you help." A booming voice filled the room just as Michalko was about to open the meeting. "We'a need'a you help," the stranger yelled, frantically waving his arms in the air while using his massive body to shove his way through the crowded room. "Lattimer is'a ready to strike! Ario too!" A chorus of shouts and whistles greeted the announcement. "We make'a Pardee listen to us," the Italian kept saying above the uproar in the room. "We'a need'a you help."

Most of the men from Harwood had not been part of previous marches and had not seen the deputies with their Winchesters. Over half of the miners were not American citizens, but John Fahy had told them that in America they had the right to peaceful assembly, and their marches would be protected by the law. "When you march, do not carry weapons and be careful not to antagonize the authorities," he had warned them. A vote was taken, and the miners agreed to go to Lattimer the next day. They would show their support for the Lattimer miners.

John Eagler, one of the Harwood miners, sent word to McAdoo asking for support by joining them in the march to Lattimer. Andrej Sivar went with others in search of American flags.

Calvin Pardee, the president of A. Pardee and Company, wanted the strike broken and operations resumed. He had no sympathy for the foreign laborers caught in a labor glut and refused to meet with them. His son, Calvin Pardee Jr., and nephew Ario Pardee Platt, the manager of the Lattimer Company store, were among the deputies. Sheriff Martin understood what was expected.

Chapter 12 - 1897

September 10

Anna

For me, September 10, 1897, had begun like so many other days in Ario. The house was quiet, dark, and a welcome breeze drifted through the open window. Stefan was asleep beside me, the smell of him familiar, soothing. Caressing his shoulder and back, I could feel the scars that now covered his body. The worst was the place on his shoulder where the pick had landed, but there were others. Small cuts from the jagged rocks that would heal in time, but some, deep and ugly, would forever be a reminder of the hazards of work in the mine. He never complained, but when I washed his back and massaged his shoulder, I could see his face soften and feel his muscles relax. It gave me so much pleasure to bring him comfort.

Barefoot, as always, I walked to the kitchen and opened the door to the porch. Stars, uncountable in their numbers, filled the pitch-black sky, transporting my ever-vivid imagination to the place in heaven where angels and the souls of the departed spent eternity. The hill behind our home appeared as a black shape that seemed ominous or protective, depending on my mood. On that morning, I welcomed the cool night air that replaced the suffocating stagnant air in the small kitchen. I didn't linger at the door for long. The coals in the stove needed to be stoked and the coffee prepared.

Cyril and Jacob came to our house that morning to talk to Stefan. They were on their way to Harwood to join the marchers who were coming to Lattimer. It was agreed, to my relief, that Stefan would stay in Ario to encourage the miners of our colliery to strike.

I remember Cyril coughing, a deep, ugly cough that turned his face red and caused his eyes to tear. Adriana had told me his cough was getting worse and kept him awake at night. It was more than a ten-mile walk round trip. I was sure Adriana was not happy when her husband told her he would join the marchers. Even for those of us who were healthy, it was not an effortless walk.

Cyril and Jacob finished their coffee and walked out the door. Stefan lingered for a moment to hold me in his arms. "By tonight, we will have shut down Pardee, and he will need to listen to our demands." When he left, I held my rosary in my hands, finding comfort in the wooden beads and the familiar prayers.

"Zdravas', Maria, milosti piná. Hail Mary, full of grace." I closed my eyes and pictured the linden tree in our village back home and the statue of the Holy Virgin standing in front of the church.

"Pán s tebou. The Lord be with you." I was sure Emil would be with the marchers.

"Požehnaná si medzi ženami a požehnaný je plod života tvojho, Ježiš. Blessed are you among women and blessed is the fruit of your womb, Jesus." I thought of my children and Emil's new baby.

"Svätá Maria, Matka Božia, pros za nás hriešnych. Holy Mary, mother of God, pray for us sinners." If the Lattimer miners walked out, the men of Ario would do the same.

"Teraz I v hodine smrti našej. Now, and at the hour of our death. Amen."

Adriana

The world outside was still dark as Adriana slipped from the comforting arms of her sleeping husband and quietly walked toward the kitchen. It had been well over a year since they had been evicted from Ario. Cyril worked in the Lattimer mine, but only as a laborer. The supervisor felt this would be an example to any other miners who caused trouble. Eventually, with the help of their sons, Cyril and Adriana left the small shanty in the outskirts of Lattimer and were now renting a double-frame house on Main Street.

With sleep still in her eyes, she barely noticed that the mahogany night sky was turning a softer shade of gray. Familiar night sounds, the snort of a deer, the scream of a raccoon, and the flutter of an owl's wings went unnoticed. The house was quiet except for her husband's muffled snoring. The children were still asleep.

Barefoot, with her shawl around her shoulders, Adriana walked into the kitchen and lit the solitary kerosene lamp that sat waiting on the kitchen table. Her strong, muscular arms were visible below the short sleeves of her calico dress, and a white apron was tied around her ample waist. She packed tin lunch pails for her husband and sons. There would be no ham or kielbasa today, but she had apples from Mrs. Novak's garden and slices of dark rye bread from the large loaf she had made the day before.

Her face was creased with worry this morning, and she looked tired. Her body tense, her mind racing, sleep had not come easily the night before. Adriana closed the last of the dinner pails with unnecessary force. She had quarreled with her husband the night before.

"The strikers from Harwood will be here tomorrow," he had informed her. "When they arrive, Lattimer will go on strike."

At first, Cyril's pronouncement had filled her with hope, and even excitement. The men from Lattimer would join the strike that had spread through the region.

"I'm going to Harwood in the morning and Jacob is coming with me."

"You cannot go to Harwood." Adriana was shocked by this declaration. "You are not well."

"I'm fine." Cyril was defiant as he struggled to control the cough that was ravaging his body.

"Jacob can go. You need to be here. You need to be here for the boys." Louis and John were working in the mine, and Patrik was still in the breaker. "They will want to join the strike."

"Yes, I'm sure they will."

"Please, Cyril, please don't go."

"I'm going!" he had shouted as he slammed the door and walked into the night. When he returned, Adriana pretended to be asleep.

"Jacob," Adriana called, standing at the bottom of the stairs, wiping her hands on her apron. "Coffee is ready." She could hear his footsteps as he walked across the room. *By this afternoon he will be among the strikers,* she thought with a mixture of pride and fear.

"Goddamn!" The voice came from the room next to the kitchen, where Cyril was sleeping. Adriana knew her husband's foot had once again experienced a painful encounter with the trunk that stood by the side of the bed. It happened nearly every morning.

"Goddamn trunk!"

"I moved it weeks ago, remember?"

"Put it back where it belongs," he commanded his wife, but he knew it would not happen.

"Mornin', Matka. Is it the trunk again?" Jacob had bounded down the stairs and now held a mug of black coffee.

"Yup, it's that goddamn trunk again. Keeps bumpin' into his toe." Adriana could not help but laugh, her anger and apprehension of Cyril joining the Harwood strikers momentarily vanquished.

"Move the damn thing back where it belongs," Cyril grumbled as he came into the kitchen.

"I'll see," she answered, without any intention of moving the trunk back in front of the bed. "Come, sit. Eggs are ready."

The family sat around the table, as they did most mornings. But this morning there was an unusual quiet in the room. Even little William seemed to understand that something of importance was about to happen.

"Jacob, tell your father not to go."

"He is determined ma."

"But he's sick, Jacob."

"I'm going with him ma. I'll watch him."

"Can we go too?" Louis and John said in unison.

"No!" Cyril and Adriana were adamant that would not happen. It would be a long walk to Harwood and back.

"Will I be going to school?" Elizabeth asked.

"Yes. There is no reason not to."

"Give this to Anna for the children and give my regards to Stefan." Adriana handed Cyril a bag of coal candy she had purchased in the company store. Cyril and Jacob were planning to see Stefan before leaving for Harwood. The miners in Ario needed to know of the plans for the march. She was still angry but there was nothing more to be done. Her husband had made up his mind.

"Sure." Cyril took the candy, stuffed it in his pocket and reached for his hat. He was ready to leave.

"Can I ask you one last time to stay in Lattimer?"

"No!"

Adriana stroked her husband's cheek and rested her head on his chest. There were no more words.

"I will take care of him, Matka," Jacob whispered, kissing his mother on the cheek and giving her a reassuring hug.

"Go, then. I need to tend to the children."

Cyril and Jacob walked down Main Street with wide, confident strides, passing the superintendent's office, the company store, the mule barn, and machine repair shop. They waited a long time for this day and did not share Adriana's apprehension. By tomorrow, all the mines owned by the A. Pardee Brothers Coal Company would be on strike.

Emil

As the sun rose over Buck Mountain on September 10, 1897, over three hundred men gathered on the Harwood picnic grounds. They intended to march to Lattimer, close the colliery, and force Pardee to listen to their demands.

Two flags tattered and old, were fastened to rough-hewn poles taken perhaps from a fence post that might have protected the garden of a miner's family or, used as walking sticks on the long walk to church on Sundays. The well-worn flags attached to the poles may have flown in front of a miner's home on the Fourth of July or carried in a parade to show the patriotic sentiments of the marchers. Today, however, the striking miners of Harwood counted on these flags for protection as they marched to Lattimer. Fahey told them they had a right to peaceful assembly and warned them not to carry anything that might be perceived as a weapon. The flags were a symbol of their faith in America and the rights of all who lived here.

Yesterday Edita took extra care to scrub the coal from Emil's face and trim his handlebar mustache. She brushed his dark wool suit and washed and ironed his white shirt. On the morning of the march, the miners exchanged their grimy work clothes for wool suit jackets and stovepipe pants. Emil preferred to wear a slouch hat, but a few of the men wore straw hats or bowler hats. They were dressed in a manner that, for them, reflected the dignity and solemnity of the march. They did not consider themselves a riotous mob.

Emil was awake before Edita, a rare occurrence. He checked the cradle where their infant daughter, Alica, was sleeping, her baby face flushed from sleep. *My little girl,* he thought. *You are as beautiful as your mother.* He kissed Edita, who stirred in her sleep and mumbled something he could not understand. Quietly he left the house.

Before joining the strikers, Emil wanted to check on his mules; he would not leave them in the care of just anyone. Sally, his favorite mule since moving to Harwood, waited for her wad of tobacco, while another mule, a veteran of many years in the mines, who had suffered bruises during a rock fall, waited for the carrot he knew Emil would offer him. Emil also hoped Peter Varga would be at the barn. Peter was a mule driver about nineteen years of age, who shared Emil's love for the mules. Emil knew Peter was reluctant to join the strike. He told Emil that he did not want trouble. While the other miners and mule drivers were preparing for the march to Lattimer, Emil suspected Peter would hide in the mule barn, hoping he would not be missed.

Emil entered the barn, where he was greeted by the familiar braying of the mules and the smell of fresh-cut hay. A feral cat brushed past his leg and headed for the open door. Emil saw Peter in the shadows near the rear of the barn stroking an agitated mule, whispering in her ear, soothing her. If Peter knew that Emil was there, he chose not to acknowledge him. Emil picked up a brush and began to stroke the neck of the mule. Peter gave him a cursory glance, and the two men worked in silence for a few minutes.

"I know you are afraid. We are all afraid." Emil's voice was calm and reassuring as he continued to brush the mule.

"I'm not afraid. I just don't want trouble."

"No one does." There was a long silence, broken only by the braying of the mules and a dog barking in the distance. "The mules are treated better than we are," Emil continued, while lifting a bucket of feed for the mule, who was now standing in his stall, eyeing the bucket in Emil's hands. "We are marching. We are brothers. You must join us."

Without talking or looking at each other, the young men began bringing feed to the other mules in the barn.

"I heard Fahy last night," Peter uttered. "I un'erstand." But still, he hesitated.

"You can't hide here."

"I know," Peter said, putting down the bag of feed. "I will go."

A little before noon the two mule drivers walked to the picnic area to join the others. The march started at noon.

The American flag will protect us

Edita, holding her baby, her bonnet shielding her eyes from the blinding sun, struggled to find Emil amidst the men gathering on the picnic grounds in Harwood. *There must be over two hundred men out there,* she thought with pride. She recognized John Eagler and Andrej Sivar holding American flags.

"The flags will protect us," Emil had promised.

"The flags will protect your father," Edita whispered to the child asleep in her arms.

"Michalko and Eagler are checking for weapons," she heard someone say. "See, over there. Not even walking sticks are permitted." Edita watched as a few sticks and clubs dropped to the ground. She thought she saw Peter, one of the mule drivers, dropping a stick when Michalko approached him.

Cheers erupted from the men, as miners from McAdoo came over the ridge to join them. "The flags will protect them," Edita whispered again.

Just past noon the men began to assemble four abreast in military formation. Just after one o'clock, Michalko gave the command, "Forward march!" With the American flags leading the way, and families cheering them on, the miners left the patch town on Pismire Ridge and began the march to Lattimer. The mood among the miners and the spectators was festive and hopeful. The men did not know that someone from Harwood had telephoned Sheriff Martin. They also did not know that the sheriff and his well-armed deputies would be waiting for them when they reached Hazleton.

"Emil!" Edita shouted, waving to her husband as he marched past her. "Stay safe."

"Cyril! Jacob! Over here!" Emil had spotted them among the men who joined them at Crystal Ridge. The men joining the marchers were greeted with cheers, and the column continued its forward march with renewed determination.

"This is Peter. He drives the mules for me."

"Then you are a good man, Pete. Emil only lets the best go near his mules," Cyril said, shaking Peter's hand.

The men walked in silent solidarity for a while until Peter took a photograph with crumpled edges from his jacket pocket. He had just wanted to glance at the image, but Jacob saw him before he could return it to his pocket.

"Who's that?"

"My girl," he said, handing the photograph to Jacob. The girl, dressed modestly in the traditional scarf covering her hair and tied neatly below her chin, was lovely. Her wide skirt that reached to her ankles was covered with a white apron trimmed in lace. A richly embroidered vest made it obvious that she was wearing her best clothes for the picture. "We will get married when I have saved enough money."

"Marriage is good," Emil said with a smile. "My wife will have a beer and kielbasa ready for me when I get home."

"Maybe even a bath," Jacob teased.

"Maybe." Emil laughed. He imagined leaning over the wooden wash basin while Edita poured warm water over his back and her strong hands caressed his shoulders.

"For me, it will just be the boarding house with the bed I share with Martin and Henrich," Peter lamented.

"Better put this away," Jacob chimed in, handing the picture of the girl back to Peter. "We need to focus on right now. Thoughts of women and love will come later."

"There must be nearly four hundred of us," Emil observed. They had slowed their pace, allowing Cyril to keep up with them, and had drifted to the middle of the column of marchers. "I can barely see the flags," he lamented. He would have preferred to be among the leaders of the march.

Anna

After Cyril and Jacob left to join the marchers, Stefan went to work. I gathered the children in the kitchen. "We will all stay home today," I informed them.

"Is it about the marchers?" Stephen asked. He was nine that year, and he had been listening to the men. I am not sure he understood everything, but he was intuitive, and I know he felt the tension, the anger, and the fear that consumed the adults around him.

"It is just better for us to stay here today," I explained, and he accepted that with a shrug. He was more than happy not to go to school.

"I have some apples," I announced, hoping to change the subject. "I believe I can find some lard and sugar."

"Apple pie," chimed in Rose.

"Pie," little Robert echoed in his tiny voice.

There was happiness in the kitchen that morning. It was almost like a holiday.

About two in the afternoon an ominous shiver coursed through my body. Something evil was about to happen. "Jesus, Mary, and Joseph protect us," I whispered as I made the sign of the cross.

Rose noticed. "Matka, what is it?" She was looking at me with an intensity beyond her years.

"Nothing," I assured her, giving her a hug. I did not voice my fear. I did not want to frighten the children.

McKenna's Corner

Cyril pulled a handkerchief from his pocket and wiped the sweat from the back of his neck. They had been walking for what seemed, to Cyril, like an eternity. The day was hot, the sun blinded him, and he was having trouble breathing. *Coal in my lungs. I am like an old man.* He was only forty-one, but twenty years in the mines was taking its toll. *Just need to get up this damn hill.* There would be water at McKenna's Corner in West Hazleton.

"Let's slow down," Emil suggested, nodding back at Cyril. "Give him a chance to catch up."

"We can rest here for a bit," Jacob called back to his father. "This hill is tough."

"No!" Cyril's face was crimson. He choked on the black phlegm that rose from his lungs. "Go ahead. I jus' need a minute. This damn cough."

"We should stay together."

"Go ahead, I tol' ya. An' not a word to your mother. I'll catch up."

Reluctantly, Jacob, Emil, and Peter left Cyril sitting on a rock near the side of the road.

"He should not have come," Jacob confided. "We tried to stop him, but he is stubborn."

"Stubborn, like all old miners," Emil acknowledged with a sad smile. He liked Cyril and had been friends with Jacob since they were boys.

"Miner's lung, the doctor told us, but he won't give in to it." Miner's lung, also called Black Lung, was a fate common among those who worked in the mines. "I told him I would go on the march and he should stay with the Lattimer miners." Jacob's voice was laced with worry when he spoke of his father.

The day was getting warm, the sun merciless, but the strikers were undeterred in their resolve to reach Lattimer. They turned onto Wayne Street in West Hazleton, the promise of water and a chance to rest just ahead. The landscape was familiar, unthreatening. Most had made this walk to Hazleton before. A culm bank, a large black mound of discarded rock and dirt, was on the right of the column. The men walked past it without concern. It was just a part of the dismal landscape that surrounded Hazleton. If they heard the squeal of brakes from a trolley on the other side of the culm bank, it went unnoticed.

Men in business suits, the sun reflecting off their rifles, appeared on the top of the bank. Seconds later, whooping and shouting with a terrifying display of force, the deputies clambered down the dusty, slippery mound of discarded coal and slate.

"Deputies." The word reverberated through the column of marchers.

"Sheriff Martin's men."

"They're gonna try and stop us from reaching Hazleton."

"Let them try."

"Me no stop!" an Italian shouted.

"Ario Platt," Emil mumbled, recognizing the general manager of the Pardee Company Stores. "Arrogant bastard," he smirked as he watched Platt slide down the bank. *He'll get a taste of coal dust,* Emil thought, picturing Platt's hands black with coal dust, and his expensive clothes smudged with dirt.

The deputies shoved their way through the column, using unnecessary roughness. During the trolley ride, boisterous talk of shooting Hunkies and teaching them a lesson had amplified their fury. Ario Platt was particularly angered at the sight of the American flag being carried by the miners. He considered this an affront to his ancestors, who had been in this country for generations.

A deputy pushed Jacob aside with the butt of his rifle. "Wha' the hell!" Jacob shouted and raised his arm with a closed fist. The deputy aimed his rifle, his hand on the trigger. Jacob's eyes flashed with defiance, and the deputy's glared with anger. Jacob unclenched his fist, and, with a final shove and a smirk, the deputy moved away.

Another deputy pulled at Peter's shirt, spinning him off balance. The photograph Peter was clutching fluttered to the ground as his mouth fell open and his eyes bulged with fear. "Better go back home, boy." The deputy's voice was deep with loathing as he roughly pushed Peter out of the way. "There's gonna be trouble."

Emil bent to retrieve the torn and muddied photograph. "Keep walking. They can't stop us," he tried to reassure the shaken boy. "The flag will protect us."

The moving column slowed to a stop. "What is happening up there?" The question was being asked by men who could not see the front of the column.

"Sheriff Martin's men are lining the road."

"Ario Platt ripped the flag from Michalko's hands."

"The sheriff is reading a proclamation. Says we can't go any farther. It is against the law."

"They can't stop us. We are going to Lattimer." The words echoed through the column as the strikers continued to push forward. *Crack!* The startled men stopped moving. The sound of the rifle baffled the men, as they had not expected trouble. They were unarmed. It was a peaceful march.

The rumors passed through the crowd in waves. It was frustrating for the men who could not see for themselves what was happening at the front of the column. "The deputies are blocking the road. Juszko's been arrested. His arms are bleeding."

"Ed Jones, the West Hazleton Chief of Police, is here."

"Heard he was sympathetic to miners."

"He's arguing with the sheriff. Says we have a right to march."

"Damn right we do."

In the end, the chief of police directed the strikers to march around the edges of West Hazleton and not through the city. Slowly, the column began to move once again. Only one flag now led the marchers as they moved up North Broad Street, through West Hazleton toward Harleigh. As Emil and his friends passed McKenna's Corner, they saw bits of fabric in the dirt, pieces of the American flag that had flown moments ago leading the marchers. Platt had torn the flag to shreds and broken the stick across his knees. Emil picked up a strip of the dirty red fabric and tied it around his neck. Peter and Jacob did the same.

The angry and tired deputies boarded the trolleys that would take them to Lattimer. They would stop the Hunkies there.

Hazleton to Harleigh

It was about two o'clock in the afternoon when John Laudmesser, the keeper of the Farley Hotel in Harleigh, decided it was time for his afternoon cigar. His wife was busy in the kitchen, and the boarders were at work or asleep. *I won't be missed.* As always, he settled comfortably in the rocker on the wooden front porch and lit his cigar and waited for the trolley that would pass by the hotel on its way to Milnesville. The trolley always offered a pleasant diversion as he observed the passengers, men in business suits, women with their hats of every variety, sometimes children who would wave to him through the open windows. This time was ominously different. The passengers were holding Winchester rifles. *Deputies,* Laudmesser thought.

He had heard the rumors. Strikers from Harwood were planning to march to Lattimer. "They're planning to shut down the Lattimer and Ario collieries," an excited boy who worked at the hotel had informed him that morning. "My pa, he works at Lattimer. He said Sheriff Martin would be sending deputies for sure. Pardee will see to it." *Not here,* Laudmesser thought, as he eyed the men in the trolley. *We don't need trouble here.* But he was silent, inhaled his cigar, and waited.

"Here they come!" Laudmesser leaned forward in his rocker to get a better look. A somber column of tired men, dressed in drab black suits and white shirts covered with dust, were rounding the bend in the road. "That's a lot of them," he remarked to himself as he watched the endless column of men marching behind a tattered American flag. "No weapons," he murmured with relief. "The deputies won't shoot unarmed men."

Emil splashed the cool water from the pump on his face and the back of his neck, washing away the dirt from the road that had mingled with his sweat. He wanted to linger longer at the pump, but there were others, just as hot, just as thirsty, waiting behind him. They had been walking for hours and finally reached Harleigh.

The leaders of the march were huddled together near the porch while the rest of the men milled around in small groups, talking, smoking their pipes, and warily watching the trolley parked in front of the hotel.

Emil joined Peter, Cyril, and Jacob.

"What do you think they are talking about?" Peter nodded to the leaders of the march huddled in consultation.

"Don't know, but glad to sit for a while." Cyril, his hacking cough dormant for the moment, had settled himself on a rock near the side of the road.

"You alright?" Jacob was worried about his father.

"Yup. Never better."

Emil looked warily at the trolley parked in front of the hotel. The men in the trolley, flushed from the heat, were mostly clean-shaven, except for what appeared to be well-tended mustaches. From their plug hats and fancy suits, it was obvious to Emil that they were bankers and shopkeepers. "Waiting for us to move," he mumbled.

"Let them wait. They can just smolder in that steel box." As always, Cyril was defiant. Emil counted the windows of the trolley, eleven on each side. "There are at least forty-four men with rifles."

"Maybe they will just give up and go home." Peter, still not sure why he had agreed to come, was searching for a way out of this predicament. He looked at the picture of his girl and wondered if he would live through this day.

"They won't shoot," Emil reassured Peter. "Just want to give us a scare, that's all. When this is over, they just want to go home to their families, same as us."

A decision was made by the eight men huddled in front of the column. The flag was lifted, the men fell into line, and the march to Lattimer resumed.

Laudmesser, still holding his cigar, leaned against the porch railing of the inn, observing the drama unfolding before him. He watched as the strikers once again assembled their ranks and resumed their march to Lattimer. As they passed the porch, he began to count them, one hundred, two hundred. Later he would tell authorities there were four hundred twenty-four marchers that day.

The trolley, which had sat benignly on the tracks, now began to move slowly, ominously, alongside the marchers. Emil felt evil emanating from the steel frame of what should have been an innocuous presence. He could clearly see the faces of the deputies and was sure he heard one of them say he would be shootin' Hunkies today.

Adriana

Around two that afternoon, some men on bicycles brought news to Lattimer. The strikers were at Harleigh, and the deputies were coming on trolleys from Hazleton and Milnesville. Many were afraid the foreigners would come with sticks and clubs and force men and boys to join them. Others thought there might be gunfire. Frightened women called to their children and barred their windows and doors. Adriana wasn't afraid of the strikers; it was the deputies with their rifles that worried her.

The breaker whistle blew. The miners were close, and Elizabeth was not yet home from school.

"Stay in the kitchen with the little ones," Adriana told Helena, her six-year-old daughter. "I need to bring Elizabeth home."

"Matka, will she be all right?" Helena, a precocious child, understood that something dangerous was about to happen.

"I will bring her right home. No need to worry. Now, mind Iva and William. Here is some candy you can eat while I am gone." Adriana gave Helena two small pieces of hard candy.

"Will they shoot us?"

"No! No one shoots children."

"Will they shoot Jacob and Father?"

"No, of course not." Adriana wished she could believe life was that simple.

"I want to come." Three-year-old William walked to the door to join his mother.

"No, you need to stay here with Helena." The little boy started to protest, but Helena firmly took his hand.

"We will be all right, Matka."

"That's my big girl."

As she closed the door behind her, Adriana thought of Patrik working in the breaker and John and Louis in the mine. She was sure her boys would join the strikers when the men reached Lattimer. "Cyril and Jacob will keep them safe," she reassured herself. The alternative was not thinkable.

Main Street was unusually quiet as she hurried to the schoolhouse. The women and children were in their barricaded homes, and the men and older boys were in the mines and the breaker. A few curious people were scattered around, and she could see women peeking from upstairs windows. Adriana walked as fast as her massive form would allow, her thoughts focused on reaching Elizabeth before the trouble started.

When she reached the trolley tracks, she looked up the hill at the schoolhouse. Miss Coyle and Mr. Guscott were dismissing the children. With her red hair, ample bosom, and striking features, Miss Coyle was easily recognized, even from this distance. Adriana liked Grace Coyle and especially liked her mother, Mary Coyle Gallagher. Mrs. Gallagher, a stubborn Irish woman, was known to speak her mind. *I heard her argue with the store clerk about her debt. She took no nonsense from that young man. I see much of myself in her.*

"Matka!" Elizabeth called as she ran down the gently sloping hill. "Matka! The strikers are coming! The strikers are coming." Elizabeth was breathless when she reached her mother. "Will Father and Jacob be with them? Will the deputies send them away? What will we do if they send Father and Jacob away?" The questions came in quick succession, not leaving time for her mother to answer.

"No, the deputies will not send them away." Adriana looked down at her daughter, hoping her expression was reassuring. "Hurry, now. Iva will wake up soon and will be hungry." Adriana took her daughter's hand and led her past the gumberry tree and up Main Street toward home.

"Will the miners have clubs?" Elizabeth had trouble keeping up with her mother, but still, the questions kept coming. "Will they be shouting?"

"No, Father told me they would not have clubs. Hurry now."

"The deputies have guns." Elizabeth had heard her father talking with Jacob. "Will the miners have guns?"

"No! Jacob told them not to bring guns. You know everyone listens to Jacob." Elizabeth nodded. She loved and admired her much older brother. She was quiet for a minute or two, thoughtful. And then she told her mother about Jimmy.

"Jimmy tried to scare me." Adriana stopped walking and looked down at her daughter. "He said the deputies would shoot the dirty foreigners, and then he pretended to shoot me. He shouted at me to fall dead like all the foreigners. I started to cry, but Miss Coyle came to save me."

"I will speak with Miss Coyle tomorrow and thank her for taking care of you. But you must remember that the miners, including Father and Jacob, are brave, strong men doing what they know is right."

Finally, at home with her youngest children, Adriana sat and waited.

Anna

The painful memory of that day will be with me forever. It was about 3:30 in the afternoon, on September 10, 1897. I was sitting on the stoop in front of my home, watching the children play. The pie we had made that morning sat on the kitchen table, its inviting aroma filling the air. "Tonight, after dinner, my family will be together, and we will feast on that pie," I remember telling myself just before the shrill scream of the breaker whistle sent a chill through my body. Something terrible had happened. There was trouble in the mine, or at Lattimer.

"Massacre!" I can still hear the shouting in the street. "There was a massacre at Lattimer. The sheriff ordered the deputies to fire."

Lattimer

Close to three in the afternoon the column of strikers neared their destination, the mining town of Lattimer operated by the Pardee Brothers Coal Company. The tiny mining village would be visible when they reached the crest of the hill.

Jacob, now twenty years old, had worked in Lattimer since his family had been evicted from Ario. He knew the roads, the breakers, the mines, and the men who worked there. The miners in Lattimer and Ario were ready. By tonight, all the collieries owned by Calvin Pardee would be on strike.

Lattimer! His home. He pictured his mother, proud and sympathetic toward the strikers, on the front stoop with a broom, watching for them. She would fight the deputies if they threatened the marchers. "Your mother is not afraid of anything or anyone," their father often told his children.

Jacob's brothers, John, the spragger, and Louis, the nipper, had wanted to march with the Harwood strikers, but their father had forbidden it. "You are needed here," he told his boys over their protests. For a moment Jacob chuckled, thinking of his spirited younger brothers and the mischief they would cause when the mine workers walked out and the mine closed.

Patrik, the youngest brother working in the mines, was more reticent. Jacob pictured him bent over the coal in the breaker, his small fingers callused, bleeding, and black with coal dust. *Patrik should be in school,* Jacob thought with a heavy sigh, not for the first time. *He does not belong in the mine.*

And then, there were the little ones. Elizabeth, at this hour, should be in school. Jacob was concerned when he saw the teachers standing outside the schoolhouse watching the deputies. "Be safe, Elizabeth."

When Jacob had left his home that morning, William, a few years younger than Elizabeth, was marching around the kitchen with a big stick. "I will take care of Mother," he had proclaimed to Jacob and their father.

"We are counting on that." Cyril laughed while tousling the hair of his youngest son.

Iva, just a toddler, was oblivious to the ominous events about to transpire. Her tiny pink feet had pounded on the bare wooden floor, imitating William as she followed him around the kitchen.

"Almost there," Emil said to Peter, hoping his voice was reassuring. The boy looked pale and ready to run away. "Lattimer is just beyond the crest of this hill." Peter did not answer, his eyes riveted on the men in front of him, drawing courage from their determination. Emil and Jacob looked stalwart as they climbed the hill. "Almost there," Emil said again.

"We need to turn back." They had reached the top of the hill, and Peter saw the deputies, with their rifles and shotguns, blocking the road to the Lattimer breaker.

"Keep moving. We have a right to be here," Emil persisted, putting his hand on the boy's shoulder.

"Over there, on the hill, the teachers are standing in front of the schoolhouse." Jacob had recognized the schoolteachers, Mr. Guscott and Miss Coyle. His sister often said how much she liked Miss Coyle. She never had anything nice to say about Mr. Guscott. "They must be expecting trouble. Too early for the children to be sent home."

"Someone is giving orders. See! By that tree!" The deputies who had been blocking the street were now moving to the fences on the left side of the road. The trolley line was on a berm on the right side of the street.

"We will be trapped," Jacob whispered to Emil, and he began to plan for an escape if the deputies started shooting. The schoolhouse, about one hundred yards to the right of the road, might offer protection. They could hide behind the trolley on an embankment next to the road. There was also a ditch that might provide some cover. Jacob had an advantage because he lived here. He knew the terrain well. *We could run over there if they open fire,* he thought but did not divulge his plan.

Without warning, the column began to slow.

"Why are we stopping?" Peter asked, trembling.

"Keep moving," the man behind him shouted, pushing the boy forward. Peter was trapped between the stalled marchers in front of him and those pushing from behind.

"The flag is gone!" someone shouted. No one was sure what had happened, but the flag was no longer there. They were too far away to see the confrontation between the sheriff and the leaders of the march. They did not hear the sheriff's order to disperse.

"Keep moving."

The column began to surge forward again. Emil was sure he heard someone shout, "Fire!" Reflexively, he turned toward the sound of a rifle being fired on the left of the column. "No!" The words were spoken just as a volley of gunfire exploded, and the air was filled with the acrid smell of gunsmoke. Agonizing screams from the wounded and dying made everything surreal.

"Run!" Jacob shouted as a bullet ripped through his hat at the same instant the miner in front of him fell to the ground. Dirt and fragments of stone were thrown into the air from the impact of bullets that found the road instead of human flesh.

Emil reeled backward from the force of the bullet that tore into his shoulder, shattering the bone. His legs were no longer his to command, and a comforting darkness enveloped him. He did not feel the strong arms that caught him and dragged him away.

Cyril, who had stopped to rest at Harleigh, had reached the crest of the hill above Lattimer. He saw the miners approaching the deputies who were blocking the road. *They can't get through!* Cyril watched with growing fear and desperation as the first rows of marchers walked toward the deputies. He thought he saw Sheriff Martin about to confront the men. *Let reason prevail,* Cyril prayed.

The column started to move again. Cyril struggled to see his son but could not find him among the sea of black suits and hats. The deputies raised their guns to their shoulders and were preparing to fire. "They won't shoot. Please, God, they won't fire."

He heard the rifles and saw the gray smoke, and he shouted to his son to run. He watched with anguish as a man who had reached the trolley tracks writhed in agony as his body fell to the dirt. A few men reached the brush along the side of the road before the bullets racked their bodies, and blood and torn flesh splattered in the air. A man dove into a drainpipe. *Please, God, help him.*

Run! A silent scream caught in Cyril's throat as he watched a man running, stumbling, almost reaching the safety of the schoolhouse. A deputy moved forward and took aim at the man running up the hill. "Run!" This time it was a primal scream. A bullet found the man's back, and he arched forward, his arms outstretched as he fell to the ground. Another man, running close behind him, stumbled forward, grabbing his leg before he fell to the ground. He began to crawl up the hill toward what he hoped was the safety of the schoolhouse. Others ran to the trolley but fell along the bank. Still, others ran toward a thin line of trees. Cyril watched in horror as another deputy moved to better position himself to shoot. "Jacob! Jacob, run! Oh, Lord have mercy, spare my son." How long the shooting lasted he could not say—a minute, five, hours? Time stood still.

When the guns fell silent, his son's name on his lips, Cyril ran down the hill toward the carnage. Other miners were running back up the hill toward Harleigh. "Have you seen my son?" he pleaded, grabbing the arm of a man who was covered with splattered blood. "Have you seen Jacob?"

Adriana

Adriana was at home when she heard the first pop of a rifle, then another. It was not just one gun but, many. A barrage of gunfire. It was loud, continuous, and frightening and then it was quiet. Elizabeth and Helena began to cry and ran to their mother. William raised his stick in defense of his family.

Adriana wrapped her large, strong arms protectively around her babies. She did not want them to see the fear in her face. "It will be all right," she whispered, her voice cracking just a little. "You will see, everything will be all right." For a long moment, the mother and her children clung together. "I need to find your father and Jacob. You must stay here and wait. Do you understand?"

"I wanna come too. I wanna help."

"No, stay here, William. Protect your sisters." Satisfied that he was needed, William stood tall. Then, giving his mother a military salute like the soldiers he had seen in parades, he took a position next to Elizabeth. He was ready for combat.

Adriana's massive body ran clumsily down the road, her skirts hindered her movement, her breath labored with the unaccustomed exertion. She did not stop when her callused feet were cut by a jagged rock in the road. Droplets of blood marked her path unnoticed. Men, women and children poured into the street tripping and scrambling toward the sound of the gun fire.

Adriana's fear intensified when she heard the whistle of the Lattimer ambulance. "Cyril. Jacob," she screamed. Her face was flushed as she ran, her breath labored, her heart beating so fast she thought it would burst. People around her were shouting, frantic and panicked. There was confusion and fear about what they would find.

"Bring water," someone shouted.

"Sheets, towels," a woman called to her. "They need them for bandages."

"Blessed Jesus, somebody bring water!"

Reaching the gumberry tree at the fork in the road, the scene in front of her unfolded as if in a dream. No, a nightmare. The call for water seemed to linger in the air mixed with the acrid smell of gunpowder. She watched in horror, as two men carried a lifeless, bloodied body to a trolley. A man with a dazed expression, his shirt covered in blood and his limp arms hanging by his sides, asked her for water. She had none to give.

Along the fence, another casualty, with an improvised bandage around his head, was being propped up on a fence. "Jacob?" she cried, her eyes scanning the man's face. But it was not her son. A derby hat was lying on the ground, splattered with blood. "Cyril." The name lingered on her lips as she stared at the hat, unable to move.

The hill leading to the schoolhouse, where she had met Elizabeth just a short while ago, was littered with bodies, some lying still, lifeless, others writhing in pain.

Adriana watched some of the deputies dropping their rifles in a pile. Others, laughing amongst themselves, carried their rifles idly at their sides while boarding a trolley. *How can they be laughing? Do they not see what I am seeing?*

A man standing near the linden tree, looking shocked, handed his revolver to another. She was surprised, recognizing the sheriff from his picture in the newspaper.

Other deputies smoking cigars, walked among the carnage without compassion or guilt. She watched as Miss Coyle tore her petticoat to bind a wound, while Mary Septak carried a bucket of water to quench the thirst of a dying man.

"Cyril! Jacob." Her voice was loud and shrill as she ventured into the nightmare, looking for her husband and son. She picked up her skirt and pushed her way through the crowd of women and men who were assisting the wounded or carrying the dead. "Have you seen my husband? Have you seen my son?" The shocked faces that looked back at her just shook their heads, no.

"Adriana!"

"Cyril!" He ran toward her with a hardened expression on his face and blood on his shirt. "Cyril." In an instant, she was in her husband's arms. "Jacob! Where is Jacob?"

"I-I don't know. Jacob and Emil went ahead. I couldn't keep up." Cyril stammered the words out, overwhelmed and bewildered. He felt powerless in the face of such misery and carnage. He needed to find his son, he wanted to comfort his wife, but he did not know where to start.

News of the massacre reached Ario. The breaker whistle sounded an alarm, church bells clanged a warning. There was trouble. "Lattimer!" Anna heard people shouting. "There was a massacre in Lattimer!"

The Road to Lattimer

Everyone in Ario headed for Lattimer. The road was filled with wagons, horses, barefoot women, men and boys from the mines and the breakers.

"Stephen, stay here, watch the children," Anna shouted to her frightened oldest child, standing in the doorway. "I need to find your father."

Stefan was riding in a produce wagon when he saw Anna. "Here, Anna," he said, reaching for her, helping her into the wagon.

"Cyril? Adriana?" Her face and words were filled with worry for her friends. "A massacre, Stefan. A massacre."

"We will find them, Anna."

It was a short distance, just under two miles to Lattimer, but, to Anna, the time in the wagon seemed like an eternity. "Holy Mary, Mother of God, pray for us."

Reaching Lattimer, Anna and Stefan stood frozen in place as they tried to make sense of the scene before them. Chaos, blood, screams of agony—the smell of war!

"Adriana!" Anna spotted Adriana and Cyril. "Adriana!"

"We can't find Jacob. We can't find Emil." Adriana was screaming as she ran to her friends.

"I couldn't keep up!" Stefan listened as Cyril explained how he had been separated from Jacob and Emil.

"We can't find them!" Adriana said, her voice shaking.

"We'll find them." Stefan's voice was calm, steady. He was a soldier once again. "Anna and Adriana, go to Hazleton. Go to the hospital. Look for them there. Cyril and I will look for them here."

The road to Hazleton was crowded with drays and wagons and ambulances carrying the wounded to St. Joseph's Hospital in Hazleton or to funeral homes. Adriana and Anna, arm in arm, supporting each other, joined the mournful procession.

The walk to Hazleton

Adriana's thin, gray-streaked hair hung in damp strands down her neck and back. Her face flushed, her lips clenched, her eyes flashed with fury. The hem of her skirt was covered with blood and dirt from the street in Lattimer, and her feet were black from the coal dust on the road. Her body was slightly bent forward as she willed herself to move faster up the steep hill leading to Hazleton.

"I am sure Emil and Jacob are all right," Anna offered, trying to reassure her friend. "We will find them."

"We will find them," Adriana echoed, her voice hard.

The women were surrounded by a cacophony of sounds: thundering of horses' hooves, the whoosh of an ambulance, voices that were angry, worried, moaning, and mournful. Carts, wagons, ambulances, men on horseback, hurried past them. A wagon, filled with wounded men, swerved dangerously. Another wagon barely avoided a collision with an ambulance headed in the opposite direction. Horses were spooked by the chaos. Sticky, thick blood dripped from carts and ambulances that carried wounded to Hazleton Hospital. The blood, mixed with the dirt on the road, added to the nightmarish scene. Women clutching children or holding babies followed wagons to the morgue, hoping that their husbands, fathers, and sons were not there.

Adriana seemed oblivious to the commotion. She could not offer help or consolation to the mourners; her only thought was finding her son. "Jacob." She uttered her son's name like a prayer. "Jacob."

The noise was deafening as Anna and Adriana reached the city. Thousands of citizens from Hazleton and surrounding communities lined the sidewalks. "What happened in Lattimer?" Horrified people milled in the streets. Sorrow, shock, anger, and despair hung like a dense cloud in the air. A sorrowful procession of men and women followed wagons that were taking the dead to the morgue or to Bonin or Boyle Funeral homes. They would soon be called upon to identify the bodies of their husbands, brothers, sons. "Perhaps there has been a mistake," women pleaded, clutching the arms of friends or strangers. It could not be their husband or son in the cart headed for the morgue.

"We'll go to the hospital," Anna urged. She did not want to take Adriana to the morgue or funeral homes. At least not yet. "If Jacob is wounded, he will be there."

It took what seemed to be hours to get all the dead and wounded into conveyances that would take them to Hazleton. The people left behind at Lattimer were stunned, saddened, unable to understand what had happened. Cyril and Stefan joined the multitudes going to Hazleton. They would join their wives at the hospital after checking the funeral homes and the morgue. Emil and Jacob were still among the missing.

Police guarded the entrances of the Hazleton State Hospital as anxious men and women struggled to get inside. Adriana was not deterred, pushing her body through the crowd she used her elbows to give her leverage against men and women just as desperate as herself.

"Let me in!" she screamed at the policeman who blocked her way. "Let me in! My son is in there."

But the policeman stood firm. "Move back!" he ordered, lifting his billy club across his chest. He did not want to use it, but he had his orders.

Anna grabbed Adriana and pulled her away from the door. "If they arrest you, then you will not find Jacob." Reluctantly, Adriana turned away from the door, her body drained from emotion; for the first time in her life, she felt she could not be strong. "You need to wait," Anna soothed. "Take a breath. We will know soon."

Adriana turned back to the door of the hospital, but Anna had a firm grip on her arms. "Soon, Adriana. I am sure they will let us in soon." Her voice had a confidence she did not feel.

"Jacob!" The words were a soft whisper as Adriana's body relaxed. "Jacob!"

Jacob was standing on the steps of the hospital. His clothes were covered in blood.

"Jacob!" Adriana shouted as she broke free from Anna's grasp and pushed her way through the crowd toward her son.

"Matka." His voice was soothing as he took his sobbing mother into his arms. "It's all right, Matka. I am all right."

"Emil? Where is Emil?"

"A bullet went through his shoulder. The doctors have seen him, and now he is asleep."

Anna felt a wave of nausea envelope her. Jacob's arms caught her before she fell on the steps of the hospital.

"I'll take both of you home," Jacob offered.

"Yes, take us home."

Stefan

Cyril's face crumbled into lines of despair as he stood among the carnage. He watched as a stranger, using an improvised stretcher, carried a limp, bloodied body to a waiting trolley. He knew the lifeless eyes staring up to heaven would haunt him for a lifetime.

"Jacob," he whispered, thankful that the man on the stretcher was not his son. He had seen mutilated bodies before and had heard the anguished screams of men whose flesh was torn and mangled. The suffering of wives and children as their men were carried from the mines was all too familiar. Still, what he was seeing today was incomprehensible. How could there be so much hatred, so much evil?

"I'll go there." Cyril pointed to the hill that led to the schoolhouse. Stefan just nodded his agreement.

Cyril's legs barely responded as he forced himself to make the climb. He stopped to turn over a body and was ashamed at the relief he felt. It was not Jacob. He walked past Miss Coyle. She was tearing her petticoat to bind a head wound. Cyril ignored cries for water; he had none to give. As he approached the top of the hill, his focus was on the schoolhouse, which was riddled with bullets. Just that morning, innocent children had been there. How would they heal? How would any of them heal? He did not look back and did not see that Stefan had not moved.

It was the dirt, the dirt drenched with fresh blood, that brought Stefan back to a world he thought he had left behind. The cries of the dying and wounded faded into the background, replaced with the cry, "Allahu Akbar!"

He felt the weight of the weapon he had carried when he was a young soldier. The body on the ground in front of him now wore the uniform of a soldier belonging to the Austrian Army. "Why could I not have saved you?" he asked the man on the ground, covered in blood. "We were careless, we ignored the danger."

The woman in black was there, kneeling in the dirt, her black robes covered in scarlet blood, her dark eyes vacant. "I will do better," he vowed as the apparition drifted away. "I will do better." With that, he joined the others in carrying the wounded to the waiting ambulance.

They met Adriana, Anna, and Jacob, walking along the road that led to Lattimer and Ario. Anna, tired, was holding Jacob's arm. Adriana walked next to them, her face frozen in defiance, her stride strong and erect. Her grief had been vanquished, and she was now ready to battle with the perpetrators of this gruesome crime.

"Jacob," Cyril cried in relief, reaching them. "Jacob, are you all right?" There were splatters of blood on Jacob's clothing and sadness in his eyes.

"Yes, Father. I'm unhurt."

"They were at the hospital," Adriana blurted. "Emil will be all right. Edita is with him." She was speaking so rapidly, the words melded together, but their meaning was clear. Emil and Jacob were alive.

"There were so many people." Anna could hardly speak as she relived the tragedy she had witnessed. "Blood dripped from wagons; horses were frightened. I was sure we wouldn't see them alive ever again." Anna was trembling, her voice shaky as she held Stefan's arm.

"Everyone is angry with the sheriff and the deputies." Jacob had heard the talk in the hospital. "There will be a meeting tonight on Donegal Hill. They say Father Aust will be there, and so will Fahy."

"I'll be there," Stefan pronounced.

"I'm going too," Adriana declared, challenging anyone to stop her.

"No, you will not." Cyril's voice was firm as he confronted his stubborn and opinionated wife. "Take Anna home, and then go to the children."

"I'm going." Adriana was defiant as her eyes met Cyril's. It was not often she lost an argument with her husband.

"Anna needs you. The children need you."

"But—"

"No!"

Jacob took his mother's hands. "Matka, please go to the little ones. They need you."

"The children." Reluctantly, Adriana agreed to go home. She would bring comfort to the children tonight, and tomorrow she would meet with Mary Septak. The world would see the power of Slovak womanhood.

Cyril, Stefan, and Jacob were among the two thousand people, Americans and foreigners, gathered at the old baseball field on Donegal Hill in Hazleton on the night of the massacre. There were speeches in Slovak, Hungarian, and German. Voices spoke of the suffering of the miners and the injustice that took place at Lattimer. The Reverend Spaulding, a Protestant pastor, implored them not to break the law and promised that justice would be done. Others spoke of the responsibility to assist the victims and their families.

John Fahy, the representative of the United Mine Workers, was there and the crowd shouted his name. They were ready and eager to listen to him. Fahy stood before them, speaking slowly so he would be understood by those with limited English. He spoke of the need to stay peaceable and to organize. "The union will be there to help," he promised them. His voice was strong, his manner convincing. "Together, we will work for a fair wage, the end to company stores, a lowering of the cost of blasting powder. Unity and solidarity will make us strong."

A group of Irish Americans stood near Stefan. The animosity and suspicion that existed between the foreigners and

Americans began to dissipate. The American miners were looking at the foreigners with new respect.

"Spolu—together," Stefan volunteered, offering his hand.

"Together," the Americans answered.

Everything changed the day that nineteen men were murdered, and thirty-nine others wounded in Lattimer. The American miners now understood that the immigrants were not docile laborers willing to work under inhumane conditions. In the days to follow, fifteen thousand anthracite miners, American and immigrant, joined the United Mine Workers. Mines throughout the region were shut down, including the mines owned by the Pardee Brothers.

Feeling the animosity of the people of Hazleton, many of the deputies went into hiding that night and did not return for weeks. The owners of the coal companies feared retribution from the miners and requested that the governor send the National Guard to Hazleton. That night, the sentiment among the people assembled on Donegal Hill, and most of the residents of Hazleton, was that the State Militia would not be needed to maintain order. Nevertheless, by daybreak, the Ninth Regiment of the Pennsylvania National Guard arrived in Hazleton.

Stefan walked home that night with conflicting emotions. He could not shake the images of wounded, dying men on the street of Lattimer, but he had hope that things would change, and that he could be a part of that change. He would talk to Father Aust about raising money for the prosecution of the deputies and to help the families of the victims of the Lattimer massacre.

Five days after the meeting on Donegal Hill, the *National Prosecuting and Charity of the Lattimer Victims* was established, and Father Aust was elected president of the committee.

Chapter 13 — 1897-1898

The Days After

Anna

The Sunday after the massacre my family walked to Hazleton for the first of the funerals. Everyone from Ario, Lattimer, and Milnesville who could make the journey, and did not have money for a trolley, was on that road walking with us. We walked in quiet, mournful solidarity up the Hill to Hazleton. Even the children, sensing the enormity of the day, were subdued.

Reaching the top of the hill, we heard the brass band playing the mournful death march, and my heart raced in time with the sorrowful dirge. Many cried as we pictured the draped wagons carrying the bodies of four men from Harwood to Saint Joseph's Slovak Church.

Newspapers would later say it was the most lavish procession the city had ever seen. Four burial societies accompanied the wagons: Saint Joseph's National Slovak Society resplendent in uniforms with white, blue, and red sashes across their right shoulder. The Italian St. Peter and Paul's Society wore extravagant blue uniforms with gold braid; and the Poles in simple gray uniforms carried long sabers.

With four caskets and thousands of mourners, there was no room for us inside the church. We stood with others on the church grounds, listening to the organ playing and the choir singing "Ave Maria" through the open windows of the church. We listened as Father Aust told us to trust in God. All knelt on the grass, the street, the sidewalk as the priest consecrated the host and the souls of the departed were given up to the Lord.

Ten-year-old Stephen lost his childhood innocence that day. As we stood outside the church, his face was solemn like his father's. In the days that followed, Stephen studied the pictures in the newspaper, showing the deputies with their rifles firing on men, men dressed like his father. The marches and strikes and deputies with rifles had made an enduring impression on the little boy. He now understood what it meant to die. I was sure he would never forget what happened at Lattimer.

Rose saw me crying that night and wrapped her delicate child's arms around me. "It will be all right, Matka," she said, trying to console me. She was still such a little girl, her arms so frail, but she held me as tightly as her strength would allow. I'm not sure she understood everything that was happening. What does a child know of the hatred that can be in a heart? All she knew was that she could see the anguish on our faces, the uncertainty and fear in the voices of the adults around her.

With all the talk of guns and shooting, little Robert found a stick and marched around the house, pretending he was a miner going to kill a deputy.

Stefan stayed in Hazleton that night. There were more meetings. I took the children home.

The funerals were behind us, but our lives were still filled with grief and a sense of hopelessness. Over ten thousand miners were on strike; the mines were closed, the breakers silent, and smoke did not rise from the boilers. The laughter of children was not heard in the streets, and the women spoke softly, mournfully, wherever they gathered.

Stefan

Stefan listened to Father Aust and others advising everyone to be careful not to provoke the authorities. Unlike many others, Stefan was confident that justice would be done. He became a member of *The Prosecution and Charity Committee* and helped to raise money for the families of the victims and for the prosecution of the deputies.

A week after the funerals, he joined a sullen group of men sitting on the porch outside the company store. They were the men who worked with him in the mines, the men upon whom he depended if something went wrong.

"They were our brothers," one of the men was saying. "We owe them justice."

"I knew Cheslak and his wife," another whispered. Cheslak was killed at Lattimer. "What is to become of her now?"

"Futa came from my village in Slovakia. My mother was his mother's sister," another shared. "He was only eighteen."

"Vengeance!" a man known for his temper shouted.

"The law will be on our side, and the sheriff and the deputies will be punished." Stefan's confidence quieted the group.

"I don't believe it! Not for a moment," the man with the temper alleged.

"Even the Americans are angry," Stefan continued, undeterred. "All of Hazleton mourns with us."

"Not all! Does Calvin Pardee care? Has he shown remorse?"

"My son worked in the Harwood Colliery. He was wounded at Lattimer. Will there be justice for him?"

"Some of the deputies have fled the city."

"They will be found and brought to justice."

"Father Aust is starting a fund for the prosecution," Stefan asserted. "I was at a meeting. Money is being raised."

"The deputies are still not in jail."

"They will be arrested, and there will be a trial. We will win."

Not everyone was convinced.

Anna

Adriana, my dear friend, was willful, compassionate, and had a strength everyone admired. She was my friend. My dearest friend. In our old age, we would sit on the porch, watch our grandchildren play in the street, and reflect on our lives. She often told me how she would visit the Gypsies as a child. Her parents forbade it. We all knew they were thieves who stole little girls. But Adriana saw the good in them. "They loved life," she would tell me. "They would sing, dance and wear colorful clothes. Sometimes I would bring them scraps of food and old blankets we no longer needed. In return, they would sing for me. Sometimes the songs were melancholy and told of lost loves, others would be exuberant, and the men would swing me around in time to the music until I collapsed with laughter.

"I was stubborn," she admitted, but there was no regret in her voice.

"You still are." We would laugh together, each with our own recollections.

Days would pass before we had an opportunity to meet again but when we did the story would often begin with her desire to come to America.

"America, it meant adventure, hope, an escape from the tedium of my life." It wasn't difficult to picture the young Adriana, rebellious, willful, daring. "My mother did not think much of my aspiration and it seemed an impossible dream until Cyril ventured into our village.

We sat in the moonlight looking at the stars and Cyril told me of his plans. Suddenly everything was possible." She was courageous, my Adriana. "I grew to love him, you know." Seeing her sorrow, I reached for her hand. Cyril died of black lung, and we all missed him so very much. We would sit then and rock in our chairs and remember young love.

On other days we talked about the challenges we had faced.

"Remember Murphy and his gang?" I certainly did! She loved to tell the tale, and her face would beam with pride.

"Tell me again." The story would be embellished with each retelling but that didn't matter. We were old, you see, and all we had were our memories. "They came to evict us." Her eyes glared with anger as she relived the shock and fear she had felt. "I fought back, a tigress protecting her family. I scratched the policeman's face. Jake tried to stop me by grabbing my arms. So, I kicked him!" Adriana would always laugh at the recollection. Adriana, I miss your laugh.

"I broke the bone in his shin when I kicked him," she continued, her eyes twinkling with delight. "He limped for the rest of his days, you know," she said with the voice of the righteous. She was David conquering Goliath, and, for a moment, her eyes lost the cloudiness of age and she was once again a young woman. "They told Cyril to control his wife, but my Cyril knew better than to try."

"You even defied the soldiers who came to Hazleton during the strike of 1889," I prompted her.

"Yes, the newspapers called us the *Slavic Amazons*." The memory was always followed by a chuckle, and her eyes once *again sparkled with the fire that had burned inside of her all those years ago.*

I must confess, I didn't march with the women that day, or ever. I wish I had their pluck. My excuse: I was pregnant and afraid. Katarina didn't march either. She stayed home during those difficult days. Her husband, Jan, did not support the strike and, protected by soldiers, went to work in the mine each day. Stefan and Cyril called him a scab.

The Slavic Amazons, their story should be told. We all need to remember these women, their courage, determination, and their strength. They supported and encouraged their men.

Adriana and the Slavic Amazons

Sunlight streamed through the open window, banishing the morning shadows from the tiny kitchen. There was a lingering smell of bacon grease, fresh-baked bread, and stale cigars, but it went unnoticed by the men and boys who stood near the door, anxiously waiting to leave. Adriana, with her hands on her hips, a white apron in place, was in the center of the room appraising her husband and sons. They knew they would not be allowed to leave the house until she was satisfied that faces were washed, ties adjusted, and hair neatly combed. It was a familiar ritual, repeated on Sundays and special occasions since the boys had been toddlers. This was an important day. A committee of miners made of three Slavs, three Americans, and three Italians had been sent to present their grievances to Mr. Pardee, the owner of the Lattimer mines. Today they would hear his answer.

Adriana's husband, Cyril, tugging at the stiff collar of his shirt, stood in front of the door, waiting for his wife to fix his tie and button his vest. His large, callused hands, which were skilled with the miner's pick and setting explosives in the mine, could not master the art of moving buttons through buttonholes or arranging the folds of a tie.

"Stand still!" Adriana commanded as she buttoned Cyril's vest and adjusted his tie. "*Reprezentatívne,*" she approved while removing some lint from his shoulder. "Presentable."

Jacob, holding his hat in his hand, gave his mother a mischievous kiss on her cheek as she adjusted the bow tie he was wearing. "*Reprezentatívne.*" Jacob had passed inspection.

John was next. At fifteen, he towered over his mother, who needed to stand on her toes to reach the strand of hair that had fallen out of place. With amusement, she inspected the thin mustache that had appeared on her son's face. "*Reprezentatívne.*"

Louis, thirteen, and twelve-year-old Patrik tugged at their collars and squirmed in their hand-me-down jackets. The delay to inspect clothing, was unnecessary, a waste of time. Louis tried to control his restless body by watching a spider crawling across the ceiling, while Patrik inspected the soft miner's cap he held in his hands.

"Louis, Patrik, look at me," Adriana commanded, the sparkle in her eye belying her otherwise stern expression. "Yes, Matka." The boys stood at attention. They had felt the sting of their mother's hand and their father's belt, and they did not want to experience that humiliation on this important day.

"Stay close to your father," Adriana commanded. Patrik would obey, but she worried about Louis and his propensity for finding trouble.

"Yes, Matka," the boys replied in unison.

"Now, go. All of you, go."

"I'm going too," three-year-old William announced, positioning himself in front of his father.

"When you are older you will come with us."

"Please, now. I am big. See." The little boy stood as tall as his tiny body would allow.

"William," Adriana interceded, taking the child's hand. "You cannot go this time."

"Next time, William. Stay here and take care of your mother."

"Will the deputies be there?" Elizabeth asked, her eyes wide with fear. She had heard the deafening crack of the rifles on September 10 and had seen the caskets of the dead. Above all, Elizabeth had seen the bandages on Emil's shoulder when he had been released from the hospital.

"No, no deputies," Adriana reassured her daughter.

Cyril and his sons mingled with the other men in front of the company store. They were hopeful as they waited for Augustus W. Drake, the Lattimer superintendent, to bring them the answer to their requests.

Louis was the first to see the cloud of dust that appeared at the fork in the road. A thunderous roar shook the earth as squadrons of cavalry, sunlight reflecting off their sabers, charged toward them. The soldiers carried rifles and pistols and wore cartridge belts heavy with ammunition. Patrik wanted to run, but not a man around him moved. He looked back at his father, who was standing tall and strong, a confidence in his expression that had been missing since the massacre. The cavalry's orders to intimidate the striking miners had failed.

Mary Septak, a buxom woman with heavy, furrowed eyebrows, dark eyes, and high cheekbones, was standing on the porch of her boarding house when she saw the cavalry approaching. Her old rickety porch shook from the pounding of the horses' hooves, but there was no fear, only anger, on her face. Mary Septak was well known in the region as an outspoken supporter of miners' rights. With her harsh tongue and brisk manner, she was both feared and respected by those who encountered her.

Young men and boys who were alone and far from home found refuge at Mary's boarding house. They slept two in a bed, crowded into the two upstairs bedrooms. She could not turn them away. Even the kitchen had a bed, where men on the night shift slept fully clothed during the day, while Mary and her husband slept there at night. Mary cared for them, cooked for them, and loved them. These young men filled a void in her life caused by the death of nine of her ten children. She watched her young boarders go to the mines and the breakers each day and understood the hardships and dangers they faced. In the days that followed the massacre, she fought for all the men who worked in the mines and especially for her beloved husband.

The door to the company store opened, and Drake, the Lattimer superintendent, stood in front of the patiently waiting men. Drake felt no empathy for the men assembled in the street. He had a job to do.

"Mr. Pardee has informed me," he paused for effect, "there will be no increase in wages, and the price of powder will remain the same." He paused again as his words were translated for those with limited English. The crowd began to grumble, and his voice grew louder. "There will be no change to the policy governing the company store, and you will still contribute to the company doctor," he continued, ignoring the growing agitation among the men. "Mr. Pardee is being generous since those on the grievance committee will not be fired."

"Strike!" someone shouted. "Strike!" The word resonated through the crowd.

"Now, listen to me, you have nothing to gain by staying out of work," Drake shouted at them. He could not understand why they could not accept the sensible offer made by Mr. Pardee. "Will you come back to work?"

"NO!" Mary Septak heard the men shout.

Adriana, pacing the floor of her kitchen, waited impatiently for news. What was the answer from Pardee? Would the men be returning to work, or would the strike continue? Would there be food to feed her children? Would they be cast out into the street? What was taking so long?

Little Iva was playing in her crib, and William was asleep on a blanket he had dragged from his bed. The "sword" he would use to protect his family was still in his hands. The little girls, Elizabeth and Helena, were occupied by a secret game known only to them.

"Elizabeth!" The little girl looked at her mother in surprise. There was an unfamiliar tension in her mother's voice. "Take care of the children," Adriana said, wrapping her shawl around her shoulders and reaching for her scarf as she gave the command to the little girl. Elizabeth nodded. It was not at all unusual for her to look after her younger siblings.

A boy, his hat in his hands, was running up the street. He was coming from the direction of the company store and had news.

"What happened?" Adriana agitatedly demanded of the boy when she reached him.

"They rejected everything."

"Wages, cost of powder, company store, everything, rejected?"

"Yes, everything."

"What about the grievance committee?"

"They can keep their jobs. That was the only concession."

"Adriana!" Cyril and Jacob were walking toward her. Her expression told them she had heard the news.

"The men were united." Cyril's face was grim as he spoke the words. "We will not go back to work."

"Good!" Adriana was ready to fight.

Mary Septak stood on her porch, her wooden sword in her hand, speaking to her friends and neighbors gathering in the street. "My man works hard." Her powerful voice was filled with emotion. "My man loves me." Adriana, standing with the others, knew this to be true, for she had often seen fond glances exchanged between Mary and her husband. "I love my man, and I will join him in this fight."

"Our men have been treated like slaves!" Adriana shouted, her husky voice gaining everyone's attention. Her words precipitated an outcry from the women who had been listening to Mary.

"Starvation wages," a woman standing next to Adriana called out.

"My children are hungry!" a woman with a child on her hip pleaded. "My husband works hard, but it isn't enough."

"Mine too."

"Then we will fight alongside our men." Mary raised the crude wooden sword she held in her hand, and the women cheered. "We will join the men in their struggle. We will not let the mines open, and we will confront the soldiers. They will see the strength of Slavic womanhood. We will be a force to be reckoned with."

Adriana was one of the one hundred fifty women who marched across the Lattimer strippings on the morning of September 15, 1897. Their intent was to shut down the mines at Lattimer by preventing the men from going to work. The women were carrying sticks, clubs, rolling pins and bean poles to challenge the armed soldiers sent to protect the mines.

They were ordinary women wearing drab calico dresses, the hems rimmed in mud and dust. Some wore old sturdy shoes, bought at great expense at the company store. But many walked barefoot, their feet black with coal dust. A few of the women wore scarves, as they had done in Europe, while others had their hair tied in severe buns that spoke of women who had no time for vanities. They were mothers, some young, with babies on their hips, others with gray hair, who walked a bit slower, but with the same determination as those who had not weathered so many hardships.

The women, whom the newspapers would later dub the Slavic Amazons, marched down the streets of Lattimer toward the strippings. They whooped and hollered, raising quite a ruckus, while the families of the miners cheered them on. At first, the soldiers of the Thirteenth did not try to stop them as the women raised their weapons and moved toward them. When the cavalrymen arrived, they used their gun muzzles to drive the women from the field. Not easily frightened, the women climbed up a culm bank. Mary, waving her sword, shouted for them to share their ammunition. "We'll show you a devil of a time," she promised.

The march through Lattimer was only the beginning of the trouble the "Amazons" would cause. They raided the collieries at Honey Brook, Bunker Hill, and McAdoo, shouting at miners to stop work, knocking tools from their hands, and pelting them with rocks. Soldiers, guarding the mines, were baffled by the women who were hurling sticks, stones, and chunks of coal at them. The women had no fear. The newspapers reported that Big Mary, holding her wooden sword, had charged against soldiers with bayonets.

The militance of the women helped to bring about some concessions, including a modest pay raise. Gomer Jones was replaced. The United Mine Workers grew stronger. The miners now had an organization with which to fight the coal barons. The women returned home to care for their families, and the men returned to work.

Anna

Our lives did get a little better after the strike. We still lived in Ario. Ario had become our home, there was no need to move. Stefan brought home a little more money, and we could rent a better house, this time on Broad Street. A hill behind our new home was covered with trees that turned crimson, gold and orange in the fall. There was space for a garden on the side of the house. A well was just across the road and the outhouse in the backyard was for our use only. What luxury! It was not unusual for women in the patches to walk a mile or more for water and outhouses were often shared by neighbors. Providing clean water and sanitation for the families was not a priority of the owners of the coal towns.

The new house was not fancy, mind you, just a typical two-story wood-frame miner's house. The shanty on Back Street that had been our home for the past nine years was now home to new immigrants. The children liked to play in the vacant lot next to our new home. My grandchildren play there still.

But that was not the end of the story. There were those who promised us that the sheriff and his deputies would be tried and punished. Fall had passed, and it was during the cold, dark days of winter that the trial of the deputies began.

I didn't go to the trial. It was in Wilkes-Barre. I did not have the money to take the train and the children needed me. I read about it in the Hazleton Standard *and everyone was talking about it. Adriana told me how the defense prevented testimony that would show the deputies planned to kill the miners. "They will go free!" she asserted but I didn't believe her. "How could they be found innocent?" I didn't understand all the legalities the way Adriana did, but she predicted the verdict long before the rest of us.*

We all wanted to forget the trial and how it ended. But, from time to time, Adriana and I talked about Miss Coyle the schoolteacher. We heard that she had seen the shooting from the steps of the schoolhouse and was a valuable witness for the prosecution. "The strikers were marching peacefully," she testified, "and there were no weapons of any kind."

According to the newspapers, she had told the Zeirdt boys they were "bums," and they were. Confronting another deputy, she scolded him, saying that there was nothing glorious in what he had just done. She swore to the court, "I saw him, Deputy Hess. He was kicking a man who was wounded."

Our Emil was a witness. We were all so proud of him. Like so many others he did not hesitate to show the jury the wounds he had endured.

The Trial

Emil was in Wilkes-Barre for two weeks, and the walk to the courthouse each morning had become a monotonous routine. His head bent against the stinging sleet and wind, he walked with a rapid stride to the Wilkes-Barre courthouse. Today he would give testimony in the trial of Sheriff Martin and his deputies. He would be the first witness of the day and was instructed to wait in the corridor of the courthouse until summoned.

The shoulder that had been shattered by the deputy's bullet ached from the cold, he was hungry, and, most of all, he missed his family. There was no money for the train, so he stayed in Wilkes-Barre. In letters home, he never mentioned the crowded, dirty boarding house where he slept. The dollar a day he was paid by the court barely paid his expenses. Anything that was left he sent home to Edita.

Curious spectators and newspaper reporters, undeterred by the foul weather, blocked the entrance to the courthouse. They were there to see the trial of the century. Emil pushed his way through the crowd, the badge that said "witness", allowed him access to the courthouse.

A reporter from *The Press*, a newspaper in Philadelphia, Pennsylvania, asked him a few questions. Emil's English was better than most of the others and the reporter took careful notes. *Perhaps sympathetic readers would donate money to supplement the funds needed for the trial.* The reporter empathized with the miners.

Before this trial, Emil had never been in a courtroom, had never seen a judge in the robes of his office, or faced a jury that would judge if he was speaking the truth. He swallowed hard and looked to the men around him for support. There was sadness, worry, and hope on their faces as they stood in small groups, voices hushed, talking about the trial.

"Hess has been identified by a witness. No doubt about his guilt."

"He should hang for what he did."

"Not likely."

"The deputies are out without bail."

"Saw them going to the theater last night."

"Bastards."

Emil knew many of the men there, including John Eaglar, a man he respected. There had been a newspaper sketch of Eaglar demonstrating to the jury how the deputies had held their rifles and aimed them at the miners. "They held their guns like this," the newspaper quoted Eaglar. He also identified Ario Platt, who worked for the A. Pardee Coal Company, as a deputy who had been at Lattimer and McKenna's Corner in Hazleton.

John Silvar, a handsome man with dark, curly hair wearing plaid trousers, was talking with a group of miners. He had been among the first of the witnesses, and everyone remarked on his calm, unflustered demeanor under brutal cross-examination.

Emil turned as he felt a gentle hand resting on his shoulder. It was Father Aust, unmistakable with his portly size and Roman collar. His expression was serious but kind. The priest understood how these uneducated immigrants, with their limited English, would be intimidated by the skills of powerful lawyers. Many needed interpreters while giving testimony and did not always understand the questions they were being asked. Emil, when asked if he needed an interpreter, had refused.

The Road to Lattimer · 195

"You will do well today, Emil," the priest encouraged the young man who stood before him. "The Lord is with you and will give you strength. Your cause is just."

"Thank you, Father."

The large mahogany doors to the courtroom were closed, preventing access to the men in the corridor. The room was already filled with spectators, reporters, lawyers, prosecutors, and defendants. Early access had been given to a few respected ladies of the community allowing them to be comfortably seated before others were admitted. Prosecutors and defendants had entered through a side door designated for them. Prominent reporters and a few spectators, who arrived early, were allowed to enter before the doors were shut.

Reaching into his pocket, Emil touched the letter he had received from his wife, Edita. Knowing the courtroom door would open promptly at 10:00 AM, Emil moved to a corner of the corridor and read the letter again.

February 11, 1898
My dear Emil,
 It has been cold, and I worry about you. Is it warm in the house where you are staying? Do you have enough to eat? I know the money you send us each week comes from money you should use for food.
 As you know, the newspapers cover the trial every day. We heard that Father Aust read the names of the thirteen men from his parish who had died at Lattimer. How could the eyes of anyone in the courtroom not fill with tears hearing the names of those brave men who were slaughtered for no reason?
 But enough with that. We are well and have food to eat, but that is not the case for many of our neighbors. With their men away in Wilkes-Barre and unable to work, the families have no money to buy food. We help them when we can. My mother and I brought some of my canned pears to Mrs. Bosko and Mrs. Jancovik and left more at the church for the Ladies of the Rosary to give to the neediest.

> *A rumor is being spread that anyone who testifies against the sheriff and the deputies will lose their job and will be barred from work anywhere else in the region. I pray to the Lord that this will not happen.*
>
> *My brother, Samuel, wrote from Pittsburgh. He wants to know if he should come home. I told him all is well, and the trial will soon be over. He told me his wife is expecting their first baby.*
>
> *Alica, our sweet baby, misses you. She says "dada" and looks at the door, waiting for you to come home. Mother has promised to make apple dumplings for you on your return. There are still some apples left in the shed, and it would be a treat for everyone.*
>
> *I miss you in our bed and cannot wait for this trial to be over and for you to be safely home.*
>
> *I will continue to pray for all of us. The women have been offering a novena to the Blessed Virgin for a swift ending to the trial. Mother and Emma send their love. I tell our baby you will be home soon.*
> *Your wife,*
> *Edita*

The imposing mahogany doors of the courtroom opened, and Emil put the letter back in the breast pocket of his jacket. It would give him the strength and resolve he would need today.

"Emil Tesar!" a tall man with a booming voice was summoning him into the courtroom. "Emil Tesar!"

"Here, here I am," Emil called, feeling friendly, encouraging slaps on his shoulder as he pushed his way through the crowd. Reaching the door, his back stiffened, and his heart raced, but the expression on his face was one of calm resolve.

"Tesar."

"Yes, sir."

"Follow me."

The crowded courtroom was large, but to Emil, it felt as claustrophobic as a dark, narrow chamber in the mine. Every seat in the room was taken, and every available space in the aisles was filled with spectators. Everyone in the courtroom turned to look at the new witness, and Emil was sure the curious murmurs were about him. There was a commotion behind him. He heard angry voices as officers of the court prevented others from entering the room. A newspaper reporter was the loudest of them all as he vocalized his right to report the trial with an eyewitness account. The heavy door closed with a thud, and Emil was trapped as surely as though a rockfall in the mine had blocked his escape.

Emil could hear his heavy shoes pounding on the wooden floor as he walked down the aisle. He felt the eyes of the spectators piercing his being. Well-dressed men turned to look at him with mild curiosity, and women with bobbing feathers in their hats strained to get a better look. Was that disdain on their faces, mockery, or just curiosity? Emil hastened his pace and felt moisture build up in the palms of his hands.

The lawyers, and there seemed to be many of them, sat in front of the judge. Not one looked at Emil. District Attorney Martin was consulting with John McGahren, an attorney for the prosecution, while others were engrossed in documents of apparent importance.

Emil looked at the twelve men of the jury, guarded by a man with a long white beard and spectacles known as the court tipstaff. *They will listen to me,* he thought. *You can see on their faces they are interested and want to know the truth. I will talk to them honestly and tell them my story. I will tell them what I know about that day in Lattimer, and their decision will be fair.* The men of the jury were of the working class, laborers, carpenters, clerks. Two looked familiar. Where had he seen them? Perhaps at a festival at the church, or maybe a parade in Hazleton? But the majority were strangers to him. *Still,* he thought, *they are working men, like me.*

Judge Stanley Woodward, a heavy-set man with a receding hairline and a walrus mustache, was absently looking at papers on his desk. He had seen enough miners and was not curious about the young man walking toward the bench. Behind him were portraits of distinguished citizens of Wilkes-Barre, most unknown to the miners who were here seeking justice.

Emil's mouth was dry as he placed his hand on the Bible and swore to tell the truth, the whole truth, and nothing but the truth. He took his seat and looked out at the defendants, so different in appearance from the miners. The men on trial for murder were dressed and groomed in a manner that left no doubt of their wealth and status in the community. Their expressions were free from worry as they read books or the morning newspaper. Obviously bored with the proceedings they were just waiting to be released from the drudgery of the trial. Emil had heard that the deputies had shown their contempt by laughing at witnesses whose limited English caused a mistake to be made. *They feel no remorse,* Emil thought. *They are confident of an acquittal.* Editorials in the newspapers argued that the deputies were doing their sworn duty to protect the people of Lattimer from an unruly and dangerous mob. Absently, Emil rubbed his shoulder, and, for a moment, his faith wavered. He was unsure that the victims of the massacre would receive the justice they deserved.

Sheriff Martin, with his neat, curly beard and, what Emil thought, was a meek expression, was sitting by the deputies. Unlike the others on trial, Sheriff Martin looked attentive, and his eyes met those of Emil. The young mule driver almost felt sorry for him. The sheriff had made mistakes, deadly mistakes, but Emil suspected that on the day of the massacre, the sheriff had lost control of his deputies and had never intended to fire on the marchers.

On the witness stand, with prompting from District Attorney Martin, Emil told the events of the day as he had experienced them. His voice was calm and steady as he answered each question.

"No, sir, we did not have any weapons. I made sure those around me did not even carry a stick." Emil thought of Peter, who had just joined the marchers in Harwood, swinging a stick as though it were a baseball bat. The boy had understood, and with a little embarrassment had dropped the stick. Peter had written to Emil a few months after the massacre. "My dreams of a new life in America have been shattered," Peter wrote. "I am going home."

"Yes, I saw Mr. Platt in Hazleton on the day of the massacre, and I can identify him." Emil, hat in hand, walked up to the rows of deputies, and without hesitation pointed to Ario Platt. Platt, sitting back in his chair with a sneer, made no effort to conceal his contempt for the foreigner.

When asked to show his scars to the jury, Emil hesitated—there were women among the spectators, and he would need to take off his shirt. He turned to the judge who indicated he should do as directed. With an angry glance at the defendants, Emil took off his coat, then his jacket, then placed them on the witness chair. Pausing for just a moment, he turned to look at the jurors. They watched him attentively. *Yes, they must see what these men did to me,* he thought as he walked to the jury box.

Blood rushing to his face, he unbuttoned his shirt and removed his arm from the sleeve. Some of the jurors bent forward to examine the scar, but a few could not look and lowered their eyes. They had seen many such scars during the trial.

February 15, 1898
My Dear Edita,

My heart aches from missing you and our little Alica. I long to hold both of you and wait anxiously for our separation to end. As always, your strength brings me comfort.

Today, I sat on the witness stand. Despite my difficulty understanding the questions asked by the defense attorney, I think I did very well. I cannot say if my testimony mattered, but the jury, and most of the spectators looked sympathetic when I showed them my scars. It was quite different with the deputies, who did not even bother to look at me. They were far too busy reading their books and newspapers. Pardee Platt was there and I identified him as one of the deputies I saw running down the hill at McKenna's Corner. I could not testify he was at Lattimer.

I carried your letter with me today. It gave me courage and comfort.

Congratulations to your brother and his wife. We will find a way for you and your mother to go to the Christening. I miss

our own little one. Give my love to your mother and Emma. I will be home soon.
Love,
Emil

February 21, 1898
My Dear Edita,

Today I arrived at the courthouse very early and was among the spectators able to enter the courtroom to hear the defense of the accused. To be sure, I was not fortunate enough to get a seat, as many had been reserved for ladies who had entered the courtroom through a side door. Still, I do not begrudge them the seats. I felt fortunate that I was in the courtroom and not waiting with so many others in the corridors, or even outside the courthouse in the cold.

Attorney George Ferris, who was representing Sheriff Martin, made the opening remarks. I did not always follow what he was saying, but he spoke with confidence, and when I heard Sheriff Martin's name, everyone in the courtroom was silent and attentive to his words. He began, as you will read in the papers, by stressing the importance of the trial. That is one thing we can all agree upon. At first, I was heartened. He seemed sympathetic to the plight of the miners. But when I heard the words, "all homicide is not criminal," everything changed. We were no longer victims of an outrageous crime, but scheming, desperate men, a riotous mob that the deputies were called upon to control. When Ferris finished, I could see a change in the way the jurors looked at us.

Women were called as witnesses. You might know some of them, Mrs. Grace and Mrs. Brennen live in Harwood. You may have seen them at the company store, although I am sure they never bothered much with you. It breaks my heart, my dearest wife, to think how rude these women might have been to you. But I want to tell you about their testimony and how it supported the defense.

They testified, under oath, that their husbands were afraid they would be pressured into joining the strike. When they saw the strikers, their husbands fled into the woods, and the women hid their sons. Others spoke of clubs and revolvers carried by strikers. The lawyer was twisting everything. The jurors were being led to believe that these events took place on September 10. I wanted to shout "No!" but I did not speak. The judge would have told the bailiff to remove me from the courtroom. I grow increasingly fearful there will be an acquittal.

The United Mine Workers of the Lehigh region met in Harmony Hall last night. It is not too far from my boarding house. Thirty-five locals with seventy delegates were there. Imagine that! It was not so long ago that Fahy was trying to organize us for the first time. Things have changed since Lattimer.

You may have heard that Stefan was there. He was with the delegation representing Lattimer and Ario. Anna would have been proud if she could have heard him speak to the delegates. He spoke of the need to appeal to all businessmen, and workers of all classes to contribute to the prosecution fund. The trial is lasting longer than expected, and funds are running low.

I miss you and the family. A special kiss for our baby girl.
Love,
Emil

February 23, 1898
My dearest wife,

More damaging evidence against us today. I am too tired to give you details, but I am sure you follow events in the newspaper.

There will be some rest for all of us. The judge announced today that the jury is to have a bath! They are to go to the Turkish bathhouse and the tipstaff will guard them. Witnesses were not invited.

If the weather is good, I might take a walk down by the river. I could use some time alone with my thoughts.
Love,
Emil

February 28, 1898
My dearest wife

The monotony of the trial is wearing on all of us. Day after day, we go to the courthouse. Sometimes we are fortunate and can find a space in the crowded courtroom, but more often we wait in the corridors or stand outside in the cold. It's a wonder more of us aren't sick, but this trial is too important, and our testimony may be needed so we stay.

I worry about you and the family. If I had the money for the train, I would be home on weekends. Although you do not complain, our savings must be dwindling, and I fear that all of you will not have enough to eat. I pray that this dreadful trial will be over soon, and we can all return home.

Father Aust is here with us, and he helps where he can. I know the money for the prosecution is limited, but he tells me how hard Stefan works to help raise the money we need.

I long for you to keep me warm in the night and miss our little girl.
Love,
Emil

March 3, 1898
My dearest wife,
The defense called some of the deputies to the stand today. Only one, deputy admitted he fired his rifle. "One shot," he said, but, of course, he didn't hit anyone. The rest testified that they never fired their rifles. Are we to believe that? We have seen the wounded and buried our dead, yet it seems no one is responsible.

Oh, for this whole thing to be over. I want to return to work, to my mules, and to my family.
Love to all of you,
Emil

March 7, 1898
My dearest wife,
The days pass slowly, and you and Alica are often in my thoughts. I want so very much for all of this to be over and to resume our lives. Today Attorney Scarlet began the closing arguments for the prosecution. At times, he spoke quietly to the jury, and I strained to hear him. He reminded the men of the jury to be free from prejudice. Could they be? At first, I was hopeful. I watched their faces, and they were attentive as Scarlet spoke. Scarlet told the jury, "The deputies had a

prearranged plan to murder." I looked at the deputies and imagined them with their rifles aimed at me. Fire. The words echoed through my head, panic gripped my body, and I was once again at Lattimer. Was my mind playing tricks? I could smell smoke from the rifles and heard again the screams of the wounded and dying.

It was almost noon when Attorney Lenahan was called for the defense. For the first time, I was afraid, afraid for all of us. It was not just the verdict but something else, something darker. Lenahan told the jury we desecrated the flag, the flag we carried so proudly, with such innocent trust. Was it not one of them who tore it to shreds? At first, I didn't understand what Lenahan was doing, but as he spoke of patriotism, love of country, it was clear the jury began to see us as a threat to their way of life. We were a lawless horde, foreigners who did not share their values or understand their way of life.

Watching the jurors today, I have no doubt that there will be an acquittal. I will pray for forgiveness at the anger I am feeling. The fight is not over, Edita.

Tomorrow Attorney Lenahan will continue the defense, and then, we will wait for a verdict. Perhaps I will be home before you get this letter.
Love,
Emil

Anna

The trial ended. As you know, the deputies and the sheriff were acquitted. The papers wrote editorials praising the deputies, calling them honorable men. The miners were just an unruly, dangerous mob. We knew the truth.

Things were quiet for a while. We went on with our lives. In the years we lived in Ario I gave birth to eleven babies. By 1902, only six of them were still alive. I never talked about the three babies who died in my arms while they were still infants. They are buried here in this cemetery, near where I am being laid to rest. Their graves are unmarked, as we only had money for simple wooden crosses. The crosses are gone now, the graves of those innocents forgotten.

In the years after the massacre, the union grew in strength. Johnny Mitchell was elected the union president. There was another strike, one much larger than the one in 1897. You may have heard of the strike of 1902. There was much suffering during that long strike. Strikers were evicted from their homes. Families were starving. Many left the coal towns. Jan and Katarina went back to Slovakia, while their oldest sons, Tomas and Alex, went to Ohio. Our neighbor's twin boys jumped on a freight train and headed for New York City.

"They're gone, Matka." I can still remember the sadness in my Stephen's voice as he told me about his friends. "The twins." I knew right away he meant the boys next door. They were close to Stephen in age, and the boys had played together when they were small. "They jumped the train. Goin' ta New York, I imagine."

So many of our children went on what was called "Johnny Mitchell Excursions." The boys wanted to spare their families from the burden of feeding them, so they ran away. The twins were just thirteen when they left. They were just a little over a year older than my Stephen. Their poor mother. I sat with her that night as she mourned for her children.

Adriana and Cyril stayed in Lattimer to continue the fight. Adriana supported the work of Mary Harris Jones, often called "Mother Jones" by the miners. Mother Jones made quite a name for herself in coal country, organizing labor marches and fighting for the rights of the miners. I stayed home with my children and prayed for all of us.

Men died during the strike of 1902, shot by the Coal and Iron Police, but there was not a repeat of what happened in Lattimer.

Eventually, the strikes were over, and our lives did improve.

**1911-1918
The Next Generation**

Anna

The children grew and found their own lives. My Stephen married a lovely girl from a village not too far from the place where he was born. They lived on Peace Street in Hazleton, a new area of the city. It was no longer required that a miner live in a coal town.

Stephen worked in Lattimer, while Mary stayed home raising their three children. The draft in 1918 took two of my boys into the army. They fought in France, places that we never heard of. Stephen filled out the draft paperwork but was rejected. He was born in Austria-Hungary and had not yet become a citizen of the United States.

Chapter 14 - 1886-1889

Stephen and Mary

Stephen Dusick

The carbide lamp attached to Stephen's soft cap lit the way through the murky blackness of the mine, casting eerie shadows on the black walls. His heavy, oil-streaked jacket protected him from the damp, cool air. Familiar sounds, the muffled voices of miners in neighboring chambers, and the creaking wheels of coal carts pulled by mules echoed through the narrow tunnel. Coal dust settled on his face and in his nostrils.

The musty air and the smell of moss on old timbers reminded him of the forests he had walked with his father on cool October days. As his feet sloshed through the mud of the gangway floor, he thought of the blue sky and rays of the sun filtering through the leaves of the maple and oak trees and the crunch of the pine needles that littered the ground in thick mats. But he was not sullen as he moved through the darkness. He was a miner, and he was proud of that. He would save his money and buy one of the new houses on Peace Street, and then he would find a wife.

"We're almost there." Michael, Stephen's laborer, just entered the mine for the first time.

"'Bout time," Michael answered, hoping sarcasm would hide his uneasiness. Silence followed, broken only by the sound of their boots sloshing through water and the clank of their lunch pails against their knees.

"Grab a beer tonight?" Stephen suggested. "Maybe play some poker?" Stephen's voice was calm and confident as he surveyed his surroundings.

"Sure," Michael replied, trying to ignore the coal dust irritating his eyes and the squealing rats that scurried by on a mission of import.

"This is it. Welcome to Strawberry Hill."

"Lovely!" Michael exclaimed sarcastically as he crawled into the space deceptively called Strawberry Hill. "I love strawberries."

A sticky, wet mixture of mud and coal dust seeped through Michael's fingers, and he bit his lip when a jagged stone cut into his knee.

Mary Karch

Maria Magdalena stood on the steerage deck of the *Kronprinz Wilhelm,* laughing as a gust of wind nearly captured her hat, pulling it loose from the hat pins she had used to anchor it firmly in place. Strands of her chestnut-colored hair whirled around her face, and her cheeks turned rosy pink from an unexpected spray of saltwater. She watched, with excitement and anticipation, as the morning mist that had covered the horizon began to dissipate, revealing the skyline of Manhattan. The screech of gulls as they flew over the water competed with the blasting of the ship's horn announcing its arrival in New York Harbor. The cacophony of sounds echoed through Maria's body, adding to the exhilaration of the moment. *Almost there.* It was October 31, 1911. Maria was eighteen years old.

Her tiny hands, unadorned with rings or bracelets, extravagances that were beyond her reach but not her inclination, drifted to the buttons on her coat.

"This is for you," her mother had announced, her lips upturned in a smile, although there was sadness in her eyes. "For the coat, I am going to make you," she explained, handing her daughter a tiny bundle wrapped in tissue paper and tied with string. The package contained two shiny mahogany buttons. "My daughter cannot go to New York with nothing but a shawl and a babushka. I will not allow it."

"Matka." The word was whispered, and Maria hoped that her mother would feel the love and gratitude in her heart.

The ship drifted farther into the harbor, past the Lady with the torch, and Maria joined the children who were waving to the statue. Just beyond Lady Liberty, she recognized Ellis

Island, and it looked just as it had in the postcard Mihaly had sent to her.

"We will wait for you at the bottom of the stairs," her brother, Mihaly, had written. *But where are the stairs?* Maria wondered as she watched a ferry filled with immigrants approaching Ellis Island. The building on the island was as large and intimidating as any castle she had seen in Europe. "How will I find the stairs?"

"Your ship will dock in Manhattan, and from there, a ferry will take you to Ellis Island." Manhattan. She could see the buildings clearly now. Their colors were like a tapestry, some were russet, the color of leaves in the fall, others gray like sand in a riverbed. Rooftops reflected the light of the early-morning sun, and white puffs of smoke hovered above the city like specters watching the unsuspecting humans below. Docks and piers reached out into the harbor, their long arms waiting to welcome expected visitors, while tugboats were busy with their tasks, and ferries waited for their passengers.

"Don't be afraid," Mihaly had written in his last letter. She was not afraid. He would be there waiting for her at the bottom of the stairs. She could imagine him, smiling, every detail of his appearance meticulously attended to. His thick chestnut hair, so like her own, would be held in place by the masculine ointments and oils she had seen advertised in magazines. His dark suit would be brushed and pressed; his shoes polished. Observers would not suspect he was a coal miner or a recent immigrant. He had changed his name to Michael, and, to their mother's dismay, signed his letters *Love, Mike.*

Maria was sure her sister Ilona would be there standing next to their brother, waiting to welcome her to America. Maria imagined practical Ilona wearing an unremarkable brown coat and equally uninteresting hat. Her brows would be furrowed in a frown, her eyes straining to find the sister she had not seen in three years.

A slightly worn carpetbag rested on the deck next to Maria. It contained necessities for the trip, documents she would need at Ellis Island, a few precious mementos, and a fashion magazine. Maria had placed the magazine in the bag the night before, but not until her fingers traced the lettering on the top of the glossy cover one more time. The words *Wiener Mode*, Viennese Fashion, were printed in a whimsical style that evoked a feeling of fun and adventure. Beneath the lettering, a woman of breathtaking beauty looked dreamily into the distance, her soft eyes beckoning her true love to join her for unspoken pleasures. There was a slight flush on her cheeks, and her hat sat prettily on top of her perfectly styled hair. "Will I look at someone like that someday?" Maria wondered, and hoped that it would be so, although she was not sure what was meant by "unspoken pleasures."

It was three years since Ilona had left for America, three years since the magazine had inexplicably vanished. With a guilty smile Maria imagined her sister's delight when, after the requisite hugs and kisses were exchanged, the long-lost magazine would be returned to her. The magazine, a small treasure shared by the sisters, had disappeared the day before Ilona left for America.

"Maria! Where is it!" Ilona's voice was high-pitched and aggravated as she stood with her hands on her hips, confronting her younger sister.

"What?" Maria did not look up from the table, where she was sorting the buttons and pieces of ribbon in her mother's sewing box.

"You know what!"

"Don't you think this button would be perfect on the coat Mother is going to make for me?" Maria, with a practiced look of innocence, held up a button made of a deep brown wood encrusted with tiny stones of diverse colors.

"Where is the magazine! I know you took it."

"I don't know." Maria shrugged. "Maybe you showed it to Irene and forgot to bring it home." Irene was a friend of Ilona's. "Or maybe Mother needed it. You always blame me." Maria managed to sniffle and pout in the manner of the unjustly accused.

"I saw it this morning." Ilona frowned. It was possible, but not likely, that someone else was responsible. With a sigh, she went back to the task of packing her trunk. There were more important things to deal with and anyway, clothing and styles and the lives of wealthy women were not of such immense importance.

Now the magazine, slightly more worn, the corners curled, and the images somewhat faded, was stored in the carpet bag and, after a three-year hiatus, returned to Ilona.

A shrill blast from the ship's horn announced its arrival into New York Harbor. Maria was confronted with the reality that her future was about to begin. Her thoughts raced with a mix of emotions, excitement, anticipation, a little trepidation, and a momentary loss of confidence. *Will I find work?* She was willing to work hard. *Will I find a husband?*

With a clang, the gate that had confined the passengers to the steerage deck opened, and with haste, everyone began to gather their belongings. *Soon I will be an American,* Maria thought as she lifted the carpet bag. *I will be called Mary, Mary Karch.* As she whispered the name, the wind carried her voice over the water to the city.

Mary and Stephen

It wasn't long after Mary arrived in America that her brother brought Stephen Dusick home to dinner.

"I showed him your picture, and he wanted to meet you," her brother announced. "He will be here tomorrow night."

"He's very nice, Mary. I've met him," Ilona chimed in when she saw the startled look on her sister's face.

"But I don't even know what he looks like."

"Well, I think he is very handsome. He has light brown hair and hazel eyes. He is rather shy, at least around me. But I like him."

"We shall see," Mary was still unsure about this young man who worked in the mines with her brother.

"I will make perogies," Ilona announced, and then began to make plans for the dinner.

Stephen felt awkward that first night. He did not know what to say to the petite woman who sat opposite him. Mary, on the other hand, was instantly taken with the shy young man. She could see the kindness in his eyes.

"May I take you to the Nickelodeon theater on Saturday?" Stephen asked. Mary didn't know what a nickelodeon theater was. They certainly didn't have one in her home village, but of course, she would go.

"What shall I wear?" she asked Ilona that night.

"The dress Mama made you, of course."

As she walked down Broad Street with her arm in Stephen's, Mary knew this was the man she would marry.

Chapter 15 - 1918

Stephen

"Name?" The clerk at the courthouse did not bother to look up at the man who had just handed him the draft registration card.

"Stephen Dusick."

"You live at 992 North Peace Street?"

"Yes, sir."

"You are a declarant?" Stephen stiffened as the clerk looked up with obvious disapproval. Stephen had applied for citizenship, but the process was not yet complete.

"You were born in Eglo Spisska, Austria?" The man standing before him was a bloody Hun. At war with Austria, the clerk found it hard to conceal his scorn.

"Yes," Stephen answered, keeping his voice level. He was born in Austria, he wanted to explain, but had lived in America all his life. He was ready to fight for his country.

"You are a miner and work in Lattimer for Pardee Brothers?"

"Yes, sir."

"And you have a wife and three children?"

"Yes, sir."

"Do you claim exemption from the draft?"

"No."

"You will be notified," the clerk muttered in dismissal, signing the card and placing it in a box marked "Alien." Stephen, considered a foreigner and having been born in Austria, would not be called to serve.

"My pick!" The walls of the mine had shuddered; with a roar, rocks had begun to fall from the black roof of the mine chamber. Stephen ducked his head and ran. There was no time to think, only the instinct to survive. It was not until he saw the light at the end of the gangway that he remembered his pick.

He learned that everyone who had been in the mine had escaped unharmed, yet Stephen was filled with foreboding. Something terrible was about to happen. His pick was buried in the rubble, the worst possible omen. *A foolish miner's superstition, that's all it is.* But he was not convinced. *Robert! Is Robert safe?*

His brother Robert was fighting in France. They did not know where, but they read in the newspapers of a great offensive at Ourcq and Aisnearne. Stephen had bought a map and hung it on the wall of his father's house, and the family marked the places where battles were being fought. Robert was someplace in France, but where?

Like so many of the homes in Ario and Hazleton, an American flag flew proudly on the front porch. "Your mother cries every night, and prays that the Lord will protect Robert," Stefan told his son. "It is better you were not drafted. At least she has you."

Stephen could not help but worry that his brother might be killed on the field of battle at this very moment, and all because he had left the pick in the mine. *No! Robert will be all right. I will get my pick tomorrow.* The dread he felt would not leave him. *My pick!*

He passed a house with a black ribbon on the door, and then another. A terrible illness, the Spanish flu, had invaded the city, the country, the entire world. With foreboding Stephen touched the bag of camphor he wore around his neck. His wife, Mary, had insisted on the camphor, but he would not eat the raw onion that was also believed to offer protection from the illness. "For your children," she begged him, but he would only wear the camphor.

He reached Peace Street, where his daughter, Margaret, was jumping rope with her friends. She smiled at him and waved, and he waved back, but the song the little girls were singing filled him with dread.

> *I had a little bird*
> *Its name was Enza*
> *I opened a window*
> *And In-flu-enza*

"*My pick!*" Up till now, Peace Street had been spared from the worst of the illness that had been terrorizing the city for months. He knew the rules proclaimed by the mayor. Spitting and coughing in public were prohibited, and schools, churches, and theaters were closed. He should have been wearing a mask, but it was uncomfortable, and when Mary, or the police, were not watching, the mask was in his pocket.

The homes along Peace Street were built on a gently sloping hill, and his house sat very near the top of the incline. Normally the two-mile walk from Lattimer was not unpleasant, but today Stephen found the climb up the hill to be difficult. His legs felt like lead, and his breathing was labored. *I am just tired,* he thought, as he began to cough. *My pick.* The words were ever present now, as the cough grew worse.

He knew that his sons would be standing on the porch waiting for him. Ed, five years old, and presumably responsible, would be holding the hand of his little brother, Steve, preventing a premature escape into the street. Today, Stephen imagined Mary would be with them. She would have heard that no one was hurt in the rockfall, but she would worry until he was home. *I love you, Mary. I love our family,* he thought, as he reached the house and saw them standing on the porch, waiting for him.

"My pick! I should not have abandoned my pick." He tried to shake off the fear. "It is only a superstition." When he reached the front door, his face was turning blue, and his cough was deep and tore through his chest.

"My pick, Mary. My pick is in the mine," he said to her as she wrapped an arm around him and guided him into the house.

By morning, Stephen's agony ended, and he was still.

Epilogue - 1939

The room was dark, the curtains drawn, and the air had the musty smell of age and sickness, but Anna did not notice. Her Stefan was dying.

"His kidneys are failing," the doctor had told her. "There is nothing I can do."

"It is the Lord's will," she had answered.

The priest came to administer Last Rites for her husband. He knew the family well. There had been many such visits to this little house over the years.

Anna sat in a chair close to Stefan's bed and watched as his strength ebbed and he retreated into a world which she could not enter. She took his hand, once strong and young, now marked with the bruises and blotches of an old man. "I love you, Stefan," she whispered and was rewarded by a movement in his fingers. *He can still hear me,* she thought, and her heart filled with warmth at this last sign of the affection they had shared.

Stefan knew he was dying, but he was at peace. He felt the presence of his wife and heard her voice. They were back in their village under the linden tree by the church. He saw the young girl with the green eyes, and he felt the rush of a new love that was to last a lifetime.

Another voice was singing inside the church. It was his mother, singing a hymn from his youth. "Matka." The word lingered on his dry lips. He could feel a moist towel on his face, and he was grateful. "Anna, my wife," he whispered, and he could not see the tear that had fallen on his pillow.

There were children playing outside his window. *Stephen, Rose, Robert? No! The grandchildren. I am blessed.*

"Stefan!" It was his brother's voice. He was there, smiling, walking without a limp. *You are well, my brother,* Stefan thought. His brother smiled without speaking, but there was love in his face as he held out his hand, beckoning Stefan to follow.

There were others now, the man he had killed in Bosnia, the soldier he had not protected, the gypsy boy he had refused to help. In the distance, he could see nineteen men with picks and shovels. He recognized the men who died at Lattimer. The woman in black was there with her children, but her face showed only compassion. "Forgive me."

"There is nothing to forgive, my dear Stefan." It was Anna's voice. Now, he heard the voices of his grandchildren in the yard, and then there was nothing.

Anna

There was always a struggle, that is the way of life. But there was happiness too. There were holidays, weddings, and births to celebrate. The miners were no longer forced to live in company towns or shop in the company store. My son Robert came home from the war and married Annie, a girl he had known since they were children. They purchased a house next to ours here in Ario. Rose married and moved to McAdoo with her husband, and Joseph and Rudolf moved to Ohio. But our family remained close, our love for each other strong.

So here I am at the end of my journey. I will rest for eternity next to my beloved Stefan and the children I have lost. But I can look out at the mourners around my grave and feel their love. I can see my children and my grandchildren. They are all Americans, and the past is almost forgotten, but maybe that is how it should be. The future is before them.

We were not wealthy, not well educated, and life was often difficult. Now there are new challenges. The coal mines are shutting down, and jobs are scarce. Still, I am glad my grandchildren will not need to work in the mines. Thanks to the Lord, they will not need to endure the hardships of the past.

I heard them talking about a gravestone to mark where Stefan and I will rest for all eternity. We are so far from the place where we were born, from the home we knew as children, but this had been our choice. When we married, we had a dream of a better life for ourselves and our children. That dream has been realized.

Appendix

Historical note on the Lattimer Massacre

In 1897 Lattimer Mines was a coal town owned by the A. Pardee Coal Company. (Novak, 1996) Lattimer was the location of a confrontation that was "among the bloodiest labor massacres of the nineteenth century." (Roller, 2018) Nineteen coal mine laborers were murdered there on September 10, 1897, and at least thirty-nine more were wounded. (Novak, 1996)

Michael Novak's novel, *The Guns of Lattimer*, provided the framework I used for the events that started in Crystal Ridge and culminated in the tragic events of September 10, 1897. Pasco Schiavo's book *The Lattimer Massacre Trial*, a compilation of newspaper articles, was a treasure of daily details I incorporated into Emil's letters to his wife, Edita.

The description of the village of Lattimer was edited for me by Dr. Michael Roller, an archaeologist, who participated in a research project in the Anthracite Coal Region of Pennsylvania along with colleagues from the Department of Anthropology of the University of Maryland. (Roller, 2018)

My great grandparents Stephen and Maria Dusick lived in Lattimer and Hollywood, Pennsylvania coal patch towns owned by A. Pardee & Company. My grandfather Stephen Dusick was a coal miner working in Lattimer. He died in the 1918 flu pandemic.

Historical places mentioned in the novel

Beaver Brook
Crystal Ridge
Harleigh
Harwood
Hazleton
Lattimer (also known as Lattimer Mines)
Wilkes-Barre
McKenna's Corner in Hazleton
Michalchik's Hall in McAdoo.
St. Joseph's Roman Catholic Church of Hazleton
Ario is a fictional patch town modeled after company towns of the era.

Historical Figures

This novel is a work of fiction, and the characters were created by the author. However, the following people mentioned in the book were participants in the events of 1889.

Aust, Reverend Richard: A Benedictine priest from Poland administered to the Slovak Catholics. He worked with the union men.
Boden, John: A mule driver at Honey Brook Colliery.
Martin, T.R.: District Attorney Martin, with his associates, represented the commonwealth during the trial.
Eagler, John: Slate Boss at the Harwood breaker, first local secretary of the Harwood chapter of the UMW, witness for the prosecution.
Fahy, John: Organizer for the United Mine Workers.
Ferris, George: Attorney representing Sheriff Martin.
Jones, Ed: West Hazleton Chief of Police.
Jones, Gomer: Division superintendent of the Lehigh and Wilkes-Barre Coal Company near McAdoo.
Hall, Thomas: Chief of the Coal and Iron Police for the Lehigh Valley Coal Company.

Kinchila, Jozef: A Slovak who was elected president by the miner's meeting in Michalchik's Hall in McAdoo August 16, 1897.

Martin, Sheriff James L.: Sheriff of Luzerne County. He took office in January 1896.

McGraham, John: Attorney for the prosecution.

Michalko, Joseph: President of the newly formed Harwood Chapter of the United Mine Workers.

Pardee, Ario: Founder of the A. Pardee Brothers Coal Company. He owned several collieries in the coal region, including those at Lattimer and Harwood.

Pardee, Calvin: Succeeded his father as president of A. Pardee and Company. His son Calvin Pardee Jr. was among the deputies at Lattimer.

Pardee Platt, Ario: The chief bookkeeper of A. Pardee & Co. and general manager of company stores in Hazleton, Harwood, and Lattimer. In a meeting with the sheriff, he made it clear that the owners wanted the strike broken and operations resumed. He was among the deputies at Lattimer.

Septak, Mary: A Slavic woman who ran a boarding house for miners in Lattimer. She was a forceful figure who rallied the women to support the strike of 1897. Called "Big Mary" by the newspapers, she died November 11, 1898.

Siva, Andrej: Officer of the United Mine Workers local at Harwood in 1897. He marched with the strikers on September 10 and was a witness for the prosecution.

Woodward, Judge Stanley: Presided over the trial of Sheriff Martin and his deputies at the Luzerne County Courthouse in Wilkes-Barre, Pennsylvania.

The men who died at Lattimer*

Broztowski

Česlak (Cheslock)

Chrzeszeski

Čaja (Czaja)

Futa (Fota)

Grekoš

Jurič (Jurich, Jurek)

Jurašek (Jurechek)

Kulik (Kulick)

Monikaski

Platek

Rekewicz

Skrep

Tarnowicz

Tomašanta

Zagorski

Ziominski

Ziemba

- Novak, Michael *The Guns of Lattimer*, Transaction, New Brunswick (U.S.A.) 1996

Glossary

Coal car: A small, four-wheeled vehicle made of wood or metal in which coal is loaded.

Culm bank: A small hill of coal refuse, also called a slag heap.

Colliery: A coal mine and the buildings associated with it.

Breaker: A building where coal is broken down into assorted sizes, and impurities, including slate, are removed. The waste materials are deposited in the culm bank.

Gangway: A passage in the mine.

Miner's laborer: Worked with the miner who paid him.

Nipper: A boy who took care of opening and closing the doors in the gangways.

Patch town: A company-owned coal town typically situated in a remote area.

Pillar: A column of coal left in the mine to support the roof.

Slate: Dark shale lying next to a coal bed.

Slope: An entrance to a mine driven down through an inclined coal seam.

Bibliography

Bell, Thomas. *Out of this furnace.* Pittsburg, Pa.: University of Pittsburg Press, 1976.

Coal Region Enterprises. *Coal Speak The (un) official dictionary of the Schuylkill County, Pa Anthracite Coal Region,* Marlboro, MA, 1995.

Greene, Victor R. "A Study in Slavs, Strikes, and Unions: The Anthracite Strike of 1897." *Pennsylvania History* 31 (1964): 199-215.

Knauf, Diethelm, Moreno, Barry (eds.) *Leaving Home Migration Yesterday and Today.* Bremen: Edition Temmen, 2010.

Lindermuth, John R. *Digging Dusky Diamonds, A History of the Pennsylvania Coal Region,* Mechanicsburg, PA: Sunberry Press, Inc. 2013.

Maclean, Annie Marion. "Life in the Pennsylvania Coal Field: With Particular Reference to Women." American Journal of Sociology 14 (1909): 329-351.

Novak, Michael. *The Guns of Lattimer.* New Brunswick (U.S.A.): Transaction, 1996.

Pinkowski, Edward. *Lattimer Massacre.* Philadelphia: Sunshine Press, 1950.

Roller, Michael P. *An Archaeology of Structural Violence, Life in a Twentieth-Century Coal Town.* Gainesville, Florida: University Press of Florida, 2018.

Salay, David L. Editor *Hard Coal, Hard Times: Ethnicity and Labor in the Anthracite Region,* Scranton, The Anthracite Museum Press, *1984.*

Schiavo, Pasco L. *The Lattimer Massacre Trial,* Pittsburg: Dorrance Publishing CO, 2015.

Scranton Republican, Scranton, Pennsylvania. *"Strikers Fired Upon,"* September 10, 1897, page 5.

Scranton Republican, Scranton, Pennsylvania. *"Blood Flows at Lattimer,"* September 11, 1897, page 1.

Shackel, Paul A. *Remembering Lattimer: Labor, Migration, and Race in Pennsylvania Anthracite Country.* Urbana, Chicago, and Springfield: University of Illinois Press, 2018.

Stolarik, Mark M. *A Study in Slavs, Strikes, And Unions: The Anthracite Strike of 1897.* Pennsylvania History 31(2): 199-215, 1964.

Turner, George. A. *Slavic Perspective on the Lattimer Massacre. Pennsylvania History* 96(1):31-41 2002.

Richards, John Stuart. *Early Coal Mining in the Anthracite Region,* Charleston, SC: Arcadia Publishing, 2002.

Acknowledgements

Heartfelt thanks and appreciation to my sisters: Stephanie Grossman and her husband Jed Grossman, who sat with me on many Sunday afternoons patiently listening to early drafts of the manuscript, Gloria Freel, who shared my excitement as we unraveled our family history, and Diane Dusick, whose knowledge of horses was so often needed.

To my friends who read the many drafts of the novel, thank you. My life-long friend Neva Weisskopf answered endless e-mails, always offering advice and encouragement. What patience you have my friend! Maureen Sbordone was there without fail whenever needed. Lynda Mann offered professional guidance. Susan Benarick shared my interest in the plight of the immigrant coal miners of Pennsylvania. Mary Strine was always there when I needed help finding just the right word or phrase. Sue Martin read the final draft looking for those small, but inevitable, errors. Thank you, all of you, for being with me on the journey.

In addition, I want to thank Dr. Michael Roller, an archaeologist who checked the novel for historical accuracy and my editor Chris Fenwick with Sunbury Press.

ABOUT THE AUTHOR

Virginia Rafferty is a writer of historical fiction focusing on immigration from Eastern Europe in the nineteenth century. Traveling to Slovakia and Hungary to trace her ancestry while working with a Slovak genealogist gave her perspective on the lives of Slovak and Hungarian peasants living in the Austro-Hungarian empire. Her genealogy research culminated in two novels that chronicle her ancestors' struggles as they leave their homes and settle in America.

Virginia is a retired middle school science teacher with a BA degree from Merrimack College in North Andover, MA. In 2003, she was awarded a Master of Education degree from Antioch New England Graduate School in Keene, NH. She is a member of the South Carolina Writers Association and the Appalachian Writers Association.

She is currently living in Aiken, SC, and is volunteer coordinator for McGrath Computer Learning Center, a volunteer organization that offers computer instruction to seniors.

www.virginiaraffertybooks.com

CPSIA information can be obtained
at www.ICGtesting.com
Printed in the USA
LVHW021931230321
682229LV00006B/1501